GUERRILLA GOLD

A CORSAIR NOVEL
BOOK 3

DOUGLAS PRATT

MANTA
PRESS

For Ashlee

PROLOGUE

The hot, sticky air was thick as Bella shoveled more dirt from the garden. The irrigation ditch was coming along, and the digging process crawled as she and Bernie scooped wet mud out of the trench. There was little chance of getting anything but muck in the Tapajós Basin. The river that shared the area's name supplied the small village with its water. Regular flooding assured the community that their soil remained filled with nutrients.

The settlement of São Miguel do Tapajós sat on the edge of the Tapajós River. Its population subsisted on traditional slash-and-burn agriculture combined with hunting and fishing. These practices dated back centuries in this area, although the exact dates when São Miguel do Tapajós first sprang up on the riverbanks were lost to legend. The riverside community fluctuated between 100 and 150 people. The citizens came and went, often in marital trades with other communities. However, through it all, the old ways raged on.

But if Bella Marquez had anything to do with it, she'd bring new traditions into the village. Besides the daily Bible studies that she and her team conducted, they spent most of their time helping the farmers adapt their agricultural practices. Bella employed permaculture techniques, a type of farming that could be more sustainable. Instead of deforesting the area for swaths of fields that only grew one crop, her team taught the farmers to develop polyculture gardens where multiple crops could grow. Their most successful plot now produced cassava intercropped with various legumes and tomatoes. The natural pest resistance of certain botanicals protected the others while crops like legumes refed nitrogen into the soil.

In another two seasons, the guava and açaí palms would grow fruit with minimal effort. Annual pruning took a few hours after the season, and then the trees could produce fruits for years to come. Bella had imported domesticated animals to help with the gardening. Free-range chickens devoured any bug that ventured in. Goats cleared the underbrush and provided the villagers with eggs, milk, and meat.

Bella spearheaded the six volunteers who had journeyed into the village two years earlier. The group, sponsored by Zion's Garden, was a Christian organization that operated similarly to the Peace Corps. Their work was gratifying, if not exhausting, and days like today, when she'd been toiling under the humid jungle canopy for most of the day, though wearisome, rewarded her with a finished task. This irrigation ditch would save the farmers hours of carrying water. Once they completed it, she had designs to add a water wheel and sand filtration system to process the village's potable water.

The açaí palms rustled, and Bella glanced up from her shovel to see the branches push apart, revealing Domingo's cherubic face as he emerged from the jungle. The eleven-year-old boy had grown fascinated with the team, especially with the twenty-nine-year-old Bella.

"Domingo," Bella greeted the boy with a bemused smile. The lad returned her grin with a sparkle in his eye. "Did you come to help?"

The child shook his head. "No, there are men coming," the child said in Portuguese.

"Men?" Bernie questioned, wiping a glob of mud off his forehead. The older man panted as he spoke, and Bella glanced at him.

Bernie Snyder was an American insurance agent in his fifties. He joined the group six months ago after his wife of twenty-five years left him for her dentist. Bernie had sold his agency, house, cars, almost everything before taking a flight from Phoenix to Medellin, Colombia, where he'd bought an old Jeep Wagoneer and traveled across South America. He'd met Joanne and Felipe in Peru and followed them to São Miguel do Tapajós.

Bella guessed he would only stay a few weeks before he grew tired of the hard work and challenging conditions. However, Bernie proved her wrong. He took on any task with gusto, and in the last six months, he had gone from an out-of-shape insurance salesman to a strong farmer. In fact, he dove into the agricultural concepts Bella and her team were teaching the villagers.

"What kind of men?" he questioned Domingo in his meager Portuguese.

Domingo shook his head. "Men with guns."

"Where?" Bella demanded.

The boy pointed back toward the village.

"Soldiers?" Bernie asked her in English.

"Not likely," the woman remarked. "Not legitimate ones, at least."

She drove the shovel's blade into the mud, leaving the handle jutting up out of the ditch. The missionary climbed out of the trench. Mud caked her jeans and clung to her boots. Back on hard ground, she stamped her feet, dislodging two to three pounds of mire from each foot. Bernie followed suit.

The woman's eyes narrowed, and she grabbed the shovel and marched through the brush, holding the tool like a soldier carrying a rifle in formation. Bernie chased after her.

"Bella, be careful," he warned from behind the feisty woman.

"These people need to be safe," Bella complained.

Bernie shook his head. He admired Bella Marquez. This young lady had a fire in her spirit. Bella was only a few years older than his own daughter, though. What she did was fill Bernie with regret. He wished he could be younger again and reevaluate his life. So many wasted years building an agency with a wife who had spent the last decade quietly despising him. If only he'd found a woman like Bella instead of Tracey. Someone who brought the best out of other people.

Now, as he pursued this woman through the jungle, Bernie sensed the worry at the edge of his consciousness. Men with guns were never a good sign. Except for law enforcement, it was bad, even back in the States. Men with guns sought control, either in their own situation or those of others. Bernie considered that to be true even for those supposed to protect—guns still provided control.

Bella continued to take the lead, outpacing Bernie and Domingo. She burst through the outskirts of the settlement, pushing aside the large palm leaves that shielded the small community. The forest canopy opened up on the edge of the river, where, decades earlier, the people of São Miguel do

Tapajós cleared the trees from the water's edge. In place of the arboreal giants stood an arrangement of stilted huts. An aroma of stewing vegetables and meat reached Bella before she had time to survey the village.

The locals were gathering in the center of the huts, waiting with wary eyes. The women lingered back without speaking, save a few whispers to each other. Six men from the community stood between the women and the edge of the jungle.

"Where are these men?" Bernie asked in English.

"Domingo, where are they?" Bella asked in Portuguese.

The boy didn't have time to raise his hand to point when palm leaves to the north parted. Six soldiers stepped through the brush like they'd appeared through a portal. All of them carried black rifles across their chests. Their fatigues were similar canvas pants that varied from tan to a dirty green.

A figure pushed through the other five men to stand out front. He was the only individual whose rifle hung from a sling off his back.

Bella studied the man she assumed was the leader of this gang. He had curly, oily black hair that stuck to his temple, coated with sweat and dirt. He was somewhere around Bella's age, but his days had been harder. The years had multiplied on his face as scars and wrinkles. The bushy beard and mustache matched the black hair in color.

He grinned a gap-toothed smile that sent shivers down her spine. His obsidian eyes bore into hers as if he was a demon. With careful precision, his head turned in an arc as he scanned the crowd.

"*Atenção!*" the man called out. *Attention.*

When he seemed satisfied that the group's gaze was on him, he continued in Portuguese. "We have come to give you a warning. This area is under threat of attack, and we are here to help you."

"What is he saying?" Bernie muttered to Bella.

"Shh," Bella whispered.

"We have heard that forces intend to invade your village. We are here to protect your homes. But we will need to move you immediately."

The men of the community exchanged glances that conveyed concern. None spoke up.

"Why do they have to leave?" Bella asked loudly.

The leader of the gunmen rotated his head in a slow swivel until his beady stare locked on Bella. He held his wide-mouthed grin that displayed a few blackened teeth.

"Miss, we're worried that if trouble breaks out, someone innocent will get hurt."

"Who are you?" she demanded, stepping forward.

"*Aliança Revolucionária do Tapajós.*"

"Mercenaries," Bella stated.

"Soldiers," the leader corrected. "Here to protect you and your people."

"By driving them out of their homes?"

"Better than letting them die."

Bella drove the shovel in her hand into the dirt and folded her arms. "Who is coming to kill them?" she asked, glaring at the soldier.

"A militia group from the south," he warned.

"I think the only threat is from you," she countered.

"Miss, we don't wish to hurt anyone," he assured her. However, the decaying smile and leering eyes unsettled the missionary. "Who are you, anyway?"

"We are with Zion's Garden," Bella announced. "We work with the Brazilian government."

The man cocked his head and laughed a quiet, bemused chuckle. "The Brazilian government does little to protect this village. It is up to those who are strong to defend the weak."

"Who told you they were weak?" she argued. "These people built a home here. That takes strength."

"What is your name, miss?" he questioned.

"What is yours?" she responded without answering his question.

"Mateo. Pleased to meet you!"

Bella marched toward the men from the village. "Do you want to leave?" she asked.

A few of the villagers shook their heads, but most of them cast nervous glances at the armed men standing at their border. She turned to Mateo.

"They don't wish to leave," she said.

Mateo held his smile. "They have no choice."

Bella put both hands on her hips and took a couple of steps toward the gunmen. Her gaze moved from face to face, committing their features to her memory. Mateo was the oldest of the group, and she estimated he was in his mid-thirties. The rest of the men were only boys. Three, she guessed, were under eighteen. The other two were in their twenties. All had hard stares they held on her.

"We will give you two weeks to move downriver," Mateo explained. "There is a clearing thirty miles south of here on a small creek that feeds into the Tapajós River."

The villagers now grew excitable. Murmurs erupted amongst them, but none voiced their thoughts to Mateo or his soldiers.

"What if we don't go?" Bella asked.

"Unfortunately, if you defy us, we cannot protect you."

"This doesn't sound like protection!" Bernie shouted in

English. He charged forward. "We'll reach out to the Brazilian officials and lodge a complaint."

Mateo faced a man to his left and gestured with his head toward Bernie. The boy lifted the rifle to his shoulder in one motion and squeezed the trigger. A single gunshot echoed through the trees, sending birds into flight from the boughs surrounding the village.

Bella pivoted to see Bernie drop to his knees. Blood was spreading across the former insurance agent's shirt. The man seemed to register the wound for a second before he fell face-forward into the dirt.

"No!" Bella screamed, turning and sprinting toward the fallen figure.

"This is not optional," Mateo said, no longer smiling. "We are giving you two weeks to move your village. You can head south to that cleared area or find another location. However, at the end of that time, we will return."

The six men vanished into the jungle as Bella rolled Bernie's lifeless corpse over. His empty eyes stared back at her.

1

———

Caleb thought he could use a shower. It wasn't a question—he definitely needed a shower. For the past thirteen days, Caleb had woven his way south out of Colombia while staying off the Colombia state police's radar. Unfortunately, such practices didn't lend themselves to fancy hotel suites with showers. In fact, given Caleb's current financial straits, even a fleabag motel with rats or roaches or both was out of his realm of attainability.

He'd traded the Suzuki motorcycle in a village called El Banco for a small pirogue fishing boat and four days' worth of food and fuel. The local was so pleased with the swap that Caleb realized he ended up on the worst end of the deal. At least, until the police found the man with the stolen motorcycle from Cartagena.

Caleb thought that would take some time, though. He'd already painted over the official emblem, and as long as the former fisherman didn't get in trouble with it soon, he, too, would avoid any legal interaction. If Caleb was out of the country, or at least far enough from El Banco to be discovered, then it didn't matter to him.

He journeyed up the river for three days before the small, three-horsepower outboard sputtered its last. With the current against him, Caleb's only choice was to ride the flow back ten miles to the last port he'd passed, Barrancabermeja. There, he got a few hours of sleep on the riverbank before nightfall, when he stole a Jeep and headed south again. By driving all night, he reached another town, where he slept for a short time in the rear of the Jeep. By the next morning, he arrived in Bogota, where he dropped an email to Khloe.

Khloe Evans was hiding with Caleb's daughter Amanda in Belize City, Belize. He hadn't spoken to them since he left Cartagena, and he wanted to assure them he was still alive. Caleb could call Khloe, but he'd risked that once. Since there were factions, both in the government and freelance, after him and Khloe, their preferred method of communication was a mail drop—an email account that never sent an actual email. Caleb would start a note and save it for later. When Khloe checked it, she would erase his message and respond, saving it as a draft as well.

His entire reason for visiting Colombia was to arrange for Khloe to get a new identity, complete with a passport. Unfortunately, Caleb had fallen victim to a double-cross. Now, with the airports in Colombia out of reach, Caleb had to find other ways out of the country. He didn't trust the ports in Cartagena de Indies, either.

From Bogota, he traveled another twelve hours to a village called Villagarzón along the Caquetá River. Again, he traded the stolen Jeep for transport aboard a little barge. He spent the next five days lounging, sleeping, and fishing on the deck. He helped with some labor for meals, but most of the time, he watched the riverbank flow past.

It was a long journey down the tributary to Brazil, where

he disembarked in a village called Alvarães. The township sat where the Japura River joined with the Amazon. From there, Caleb found a freighter heading toward the Atlantic Ocean.

Passage was cheap, but it consumed the rest of Caleb's money. He still had the Glock he'd taken from the dirty cops in Cartagena. Caleb knew it was a mistake to hang on to it, but he didn't enjoy moving around unarmed. Besides, he kept it stashed in the bottom of the rucksack he'd picked up in Bogota. He completed his shopping late at night on the clotheslines in a nicer neighborhood in the city. When he finished, he stuffed several days' worth of clothes into his pack.

Three other passengers joined the boat in Alvarães. The others cordoned off an area on deck and started stringing up hammocks. Buying a ticket on the freighter only ensured a ride. Private rooms and food were all extra. Most vagabonds found free space somewhere and hung up their hammocks. Caleb didn't have one, so he settled for sleeping on the hard metal floor.

The vessel had a lot of scheduled stops along the river, but its final destination was Macapá at the mouth of the Amazon. He hoped by the time he got there, he could find a ship heading back to Central America. Caleb had no way to buy his way onboard, but that was a bridge to cross later on.

Caleb stretched out on deck. It was easier to sleep during the daytime when the mosquitoes weren't swarming. They were always swarming, but at least during the heat of the day, there were millions less of them.

"You want some jerky?" Deke asked Caleb from the other side of the deck.

Caleb lifted his head off his pack to peer at the twenty-three-year-old kid who hailed from just outside Cleveland.

Deke and his buddy, Danny, were trekking South America. They had a couple of mountain bikes that they'd ridden across Peru and Brazil.

"Yes, thanks," Caleb agreed, sitting up.

Deke threw a package of jerky over the open space to Caleb, who pulled two sizeable pieces from the package before returning it. Since coming aboard, Caleb had made do with scraps for meals. He'd helped the crew clean and even given his watch in exchange for a meal, but the leftovers would hold him. When he got off this jungle cruise, he expected to be several pounds lighter.

"We're supposed to dock in a couple of hours," Danny remarked from his hammock. "What's the name of the town?"

"Juruti," Deke told him. "Hey, Rick, you want to come ashore and explore with us?"

Caleb, who'd introduced himself to the young men as Rick, answered, "Naw, I can wait it out here."

Deke shrugged. "It's no trouble. I know you're tight on money, so we'll buy you a drink or something."

"Thanks, guys," Caleb replied, meaning it, too. He'd gotten to like the two boys who'd been more than just hospitable. After all the issues he had run into, some genuinely good human spirits warmed his heart. "I'm okay."

Caleb had considered going ashore long enough to find a computer and message Khloe. He had been incommunicado for over a week now, and since he had no cell signal on the Amazon, borrowing one of the boy's phones to reach Khloe wouldn't work.

It was a challenge he struggled to get used to as he blended his old life with his new. Until last year, the intelligence world considered Caleb Saunders deceased along with his codename, Corsair. But before that, Corsair had been amongst the best assassins in the US government.

A shadowy agency called the Office of Compliance had recruited Caleb Saunders from Parris Island. The OOC operated under the Homeland Security umbrella, although it seemed the only person who knew what happened at the OOC was the head, Carl Winston. After a decade of fixing America's problems, Caleb discovered Winston had used him to pull off personal hits. When the last one had taken him to Turkey, where Winston intended for him to kill a kid and his mother, Caleb had improvised an explosion and faked his death.

With Caleb Saunders deceased, he found himself resurrected as Tom Harrod, a man who met the woman of his dreams and had two beautiful kids: Jackson and Amanda. But Corsair hadn't died, and when a pair of carjackers killed his wife and son, the assassin rose from the grave to save the only thing he had left: his daughter.

Resurrection came at a price, though. Within hours of revealing his presence, the OOC and numerous old enemies stepped out for their pound of flesh. Caleb and Amanda went underground, where they stumbled across Khloe Evans, a young woman with her own target painted on her. Now he had to get to his family to make sure he protected them.

Cartagena had been a near miss, and he found that an old enemy was turning over all the stones to come after him. Mahmoud Abbas had manipulated him so well, and Caleb worried that the arms dealer had more men in South America searching for him.

For now, he'd prefer to remain with his head down. Khloe knew the drill. He might be gone for an extended period, and she was under explicit instructions to protect his young daughter.

"Thanks, guys, I'll just hang out here," Caleb said. "If you find a paperback or something to read, I'd take that, though."

"Will do, Rick," Deke promised him.

Caleb sat up, crossing his legs. He needed some exercise, but leaving his spot meant dragging his pack around. While Deke and Danny struck him as two all-American kids, the sailors of the freighter came off more like the crew of the *Black Pearl*. Unaccompanied belongings often went missing on these river cruises, so the common practice was to carry everything at all times. While there wasn't anything except the Glock in his bag that was worth stealing, Caleb didn't want to confront questions about the gun.

Instead of walking the deck, Caleb rolled onto his stomach, proceeding to do some push-ups before rolling to his back and counting out the same number of sit-ups.

"Every day," Danny remarked, eyeing Caleb as he worked out.

Caleb just smiled at his young friend.

Deke commented, "You should do it, too, Danny-boy. Dude's in killer shape for his age."

Caleb shot Deke a glance.

"Oh, Rick, that wasn't what I meant," he amended. "My bad."

Caleb nodded with a grin. "At least I'm not a woman. You should never use that phrase with any woman."

Danny chuckled. "Yeah, d-bag. Mind your p's and q's."

"What the hell does that mean, anyway?" Deke asked.

"It means be careful what you say," Caleb explained.

Deke shook his head. "Makes no sense," he commented.

"It has to do with typography," Caleb told the pair.

"When typing, you want to ensure you are using the appropriate letter. A typed p and q look similar, but reversed. The idea is to be certain you use the correct one."

"I had no idea," Danny said. "I thought it meant 'polite questions.' Or something like that."

Caleb shrugged. "Always a good time to learn something." He got to his feet and began stretching.

"Think we can find a bar in this port?" Danny asked.

"Let's hope so," Deke replied with a grin.

"Watch yourself, boys," Caleb warned. "These river towns are mostly fine, but it's still on the edge of nowhere. You never know who might be waiting until a couple of Yanks stroll in."

"Personally, I'm hoping it's a gorgeous gold-digger looking to screw my brains out," Deke said, grinning.

Caleb felt the corners of his mouth turn up. By the time he was Deke and Danny's age, he'd completed over ten missions for the OOC. He'd crossed multiple continents with even less than he had today. Even so, he had been just as concerned as these boys were now with meeting a sexy local.

The next few hours left the boat empty. Any crew remaining on board stayed busy loading and unloading cargo. Most of the passengers followed Deke and Danny into the little port, which was comprised of an old wooden dock and a few shanty houses. This wasn't like the ports a cruise ship stopped at. Port days were only a few hours long, depending on how much cargo was off- and on-loaded.

Caleb took advantage of the quiet for some rest. The Amazon sun baked down on the vessel. He settled under a flight of stairs where the sun couldn't reach him. The shade offered a twenty-degree difference, making his slumber a bit more tolerable.

Since leaving Belize, he hadn't slept well. Caleb never did when he was on assignment. There was an edge in existing like this that never let him find peace. When he jerked awake after a couple of hours, he saw the crew getting ready to set off.

Danny and Deke weren't back in their hammocks. Every other time they'd gone ashore, their first stop before dinner was their hammocks on deck. Caleb threw his pack over his shoulder and started moving below deck to the mess hall. Perhaps the boys had stopped there for a bite first.

Two off-duty crewmen were just getting back with supplies. As they loaded the coolers with meats and vegetables, they turned to see Caleb. He had only encountered each of these two men once, and he remembered that one was named Diego.

"Have you seen the other two *gringos*?" Caleb asked the pair in Spanish.

The one he thought was Diego replied, "If they aren't back, the captain won't wait on them."

"They should be back now," Caleb remarked.

"They were the ones looking for a bar?" the other asked.

"Probably," Caleb answered.

"That's no good," he told him. "Not a good place for tourists."

"Why is that?" Caleb asked.

"Lots of cocaine around here," Diego explained. "That brings some not-so-nice people."

Caleb sighed. "Do you know the town?"

Both men nodded.

"Where would they go?"

"Little bar on the south side," Diego stated. "It would be the safest for Americans."

"Might have been nice for someone to warn them," Caleb commented.

Diego shrugged. "We don't all have time to babysit *gringos.*"

Caleb responded with a nod before leaving the two men. No point in arguing what common decency was. Passage along the Amazon came with a warning, which was pretty much: "Be very careful." The captain, crew, or ship's owner denied any responsibility. No one was going to track down stragglers, either.

At the railing on deck, Caleb stared at the small town of Juruti. He squinted, trying to make out the two young men rushing back to the dock. He saw no sign of them.

Not your problem.

Caleb had repeated that mantra a lot in recent months. Each time, he ended up making it his problem. This time, it could be as simple as Deke and Danny finding a couple of local girls and losing track of time. They could easily catch the next ship in a few days. But if Caleb missed this ship, he'd have to scrounge together enough cash to buy space on board any other boats.

Still, the boys were just boys, and they'd shown exceptional kindness to him.

A loudspeaker on deck blasted behind Caleb in Spanish and then in Portuguese. "Twenty minutes until we leave port," it announced.

Twenty minutes. Not enough time.

He scanned the streets again. No Americans in sight.

Caleb grunted, tightened his grip on his pack, and started for the gangway.

2

____

The bar in question had no name on it. No sign. Not a single neon sign for a beer brand in the window. There was one metal placard advertising Brahma lager, but the paint had turned to rust, leaving only a bare reminder that the picture might have once been a bottle.

However, there were other indications that this shack operated as a tavern. The fifty-five-gallon drum filled with aluminum cans and bottles, the six men lounging on a wooden deck with half-drunk beers and a pile of burnt cigarette ends, and the pack on the ground that looked a lot like the one Deke had pulled the package of jerky from.

Caleb eyed the men at the table. These were hard men with calloused hands and thick arms. Corsair saw more.

A man who killed with Corsair's ease could recognize that same darkness in others. Two of these men were killers. They might have all killed at some point, but that pair enjoyed it. It was an odd realization that Caleb struggled with. Corsair was an accomplished assassin, and honestly, he'd once enjoyed the act. Not the taking of a life, but like anyone who performed their job well, he'd felt a certain satisfaction when he pulled off a challenging hit. Back then, he thought he was doing a service for his country.

He questioned if this group could be described in the same way.

The man with the pack at his feet lifted his bearded face to stare at Caleb. He seemed to recognize Caleb, and Caleb watched as some switch in this man's eye flipped. Did he realize the slim odds of another American showing up now? Corsair doubted it. No, he either assumed Caleb was a friend of Deke and Danny's or just another fresh, ripe American setting himself up to be picked.

"Pardon, have you seen two American boys here?" Caleb asked in Portuguese.

The one who first caught sight of Caleb responded, "Who are you?"

Another man, one Caleb pegged as more dangerous than the rest, murmured something to the first man.

"We haven't seen them," the first man answered.

Caleb let his gaze drift down to Deke's backpack before bringing them back up to connect with the bearded man's eyes.

"What's your name?" Caleb asked.

"Why do you want to know?" the thug wondered, allowing his hand to fall to his side and rest on the hilt of a large knife attached to his belt.

"I'm curious what they'll put on your tombstone," Caleb remarked.

With the amount of gusto that Caleb expected, the man shoved away from the table, screeching the wooded feet of his chair across the wooden deck. He drew his blade and glared at Corsair.

"You want to say that again?" the man wielding the knife snapped.

"Do you not understand my Portuguese?" Corsair shot back. "I thought I was fluent."

Corsair's brashness unsettled the man, who had been seeking some solace with his friends around the table. If Corsair appraised the situation, this group—and the two de facto leaders in particular—thought they were the apex predators in Juruti.

"Don't let him talk to you like that, Thiago," one of the men urged.

Thiago lifted the blade, pointing the tip at Corsair. "I think we will let you join them," he announced.

"They're alive?" Corsair inquired.

Thiago grinned. "Oh, yes. We can still ransom them off to their rich American families. Might do the same for you."

Caleb raised his hands in surrender. "That sounds ideal. Why don't you take me to them?"

"Don't trust him, Thi," another of his group argued.

Corsair cocked his head. Thiago was wary. Corsair didn't blame him, but it would have been easier if this gang had taken him to wherever they held Deke and Danny. The boys might be alive now, but even if their families paid up, these goons would not release them. At best, they would press Deke and Danny's families for more money. If they were lucky, they could get one more payment before the parents realized their boys were never coming back. More likely, Thiago and his clan would kill Deke and Danny, leaving their corpses in the jungle somewhere to rot.

"I think we have enough with them," Thiago remarked to Caleb. "You would be too much trouble."

"Where are the Americans?" Caleb asked again. "We can still do this the nice way."

Thiago chuckled. All of his crew laughed with him. Here was a cocky American threatening a group of six men. Even if half of them were drunk, Corsair was clearly outnumbered.

"Felipe," Thiago said to one man with a nod of his head. An unspoken order to help Thiago handle Caleb.

Felipe stood up. He was the second man Corsair had identified as a murderer. The gleam of hatred in Felipe's eyes pierced through the air. The other four men watched with some glee.

"I'm going to slice you open and carve my name in your heart," Thiago growled with an evil smile.

"Can you even spell your name?" Corsair asked.

Thiago lunged at Corsair, driving the six-inch knife toward the former assassin's chest. Felipe reacted a half-second after his partner. Their timing was perfect—for Corsair.

He stepped to the left as the shiny blade whizzed by. Corsair's right hand rose under Thiago's forearm, catching the thug's arm while Corsair hooked his right foot behind Thiago's calf. A swift sweep lifted Thiago off his feet. The criminal's eyes widened as he went off the ground. In the split second of weightlessness, Corsair loosened his grip on Thiago's wrist and slid his hand up, snatching the knife by the handle.

The four men seated let out a collective "Ooh!" as Corsair stepped toward Felipe and drove the point of Thiago's knife into his throat. Surprise flashed through Felipe's eyes in the last second of his life. Corsair reversed course, pulling his right leg back and stomping down on Thiago's face. His heel crunched through the man's nose and crushed his maxillae.

Thiago didn't die as fast as Felipe. Instead, a gurgle of air seeped through the smashed sinuses. Blood filled his nasal cavities, and in a minute, Thiago would drown in it. Even if his comrades got him up, any medical treatment that might save him wasn't nearby.

The other four men bounded from their seats at once. Corsair caught the closest as he twisted toward him. His hand grabbed a handful of black hair, and the former assassin yanked the man forward off his feet. Corsair drove his head into the man's face, breaking his nose.

As the man howled in pain, Corsair twisted his body, encircling his forearm around the Brazilian's neck.

"If you don't want to watch another friend die, everyone should stop moving," Caleb ordered in Portuguese.

The closest one motioned with his hand for the rest to stay back.

"Listen, we didn't mean anything by it," the man facing Corsair claimed. "It was Thiago and Felipe's idea."

"My friends," Caleb said. "Are they alive?"

"Yes, Thiago wasn't lying," he explained. "They only wanted to ransom them to their families."

Caleb shook his head in disbelief. The kid talking looked like the youngest in the group. Early twenties, Caleb guessed. At least ten years younger than Thiago.

"Are you stupid?" Caleb demanded.

"What do you mean?" the boy asked, frowning.

"You think they planned to let them leave after taking a bunch of money from their families?"

"He said so," the kid argued.

"Thiago didn't look like the trustworthy type," Caleb pointed out. "Would he and Felipe even give you your cut? How much was he asking, anyway?"

"A hundred thousand. American dollars."

Caleb smirked. The probability was high that some yuppie kids with the means to travel abroad came from families with ample financial resources. The ransom wasn't so obscene that a good portion of Americans couldn't scrounge it together. It wasn't a ridiculous amount, like a million dollars. In fact, Corsair bet Thiago would have gotten the payoff, too. Deke and Danny, while friendly and kind, came across as well-to-do—that's the phrase his grandfather used back in Georgia.

Audrey would have called them entitled shits, but then his wife had a caustic wit at times.

"We didn't want to kill anyone," the kid stated.

"Where are my friends?" Caleb asked.

A loud whistle echoed through the streets. The freighter's disembarkment whistle. Caleb's ride was leaving now.

"There, in a house on the other side of town."

"I'd suggest we go," Caleb demanded. He motioned to the young man in front of him and his captive. "You and him," Caleb said, pushing the man he held in his arm. "Any problems, I will snap his neck, kill you, and find them myself. Understand?"

The boy nodded vigorously.

"You understand?" Caleb asked his prisoner.

The man nodded.

"Pick up that bag," Corsair told the younger one. "Walk!" he ordered when the kid had the pack on his shoulder.

The trip across town was quick. After all, it was not a large town. Caleb wondered if the community had any kind of law enforcement. If they did, it might make it difficult for him to explain a couple of dead men at the bar and his two hostages.

Those were problems he'd sort out later. For now, he wanted to find Deke and Danny and get the three of them to safety.

The younger man marched ahead. His stride increased a

bit, and Corsair warned him to stay near. When they reached the house, Caleb stopped. "Drop the bag," he directed.

When the backpack hit the dirt, Caleb ordered, "Go get my friends. If you come out alone or not at all, I'll get your name from your friend and kill you. Slowly."

The one in his grip struggled, but Corsair tightened his hold on the man's throat.

The kid nodded, choking out, "I swear, I'll be back."

"Go!" Caleb barked.

The kid vanished into the house, a cinderblock structure with metal roofing and iron bars over the windows. A metal door squealed as the young thug entered.

"Please, let me go," Caleb's captive begged.

"Might want to rethink who you cross," Corsair suggested.

"I won't ever do this again," he promised. "After all, you killed Thiago and Felipe. It was all their idea."

The door opened, letting out another squeal. Deke and Danny stumbled outside. Deke's hand raised up to shield his eyes. He blinked twice before he said, "Rick?"

"Boys, you best run for the dock. I doubt you'll make it, but who knows?" Caleb told them. "Don't forget your bag." He gestured to the backpack on the ground.

"Thank God!" Danny cried. "I thought we were dead."

"You aren't out of it yet," Caleb warned. "Now hurry."

Deke hurried over and grabbed the pack at Caleb's feet. "Rick, thank you."

Caleb nodded as the two boys ran for the port. They probably wouldn't make it, and if they didn't, the pair of Americans needed to get out of town before Thiago's friends downed enough liquid courage to go after them.

Once the boys were gone, Caleb's free hand reached

around his prisoner's front, patting down the man's trousers until he stuck his fingers into his pocket. He came out with a small wad of cash. Caleb released the man's neck, shoving him forward. The kid stood in the doorway, watching from a distance. His knees quivered as if he were ready to break into a sprint, but he only stared at Caleb.

"I'm sorry, man," he repeated in Portuguese.

Caleb fanned out the bills. It was about two hundred reals, which was only about forty dollars. He wished he'd looted Thiago and Felipe's corpses before he left them. By now, it was too late. He pocketed the man's cash and tipped an imaginary hat to the kid in the doorway.

"Stay out of trouble," he told him before sprinting for the river.

He reached the port to watch the freighter's tail chugging a quarter of a mile downriver. The two boys stood at the end of a dock talking with a local. Caleb sighed and marched toward them. As he neared, they spotted him.

"Rick, we missed the boat," Danny announced.

Dumb statement, Caleb thought, since he could see for himself that the freighter was leaving them.

"This man offered to drive us out to the ship," Deke explained.

The individual in question was about the same age as Thiago, and Caleb didn't trust him. He exuded an aura that suggested to Corsair he'd take advantage of the Americans' desperation.

"Sir, can you ferry us?" Deke asked him.

"Of course," the fellow replied. "It would cost you one hundred American dollars."

Deke nodded, reaching into his pack. "Shit, they took my money."

"Mine, too," Danny admitted. "At least you got your clothes back."

The local shifted his gaze from Deke to Danny and then to Caleb. He folded his arms, waiting.

Just then, sirens started wailing.

"We might be out of luck, boys," Caleb said.

"The cops?" Danny questioned. "They can help us."

The boat owner laughed under his breath, and Caleb shook his head. "No, I bet they are going to take offense." He turned to the man. "I have 250 reals to ferry us now."

As he listened to the sirens, the man suggested, "You sound like you want to leave right away. The police might prefer to chat with you. Are you worth more to them?"

Danny glared at him. "Dude, they tried to kidnap us."

"Ah, ransom," the man replied with a knowing smile.

Caleb groaned and hit the guy in the face. The blow stunned him, but he was a large, muscular man. One blow didn't drop him.

So Corsair punched him again. This time, the strike felled the local like he was a sycamore.

"Which one is his boat?" he asked the two boys.

"We don't know," they replied together.

Caleb glanced over his shoulder at the sound of the siren and let out a string of curse words.

3

————

Lee Hubbard climbed down the stairs from the jet. The tarmac at the Phillip SW Goldson International Airport emanated waves of heat. The Belizean sun blinded her as she reached the bottom of the steps.

A flight attendant nodded to her. "*Gracias.* Thank you for flying with us," she told the OOC agent.

Lee Hubbard didn't want to be back in Belize. She thought Corsair hadn't gotten out of South America, although it had been two weeks since anyone had spotted the former assassin. Now, her boss demanded that she return to Belize City.

Lee knew why Carl Winston required her presence there. First, he was pissed at her. She'd missed Corsair in Cartagena by hours. The ex-Office of Compliance agent had left a mark on the city, though. A group of police officers had been gunned down in a firefight. Word had filtered through the ranks of Colombia's police force, suggesting the cops were dirty. Several young women had claimed the cops held them prisoner, forcing them into prostitution.

That Caleb Saunders killed them all failed to surprise her. The more she chased Corsair, the more she learned of the moral compass he carried. Based on his work in the OOC, that guidepost was not present until after he faked his death. Lee Hubbard suspected domesticity had mellowed Caleb, but her girlfriend kept telling Lee that it was the man's deceased wife who'd inspired him to be better.

It all remained irrelevant and theoretical until she caught up to him. Winston, the head of the Office of Compliance, now wanted Lee back on the trail of Corsair's daughter and protégé. Since Lee hadn't told him that she'd found Khloe Evans, Winston ordered her to continue the hunt in Belize.

While Lee thought for certain that Caleb Saunders hadn't left South America, his exact location was still unknown. Winston's point was valid. Once Corsair got off that continent, his next stop would be wherever Amanda Harrod was.

If she was in Belize, then Caleb Saunders would return here.

How should she approach Saunders? When she reached out to Khloe, she'd offered something of a truce to Caleb. She only needed whatever evidence Caleb Saunders knew about Carl Winston. If she pressed again or somehow clued the OOC's fugitive squad into Khloe's whereabouts, any chance of wooing Caleb Saunders to her side was gone.

That required her to play the part for Winston, to look like she was searching for clues without pointing Khloe Evans and Amanda Harrod out to the team. Yet, she needed to make certain Khloe didn't bolt, causing Lee to lose the only lead she had on Corsair.

She saw Pendleton when she came out of the airport entrance. Lee couldn't remember his first name, and ever since she first met him in Mexico City, she could only picture the rat from *Charlotte's Web*. That the fugitive squad's leader sounded like Paul Lynde didn't help.

"Deputy Director," Pendleton greeted Lee.

Despite being in the position for over a year, her title unsettled Lee. She didn't revel in labels like Winston did. He wanted to be called "Director Winston," even by her, his deputy. Since Carl Winston neglected to return the courtesy, calling her only "Lee" or "Hubbard," she replied in kind.

"Agent Pendleton," she responded.

"No luck in Colombia?" the agent inquired.

She gave a half-smile. Of course there had been no luck. Otherwise, Lee wouldn't have returned to Central America. Instead, she would be on a plane with Corsair to Washington. The smugness that Pendleton put into the question irked her more, though. It was part of the culture Carl Winston cultivated in the Office of Compliance. He wanted his agents hungry and desperate to be the ones to make any headway. It created a back-stabbing environment, and Lee found both the office culture and the professional outcomes unsatisfactory. In her opinion, rewarding teamwork brought the members together. They would share resources and cover more ground.

Of course, it was up to Carl Winston, who had leveled up to a class-ten micromanager. That made sense to Lee. He had too many illegal activities flowing through the OOC to allow even one other person access. Better for Winston to route everything through him.

"What have you uncovered here?" she asked without responding to his query.

"We thoroughly searched the house we found," Pendleton replied. "We discovered some prints, but so far we haven't matched them. Not Corsair or anyone in the databases."

"Not surprising," Lee remarked. "The person who operated out of that house has been thriving outside the system for a long time."

"What makes you so sure?" Pendleton asked sharply.

"Corsair approached him," Lee replied.

"That doesn't mean he didn't make a mistake," Pendleton argued. "Everyone does at some point."

Lee nodded. "True, but people like Corsair make a lot fewer than the average criminal. I've been studying Corsair for a while, and he has always been meticulous about who he affiliates himself. The forger in this house must have been good for Corsair to come to him."

"Saunders might be desperate," Pendleton countered.

"Even when he's desperate, he's still careful," Lee explained.

"Bullshit," Pendleton barked. "Everyone makes a mistake."

"That they do," Lee agreed. "The problem, as I stated before, is that Corsair doesn't make a lot of them. That means we have to be so good that when he does, we actually catch it."

"We are," Pendleton defended.

"You haven't caught one yet."

"This guy turned him in," Pendleton snapped. "That sounds to me like Corsair messed up coming to him."

Lee climbed into Pendleton's rented Toyota. The other agent got behind the wheel.

"Are you staying at our hotel?" he asked.

"Yeah," she replied.

"I think we're going to track Corsair sooner rather than

later," Pendleton bragged. "Director Winston believes his daughter is still in Belize. Once we find her, we'll get him."

"Don't be so sure," Lee reminded him. "I've seen first-hand what that man can do to protect his daughter. Getting between him and her would be more dangerous than a mama grizzly and her cub."

"Psh," Pendleton scoffed. "He's running out of options."

Lee Hubbard shook her head. "That could be the mistake you make."

"He has nobody to turn to," Pendleton considered. "I've studied his records. We're covering every contact the man made as an agent. He'll show up at one of them."

"Or he'll show up like he did here to someone who's nowhere on our radar."

Pendleton let out a frustrated sigh. "Whoever this guy is, I guarantee we know him. We will find him in the files somewhere."

Lee marveled at the mindset of agents who had never been undercover in the field. To them, everything was by the book. Field operatives, however, improvised. Even if their superiors proved trustworthy, they took steps to protect themselves—stash houses, secret accounts, back-up plans. Most hitters had a strategy in place in case things turned south.

And those were the ones who colored inside the lines. For every patriotic agent toeing the line, there was another manipulating the system. Those who set up protocols for any contingency.

Plus, no one knew what Corsair had done during his decade-long hiatus. They could track the movements of Thomas and Audrey Harrod, but if Lee had been Corsair, she would have established a complete history for all four members of his family. They presumed he already had another alias ready for Amanda Harrod.

If Corsair had made a mistake, it was protecting Khloe Evans. Once Lee had found the forger's house in Belize, she suspected Corsair's reason for visiting was to establish a new identity for Khloe. The girl had escaped the Cincinnati mob with her own name, and while the mafia didn't have the resources of the OOC, they had eventually tracked her to Puerto Vallarta. Had it not been for Caleb Saunders's intervention, Khloe Evans would be a random American killed while on vacation.

Lee suspected the forger had planted the fingerprints that Pendleton's team found. Given the tech they'd found in the house, this wasn't a fly-by-night forger. This was a master criminal who bailed. A few false leads had bought the man extra time to get away.

But he had reported to the OOC. It was an overnight call on a non-recorded line, but the message was that Corsair was coming to Belize to kill him.

Like Pendleton, Lee had studied every job Corsair pulled. She compared them to the people he had killed since resurfacing. If the forger thought Corsair planned to kill him, then Lee suspected that was because he'd double-crossed Caleb Saunders.

It explained why Caleb Saunders was on the run in South America. Lee surmised that might be what the forger was worried about. He'd set Corsair up as a target, but when the former agent escaped, the forger realized his mistake. By calling in the cavalry in the form of the Office of Compliance, this man hoped he could either protect himself or buy time.

To Lee, both options were only wasted time. If Corsair planned to kill him, it was inevitable.

"Looks like the OOC is paying top-notch," she remarked as Pendleton turned toward a small motel-style building with a stucco exterior and terracotta roofing tiles. Had the owners cleaned or painted the building in the last decade, it might pass for a two-star establishment. In its current condition, it would fit in some of the worst neighborhoods in D.C.

"Yeah, we have all the perks. I imagine Corsair is staying in some penthouse flat somewhere," Pendleton griped.

Lee didn't respond, although that was far too extravagant for the assassin. If that were true, tracking him would be a cinch.

"Let me get settled," Lee suggested. "Then we can gather the team leaders together."

"I've got most of them on something," Pendleton pointed out, clearly annoyed that the deputy director was now overseeing his job.

"Understood," she agreed. "Let's still do it. I want to be up-to-date, and we can strategize our next steps."

She didn't need the agent to verbalize his discontent; he smeared it across his face. However, he remained diplomatic, stating, "Yes, ma'am."

Lee hoisted her bag from the rear seat, shouldering the leather case. Her overnight luggage had become over-week luggage as her stint between Central and South America lengthened. Once she got a key to her room, she dropped the bag and dialed a number.

"You made it?" Angie asked when she answered.

"Back for round two," Lee told her girlfriend.

"Carl's roving around the offices," Angie reported. "The man has got some pent-up energy."

"He's mad I missed Corsair."

"Of course he is," Angie croaked. "He'd be completely lost without you."

"Doesn't sound accurate if I can't get near Saunders."

"You will, Lee," she said. "Believe that."

Lee never told her girlfriend that she'd encountered Khloe Evans. While she trusted Angie, Lee didn't trust that no one was ever listening. After being part of the OOC for over ten years, Lee Hubbard distrusted her bosses and the entire intelligence structure. So much in-fighting had led to mutual dislike among many department heads in the OOC along with their counterparts in the CIA, NSA, and probably even the IRS. And if Winston discovered that Lee Hubbard was in contact with the government's once top assassin, she might face charges of treason.

Or worse.

"I need you to come home soon, Lee," Angie continued. "It's getting frigid in my bed."

Lee smiled. "When I get there, I'll enjoy heating things up."

Someone knocked on her room door.

"Yes," Lee called.

"We're heading down to eleven!" Pendleton shouted through the door. "We set up a conference room there."

"On my way," Lee replied. She said into the speaker, "I gotta go, Angie."

"Love you," her girlfriend told her as she hung up the phone.

4

Mahmoud Abbas stalked down the concrete pier. It had been two weeks since he'd heard anything from Salar. Two weeks since he'd spoken to the killer Corsair on his head of security's phone.

The assassin had suggested that Salar Tolazar was dead. Not that Abbas didn't believe Corsair. On the contrary, he was aware of what awaited him on the vessel.

His agent at the port of Qatar called him a couple of hours earlier. The *Tunisian Angel* had docked half an hour earlier. The freighter left Cartagena thirteen days ago, and Abbas had tracked its progress every day online.

Mahmoud Abbas had gone through considerable effort to set up the container in the freighter. While he owned the vessel through several shell companies, he was at a loss to speed its journey along. There was only so much time to cover the ocean. No amount of coercing or demanding could move a freighter faster.

Somehow, though, the crew had shaved two days off the journey. For that, he'd reward them with a bonus.

His new security detail had been Salar's second-in-command, Omar Al-Farouqi. A former member of the Qatar Emiri Guard, Al-Farouqi marched a few feet ahead of Abbas. Three more men flanked the financier. Each guard wore a black, tailored suit and carried an FN P90 submachine gun. Underneath the Christian Dior suits, their Kevlar vests added an extra layer of protection.

"Mr. Abbas is here to inspect the cargo," Al-Farouqi told the crewman at the gangway.

The boy, no older than twenty, stared dumbfounded at the security leader.

"Let him through," Al-Farouqi demanded. His tone dropped deep as he narrowed his eyes on the young man.

"Of course," the sailor agreed, stepping out of the way.

The idiot child hadn't questioned Al-Farouqi at all. Instead, he moved to the side to allow the group through. This would have been acceptable had the man known who Abbas was. Based on the reaction, the boy wouldn't have recognized Mahmoud Abbas from Brad Pitt. That meant he allowed unknown subjects onto the vessel. It was a security breach that Al-Farouqi would follow up on at another time.

For now, his task was to ferry Abbas to the *Tunisian Angel* and allow him to inspect a container. Al-Farouqi understood what to expect. He'd been working with Salar, his superior and mentor, to arrange the shipment. It had been Al-Farouqi who'd sourced the hospital bed and drugs. Most importantly, Al-Farouqi was the one who'd found the doctor to care for Corsair during the overseas passage.

Even more important, Al-Farouqi was there when Corsair had spoken to Abbas on the phone. He'd heard the assassin's voice over the speaker when he told Abbas, "You crossed a line, Mahmoud. Now I have to come across the fucking ocean and kill you."

Another member of the crew stepped toward the group. "You cannot be here."

"Where is Captain Balar?" Abbas demanded.

"On the bridge?" the crewman replied.

"I want to see him in the cargo bay immediately."

"Sorry, who are you?" the sailor asked.

"Tell him Mr. Abbas is on his way to the hold."

This time, the name triggered recognition in the sailor, who had fifteen years on the boy at the gangplank. This man was familiar with Abbas. Most individuals in Qatar were. His moniker was on too many businesses not to be recognized. Of course, those that did not have his name on them were the ones that feared him most. Mahmoud Abbas supplied arms to people across the globe. Although most of his dealings were in Africa and the Middle East, he operated around the world.

"Yes, sir," the sailor agreed, leaving the group to find a phone to the bridge.

Abbas didn't wait for the crewman's return. He started along the corridor to a flight of metal stairs that split, going up and down from their current position.

"Sir, we don't know where the particular container is," Al-Farouqi reminded his boss.

Abbas sneered. The man disliked being in the dark about anything. Normally, something like this was a trivial affair. Abbas rarely inspected any freight these days. He paid people to do that for him. Men such as Salar and Omar managed those employees for Abbas.

This, though, was another matter. Abbas didn't expect to open the container and find his quarry. He assumed the worst. Despite that, he hoped some miracle delivered a living Corsair to him, though the man recognized the lunacy of such a thing. Still, the hatred he held for the American was visceral.

After all, Corsair had killed the arms dealer's only son. That his son had, like his father, been on the wrong side of the United States meant nothing to Abbas. After all, most of the world was on the wrong side of the United States. The foolish Americans assumed their way was the only way. The right way. They simply didn't care what people in another hemisphere did or thought as long as it benefited the damned Americans.

If it was feasible, Abbas would arm all of America's enemies with enough firepower to lay ruin to the nation of plenty. Such was an impossibility. As terrorists had learned over the last thirty years, the best they could do was instill a bit of fear into a small population of Americans. On 9/11, the people of the US had quaked—for a minute. But the attention span of the average American was a day, possibly a week. Then, they went back to their daily routine of Starbucks, *Friends*, and Big Macs. Subsequent terrorist attacks hadn't proven as effective, and they'd garnered media coverage for a few days. Only, Abbas didn't think the populace of America really paid heed.

His people monitored their media. Social accounts offered "prayers," and heated outrage broke out. But those who spoke the loudest online spat the same vitriolic statements at their own brethren as they did the terrorists and immigrants.

From his outside vantage point, Abbas predicted the United States of America was on its own fast track to destruction. Not like the fall of some countries across the globe. This wouldn't be a coup or rebellion, but a civil war. The country's political structure sharply divided it, and he prayed for a civil war that led to the government fracturing and weakening.

However, even a weakened US military outgunned the next top three countries combined.

For now, the world prayed that the split seen in America turned to violence. Let the infidels kill themselves, Abbas thought.

"Sir, thank you for coming aboard," a tall, dark man said as he came down the metal stairs, carrying a tablet.

Abbas recognized Captain Balar. Although he knew Balar by name and sight, the two had never met. The businessman nodded a greeting to the captain.

Al-Farouqi interjected, "We are looking for container B-27948."

"Of course, sir," Balar agreed. He tapped on the tablet as he searched for the box by code. "Ah, here it is. Lower hold. We wanted it out of the way of any inspections."

Abbas adjusted his chin down as he stared at the captain.

"If you'll follow me, Mr. Abbas," Balar suggested.

Al-Farouqi guided the captain to take the lead as they descended the stairs. From above, it looked as if they were dropping into a dungeon. As they continued down, the dark holds appeared lighter thanks to the fluorescent-tubed lighting casting a soft yellow glow on the bowels of the ship.

"Here it is," Balar announced, pointing at a large shipping box. "We need to move this one."

"Do it," Al-Farouqi demanded.

"Of course," Balar replied before marching to a crew member to bark an order.

It took ten minutes to move the other container out of the way. When it was clear, Al-Farouqi sent the rest of the crew away.

There was a slight hum coming from the metal box. If Al-Farouqi hadn't known that the container was equipped with an air circulator and climate control, he might not have noticed the sound. The din of the ship masked the electric fans whirring in the container.

Captain Balar cut the seal on the door and pulled up on the handle. A groan emitted from the hinges as both metal doors swung out. Light spilled from inside the box. Captain Balar and the other three security men covered their noses as the stench of rotting flesh rushed out.

Al-Farouqi looked at his boss, silently asking permission. Abbas gave him a nod, and the security chief entered the container. Bright LED lights hung from the ceiling, illuminating the interior. An empty hospital bed lay on its side next to the doctor that Al-Farouqi had met three weeks earlier.

Omar Al-Farouqi knelt by the other prone body in the box. Salar Tolazar's corpse sprawled on his stomach. The odor of decay brought bile up Al-Farouqi's throat, but the man swallowed against it, forcing it back down.

"It is Salar," he announced to his boss.

"Fucking Corsair," Abbas growled.

"Who would do this?" Balar questioned.

"No one you should concern yourself with," Al-Farouqi informed the ship's master.

"Omar, let us go," Abbas declared.

"Mr. Abbas, what do I do here?" Balar asked.

Abbas ignored the question as Omar Al-Farouqi stated, "Clean it up."

As Abbas started up the steps, he looked at his security chief. His new security chief, he corrected himself.

"Omar, we must find Corsair."

Al-Farouqi nodded.

"Ifrit," Abbas remarked.

"What, sir?"

"Find Ifrit," his boss ordered.

Al-Farouqi recognized the designation. "Ifrit" was a pseudonym for an assassin and problem-solver who had become as legendary as Corsair once was. Like the American, his real identity wasn't known. At least not by Al-Farouqi, and the security leader doubted Mahmoud Abbas knew the killer's real name, either.

"Yes, sir," Al-Farouqi confirmed.

"When you do, I want him to find Corsair's every weakness. Scour his life as this Tom Harrod and cut at him until he comes forward."

"Mr. Abbas, didn't he threaten to come for you?" Al-Farouqi asked, though he already knew the answer.

"He will," Abbas responded. "Let Ifrit welcome him when he does."

"Yes, sir."

5

____

The motor whined a high-pitched scream as it raced down the river, though "raced" was a bit of an exaggeration. The nine-horsepower outboard had a broken prop, and even at full throttle, the eight-meter flat boat wouldn't go faster than four knots. The current sped them up a couple of knots, but with the freighter already speeding down the Amazon at about fifteen knots, there was almost no chance of catching up to the ship.

"I'm sorry, Rick," Deke repeated for the eighth time since they'd pushed off the little marina in Juruti. Calling it a "marina" was on par with referring to the fishing boat's speed as racing. It was a collection of wood bolted to plastic drums.

Corsair found himself only angry with himself. They were puttering down the waterway before he realized he had half a propeller. If they went back for another boat, the Juruti police would be waiting for them.

At the moment, Corsair had no options but to continue on. He hoped that the freighter would slow for a bend in the river, and Caleb and the boys might catch up.

That glimmer of hope, though, was fading. The ship the three had booked passage on was over a mile downriver.

"We won't make it, will we?" Deke questioned.

"Not likely," Caleb answered.

"Should we return to the dock?" Danny wondered.

Caleb shook his head. "I don't think we'd have the best welcome back there."

"Surely the guy you hit could come to an agreement with us," Danny argued.

"What kind of agreement do you want to have with him?" Caleb posed.

"I bet he'd take some money," Deke suggested.

"Neither of you have any money," Caleb reminded them. "And I have the equivalent of forty dollars. Not sure what that would buy me anywhere."

"What do we do, then?" Deke asked.

"Keep going," Caleb told them. "Pray that the local police don't have a boat faster than this one."

"Think they'd arrest us?" Danny asked.

"We could call the embassy," Deke stated. "There are people there to help us."

Caleb let out a chuckle. He knew what people were like at the embassy.

"What's so funny?" Danny inquired.

"You're assuming you get to call the embassy," Caleb pointed out.

"Of course. We have rights," Danny commented.

"Not here, you don't," Caleb reminded him. "Your rights end at the American border."

"Our government won't leave us here. Remember that WNBA star? They got her out of Russia."

"She was a high-profile athlete. You two are average twenty-year-old tourists."

"Still, it has to be better than getting lost in a jungle," Deke considered.

"You ever been in a Brazilian prison?" Caleb asked.

Both boys shook their heads.

"Me either, but I guarantee it's not as nice as an American one. Do you want to spend time in Sing-Sing?"

Again, both shook their heads.

"I'll get you somewhere safe," Caleb promised.

"Look, Rick, I didn't mean to sound ungrateful," Danny told him.

Deke nodded along. "Me either. Dude, you saved us. I don't know what those guys planned to do."

"Ransom you for a hundred grand," Caleb informed them.

"To who?" Deke asked.

"Your parents, maybe."

"My folks can't pay that," Deke remarked.

"Mine either," Danny agreed. "My dad's been unemployed for a year now."

"Wouldn't have mattered," Caleb told them. "If they got the money or not, you'd end up dead."

"Shit!" Danny muttered.

"There were a bunch of them," Deke noted. "How did you do it?"

Caleb smiled. "I'm persuasive," he explained.

"Bullshit. You're some kind of badass soldier, aren't you?" Deke declared.

"If so, then you better be glad you shared your jerky with me," he retorted.

"Hell, man, I'll feed you jerky the rest of your life," Danny offered.

"How about let's get out of here first?" Caleb suggested.

"Man, take me to an ATM, and I'll buy us the biggest dinner you've ever seen," Deke promised.

"Absolutely," Danny agreed.

"I'd settle for a new motor," Caleb remarked, steering the flat-bottomed boat around a clump of flotsam drifting down the river.

"Our next stop was supposed to be Santarém," Deke commented. "That was overnight."

"It's a little over a hundred miles for us," Caleb explained. "We won't have enough gas for that."

"Shit, man," Danny groaned. "What are we going to do?"

Caleb pointed to the fishing line and gear on the floor of the boat. "Unless you still have some jerky, you two need to cobble together some fishing tackle. We'll want to eat something."

Corsair suddenly lifted his head, and both boys locked eyes with him. They all heard the sound. An engine coming from behind them. As he spun around, Caleb scanned the river. After passing the bend, Juruti was out of sight, hidden by the river's curve, yet only a few miles away.

"Help?" Deke asked.

"Remember the Brazilian prison," Caleb reminded him. "I wouldn't trust any help. Besides, chances are better that it's not the police. More likely friends of the gang that kidnapped you or the guy whose boat we stole. None of those are people I want to run into. How about you?"

Both boys shook their heads again.

"We can't outrun them," Caleb commented. "We need to beach the boat and take cover."

"Where?" Danny asked.

Corsair's eyes moved along the coast on either side of the Amazon River. This section was over three miles wide. Caleb and the boys had been motoring along the southern shore, and they'd spend over an hour trying to cross the channel to the northern bank. Longer if this motor had to fight the current at all.

Caleb turned the tiller on the outboard, directing the bow toward the southern side. A single structure stood on the banks of the river. The shack rose out of the water on wood pylons and had seen better days. The metal roof showed its age with rusty designs and curled edges.

"What about there?" Deke suggested.

"You want to hide in the only building around?" Caleb asked.

Deke let his head droop. "No, that's stupid."

Caleb pointed at an outcropping of brush. The current rushed past the mangroves growing off the muddy bank. "Over there," he stated.

"The bushes?" Danny questioned. He glanced back between the shoreline and the curve in the river behind them.

"It's an inlet," Caleb explained.

"Won't they see it, too?" Deke asked.

Caleb didn't answer. Instead, he steered toward the pass. Behind him, he watched the current masking any disturbance the motor caused in the water. Had they been traveling much faster, the wake would have been visible for several minutes. With any luck, the surface wouldn't hold their trail for long.

As they rounded the outer mangroves, the other engine sounded louder. Caleb released the throttle, which had been wide open. The struggling outboard ceased its scream. He cut the motor off, silencing the last of the noise.

The flat hull coasted over the water in the small tributary.

"Oars," Caleb announced, pointing at two paddles at the bottom of the vessel.

Deke and Danny each grabbed one and started paddling. Caleb steered the boat with the tiller as the boys stroked.

"See that brush up there?" Caleb asked.

"Yeah," Deke acknowledged.

"We're going right between them," he explained.

A minute later, branches scraped across the wooden sides, and Caleb rushed forward, jumping off the bow and landing in eight inches of water. His hands grabbed the two cleats on the front and pulled the bow deeper into the leaves. When they were far enough in, Caleb relaxed. He still stood mid-calf on the river's edge.

He turned to peer through the brush. Dry land was another three hundred feet into the growth. No way to get the boat through the foliage.

"Grab what you can carry," Caleb ordered. "Don't forget your fishing gear."

As Deke and Danny scrambled around, Caleb grabbed his pack and one oar. He pointed at a handle jutting out from under the seat. "Danny, right there."

Danny reached down, removing a filet knife trapped in the crevice. The other outboard engine grew much closer, its sound echoing over the water's surface.

"We need to move," Caleb urged. He hoped the boat was out of sight, but he knew it wasn't invisible. If their pursuers noticed the same inlet, they might investigate. He had no intention of being close by if they did.

Corsair pushed through the brush as Deke and Danny followed. "Keep quiet," Caleb whispered. "Acoustics can be tricky on water."

As if in response to Caleb, voices drifted over the river.

He couldn't understand what was being said, but it was Portuguese. The people in the boat were talking over the outboard, and the sound waves traveled to them.

"What did they say?" Danny rasped.

"Don't know," Caleb replied. "Keep moving."

The boys behind him obeyed. Other than the occasional word from the other boat and the motor as it came closer, Caleb only registered the sloshing of their feet through the river.

"Aren't their crocodiles around here?" Deke asked after a few minutes.

Caleb shook his head. "Some caiman. Those won't mess with you."

"Yeah, dude. It's the anacondas you gotta worry about," Danny suggested.

"Shh," Caleb snapped.

The outboard motor sounded closer, and Caleb turned back. He raised his hand, signaling the others to get down. The other boat was in the inlet. Its operator dropped the vessel to a crawl as they maneuvered through the mouth of the tributary.

Corsair pointed southwest, motioning for them to take the lead. Deke nodded and waved for Danny to follow him. Caleb mouthed the words, "Stay quiet." Both acknowledged him with a nod.

When they were out of sight, Caleb took off his pack and hung it on a branch. He fished in the compartment until his fingers wrapped around the cold steel of the Glock 19 he'd brought from Cartagena. He removed the gun and chambered a round.

"They had to come in here," a voice said in Portuguese. "They couldn't get that far."

"What if they made it to their ship?" another asked.

"No way. That junk boat of Josia's would never catch up to it."

"Where are they?"

"Over there. That broken limb."

Caleb winced. He hadn't looked for any snapped branches. Stupid mistake on his part. Not that he'd had a lot of time, but he still regretted the oversight.

"What about that guy?" an unfamiliar voice asked. "You saw what he did to Thiago and Felipe?"

"Well, you two let him do it."

"Lucas, you weren't there. The man took both down like it was nothing."

"Idiots," Lucas complained. "Pull over there. There's something in the brush."

"It's Josia's boat."

"Find them. We'll make them pay for Thiago."

"Don't forget Felipe."

"Of course," Lucas replied. "Remember, we can still ransom the boys. Kill the other one, though."

"Right," a nervous voice muttered.

Caleb stayed low and moved east. He couldn't see the boat he'd pulled into the brush or Lucas's boat, but he knew he wasn't that far from it. As he circled around, he listened. The three men had fallen silent. Now that the outboard was off, they weren't shouting over the din.

They also believed the three Americans were on the run. As locals, they likely knew the area better than Caleb, but if they were like the rest of the bunch, that was the only advantage they had.

He noticed the first movement through the stalks—the rustle of branches. One voice grunted, followed by a hush from Lucas.

Corsair stayed crouched. The Amazonian water covered

him from the waist down. His right knee sank into the muddy bank. With the Glock extended toward the sounds of their hunters, Caleb waited until they moved through the brush.

He moved after them with slow, deliberate motions. If he made the slightest splash, he would give away his location. Caleb assumed the men were armed since they'd chosen to pursue the Americans into the jungle. If they weren't armed, the odds were an even three-on-three.

Of course, that assumed that all three men were of equal strength. Corsair had already proven he could take on a small group alone. For that reason alone, Caleb knew Lucas and his goons wouldn't have come out here unprepared.

Caleb's feet stepped in short strides, never coming above the river's surface for fear of creating drips or sloshes as he walked. He spotted the three men now through the brush. Or, at least, he saw their legs. They didn't take the same care that he did as they walked. None of them were loud, but they moved toward dry land with some hapless haste.

None of them expected to be flanked. As far as they were concerned, the river to their backs represented safety. Corsair could stand up and line up three kill shots before they realized the first gunshot sounded. Had he equipped his Glock with a silencer, it would have been the smart play. Corsair could drag the bodies away from the boats, retrieve Deke and Danny, and take Lucas's faster vessel. All of that without alerting the two young Americans that he was a dangerous killer.

However, the gunshots would be hard to mask or deny.

No, he decided to do it quietly. From his vantage, he watched the three men spread out. They were far more familiar with the terrain. Caleb wagered that Deke and Danny were still together. If the two Americans had split up, it would increase their chances of not crossing paths with the three newcomers. He watched as the three predators were doing just that, breaking up to suvey more of the area.

Caleb chose to follow the man on the left as he ventured off to the side. When the other two were out of sight, he closed on his quarry. Close-quarter kills were tricky, especially in a field like this where one couldn't blend in with passersby. This kind had to be fast and quiet—two things difficult to accomplish together.

The sun was already setting, and twilight was mere minutes away. If he waited a few more minutes, the sky would darken, casting shadows around and providing ample places to meld into darkness. For now, he had to deal with the present. He was within five feet of his target.

Corsair popped up behind the man, caught him around the neck with his forearm, and dragged him down with a regrettable splash.

"Marco?" Lucas called.

Caleb pressed the barrel of the Glock against Marco's temple. "Tell him you just fell, or I'll kill you," Corsair rasped in his ear.

"I'm okay, just tripped!" Marco called out immediately. His eyes widened as they struggled to see Corsair's face.

The assassin wrenched the man's neck. A crack resounded as the vertebrae separated. Marco slumped out of Corsair's arm, sliding into the water. A hunting knife dangled from a sheath on his belt. Corsair plucked it from Marco's side, leaving the sheath attached to the man.

On the prowl again, Corsair slid the Glock into the back of his waistband. The knife offered a quieter means to dispatch the men. Now that the other two spread out, he picked up the pace to skirt around to the man on the far right.

"Marco?" Lucas called. "Where did he go? Do you see him, Leon?"

"Marco?" Leon tried to shout, but Lucas shushed him.

"Not so loud," Lucas warned.

Caleb slipped behind Leon. Even from his cover, Caleb watched the Brazilian turning nervously in a circle as he searched for his friend.

"Lucas, maybe we should head back," he suggested with a twinge of nervousness.

"No," the leader snapped. "We need to find Marco."

Corsair erupted from the brush like a deadly jack-in-the-box. He grabbed Leon, pulling him into the water as the blade of the knife sliced across the man's throat. Leon landed face-down in the water, a gurgle of bubbles escaping through his torn neck.

"Leon!" Lucas cried. "You bastard! I have a gun."

Corsair started moving before the knife had finished opening Leon's throat. He didn't care now about splashing. In fact, he hoped the sound unnerved Lucas, sending him into a panic.

In Corsair's experience, men like these preyed on weaker individuals. They used fear to control others, and when the tables turned on them, they had no means to process the terror striking at their heart.

Lucas was no different. Two gunshots echoed over the water. He wasn't shooting at Caleb because he couldn't see him. Caleb knew Deke and Danny should be hidden and out of sight, so Caleb suspected the shots were an attempt to reestablish control.

Of course, he thought Caleb was unarmed, or at least not equipped with a gun. After all, in most matches, a gun beat a knife. But without the Glock, this match still wasn't even.

Lucas's panting rippled across the water. He was in panic mode, and that allowed for more mistakes. Caleb waited until he heard Lucas turn away from him. The heavy breathing muffled as the Brazilian faced the other direction.

Corsair rose up slowly from the brush. "Hey!" he called.

Lucas spun around to see the barrel of the nine-millimeter bearing down on him. Corsair cocked his head and pulled the trigger. Lucas fell as the bullet struck him in the face.

Caleb found his pack, put the gun and knife back inside it, and shouldered the bag before following the trail Deke and Danny had left behind.

6

———

Caleb sat up, sweat pouring down his forehead. A half-moon brightened the heavens, dimming a few stars around it. The rest of the sky glittered with the Milky Way. Caleb coughed, feeling his head pound with each hack.

The silhouette of Lucas's boat stood out on the bank below them. After retrieving Deke and Danny, the three took the larger craft and continued downriver. They hadn't spoken about what happened, but both Deke and Danny had paused when they passed Lucas's lifeless figure stretched face-down in the shallow water.

They made camp in the dark about ten miles from where they left the local thugs. Caleb put Deke on first watch, ordering him to wake Danny after two hours. They were to rouse him two hours later.

His head squeezed, and Caleb tried to pinch the bridge of his nose to ease the pressure. But it wasn't just a headache. The excessive perspiration suggested he had a fever. A high one at that.

"Rick, you okay?" Danny asked in the dark.

"Got a fever," he muttered.

"Shit," Danny snapped as Caleb collapsed to the ground, too weak to hold up his head. Danny appeared over him. "Do you need some water?" he questioned.

Caleb nodded. Every motion was like an endurance sport.

Danny started pouring water into his open mouth. Caleb had not realized how thirsty he was until the first drops landed in his mouth. His parched lips soaked up the liquid, and he tried to gulp at it.

"Slow down, Rick," Danny urged. "You'll get too much."

Danny placed the back of his hand against Caleb's forehead. "Damn, man. You're burning up."

Caleb tried to respond, but his tongue failed to function. Through the fog of fever, a single word resonated in his mind. "Malaria."

It could have been dengue fever, something Caleb had contracted over two decades earlier in the Congo. It was a strange segue for his mind to give him. Danny's face morphed into that of the doctor who'd treated him so many years ago. If he hadn't stumbled across a group of medical missionaries, Caleb would not have survived that disease.

"Deke, wake up," Danny barked to his friend. "Rick's real sick."

Caleb chuckled, or he thought about chuckling. The phrase "Rick's real sick" echoed through his mind. It came to him in a sing-song voice belted out by Gonzo from the Muppets.

The character was Jackson's favorite Muppet. The first time Caleb played *The Muppet Movie* for Jackson, his son cackled at the scene where Gonzo's plumbing truck lands on top of Kermit and Fozzie's Studebaker.

"Wait till you meet Animal," Caleb muttered.

"What did you say, Rick?"

"If you like Gonzo, you'll love Animal."

"He's funny, Daddy," Jackson replied when Animal exploded into a giant. "But Gonzo's the funniest."

Caleb ruffled Jackson's hair, and his boy nuzzled against him.

"Honey, you don't look good," Audrey told him.

"Think it's malaria?" Deke suggested, wiping his face with a wet cloth.

"Hell if I know," Danny remarked.

"It's nothing," Caleb muttered to his wife.

"It's not nothing, man," Deke corrected. "Those bastards took my quinine."

"Want some soup?" Audrey offered, stroking Caleb's clammy cheek.

"Please," Caleb moaned.

"Please what, man?" Danny inquired.

"I'll take the soup," Caleb replied.

Danny looked to Deke, who responded, "He's hallucinating."

"We need to take him to the hospital," Danny stated.

"Dude, there are no hospitals around here. We could get to Santarém, but that's a long way downriver."

"Here you go, honey," Audrey whispered, leaning over him with a spoon. Caleb opened his mouth for her to feed him.

"What's he doing?" Danny wondered.

"Thank you, Audrey," the assassin mumbled.

"Who's Audrey?" Deke asked.

"Could be his wife?" Danny suggested.

"Rick, who's Audrey?"

"She's wonderful," he rasped.

"I think we need to move him to the boat," Deke said. "If he gets worse, it might be more difficult."

"Should we head on downriver?" Danny wondered.

Deke shrugged. "I don't know," he admitted.

"Have to keep moving," Caleb groaned.

"What Rick?"

"Can't stay here," he moaned. "Water, please."

Danny poured more water into his mouth. Caleb lapped at the stream.

"Slow down, Danny," Deke warned.

"I'm trying," the other boy retorted.

"Can't let them find me," Caleb told them. "They'll kill us."

"Who will?" Deke asked. "The guys from Juruti?"

"The OOC," he muttered. "Audrey, they're coming for us."

"What's the OOC?" Danny asked.

Deke shrugged. "See what he has in his pack. He might have brought some meds."

Danny reached for Caleb's rucksack.

"No," Caleb moaned, reaching for the boy. "You can't." His hand flopped down.

"What do I do?" Danny asked, digging into the man's bag.

"If he has anything in there we can use, we need to," Deke insisted.

Danny flipped the backpack open and pulled out some clothes. The hunting knife that Caleb took from Marco bounced out and landed on the ground. Deke picked up the eight-inch blade.

"Shit," Danny said as he removed the Glock.

"I knew he must have shot that other guy," Deke blurted out.

"Rick, why do you have a gun?" Danny asked the sick man.

"Dangerous," Caleb whispered.

"What's so dangerous, babe?" Audrey questioned him.

"They'll be looking for Amanda," he informed her.

"I thought you were protecting her," she scolded him.

"I'm sorry, Audrey," he replied, tears running from the corners of his eyes. "Khloe is watching her."

Audrey nodded. "I like her," she assured her husband.

"Who is Khloe, Rick?" Deke asked.

He shook his head. "No one," he lied.

"Dude's got some secrets, Deke," Danny pointed out.

"No shit," Deke retorted. "What do we do? It sounds like someone's after him."

"We take him somewhere to get help," Danny answered.

"They might be after us, too," Deke reminded him.

"Leave me," Caleb mumbled. "Don't let them find you."

"Who are they?" Danny asked.

"He'll go after Amanda," Caleb said.

"Who?" Deke pressed.

"Rick, who are you?"

"Rick's real sick," he sang off-key in a scratchy voice. "Rick's real sick. Rick's real sick."

Caleb tried to roll away from Danny, and his hands pushed him to his feet. The assassin stood still in the moonlight, wavering. "I'll cover you," he told the two Americans.

"Cover us?" Deke repeated.

"Do you hear them?" Caleb asked.

"What?" Deke implored.

"Choppers. Winston's sending a kill team. We have to get ready."

Caleb's legs buckled, and the former government agent

dropped to his knees before teetering to the ground in a sweaty heap.

"Who the fuck is this guy?" Deke stammered. "We need to go."

"We can't leave him," Danny repeated.

"Look, if people are after him, we should protect ourselves," Deke argued.

"He came for us," Danny reminded him. "He's out here because he got off the ship to save our asses. Can you live with yourself if we left him here?"

"He killed those guys back there," Deke pointed out.

"They would have killed us," his friend pointed out.

"Who is he?" Deke wondered again.

"Our friend?" Danny suggested.

Deke curled his lip before nodding. "Yeah," he admitted.

"Let's get him to the boat," Danny told Deke. "You can rest a little longer, and then we set out at first light."

"Some sleep might help him," Deke agreed.

"Not likely," Danny remarked. "If it's malaria, he needs treatment."

"They seem like good boys," Audrey said to Caleb.

He nodded with considerable effort.

"Tom, you need to listen to me," Audrey commanded. "Get to Amanda before Carl Winston does."

"I will," he vowed. "I swear I'll protect her."

Audrey touched his skin. Her palm left a cool impression on his cheek. She wiped a strand of sweaty hair from his forehead.

"I miss you," he mumbled.

"Why?" she asked. "I'm still here."

Caleb stretched his arm up to her. "I can't touch you."

"Do you think I'd leave you?"

More tears dribbled down his face. "It was my fault. I should have saved you. Saved Jackson."

She shook her head. "You did what you needed to," she assured him.

"Rick, are you with us?" Danny's voice interrupted his vision, and Audrey faded into a mist.

"We have to get you to the boat," Deke urged. "We'll wrap up. Try to fight the fever as best we can."

"What if we dip him in the water?" Danny asked.

"How would that help?" Deke asked.

"I don't know," Danny admitted. "I remember an episode of *Dr. Quinn* I watched with my grandparents as a kid. They put people with high fevers on ice to reduce their temperature. We don't want his brain to cook."

Four arms hooked under his armpits, lifting him off the dirt. He kicked his feet, trying to find the ground.

"Dude, calm down," Danny urged. "It's us."

"Tom, they are friends," Audrey's voice reminded him.

"Where did you go?" he asked her.

"We're here," Deke assured him.

"I'm here," Audrey responded. "Let them take care of you."

"What about Winston?" he mumbled. "He'll kill them."

"Who the fuck is Winston?" Deke questioned.

"Don't worry about it," Danny ordered. "Let's get him set up, and I'll keep watch for another hour or so."

"Think the guys from Juruti are still after us?" Deke asked nervously.

"Man, Rick killed them," Danny answered.

"Rick's real sick," Caleb sang as he shuffled between his traveling companions. He lolled his head to look at Danny. "Rick's real sick."

"It's okay, Rick."

Caleb swung his neck in a large, slow arc. "I'm not Rick."

"Who are you?" Deke asked as they reached the river bank.

"Everybody," Caleb answered. "Whoever I need to be."

"That's not an answer," Deke admonished.

"Tell them who you are," Carl Winston demanded. He folded his arms across his immaculate suit.

"It's against protocol," Caleb argued.

"They are on your team," Winston reminded him.

"But you aren't," Caleb snapped. He pulled at the boys' grip, but in his weakened state, he didn't break their hold.

"I am," Camille Dubois assured him.

He nodded. "I'm sorry, Minuit."

"He's all over the board," Danny muttered as they stretched him out in the bottom of the fishing boat. "Go get those extra clothes he had. We can cover him up. Make a pillow or something for him."

"It's water under the bridge, Corsair," Camille Dubois promised, fading into a fog.

"Sleep, man," Danny urged Caleb. "We've got your back."

Caleb's eyes blinked, trying to lock onto the face speaking. "Audrey!" Caleb called. "Audrey!"

His voice weakened as two hands lifted his head. It settled on something soft. "Audrey," he whispered again before letting his eyelids close.

7

Khloe Evans stared at the draft folder in her Nomail.com account. It had not changed in days, which meant Caleb had not checked it. She opened the email and typed an addendum, adding the date and time. Even if he didn't reply, she tried to add a note every day so that when he did get online, he'd have the most updated information she could provide.

Not that what she was including was that crucial. Today, she noted they were running low on groceries. It had been several weeks since Caleb had left for Colombia, and the cupboards had been stocked with over a week's worth of food. As time stretched out, though, she found the cupboards growing bare.

Caleb had issued strict instructions, and she worked to follow them. She and Amanda stayed in the house, only leaving for brief strolls around the bungalow's small back-yard. They avoided the beach, even though it was steps away. Too many people. As Caleb had pointed out to Khloe, places like that were easy to disappear in, but also ideal locations for others to monitor.

"The OOC could tap any security feeds and run facial recognition on it," he informed her. "Do your best to stay off any cameras."

"But they're everywhere," Khloe reminded him.

"True, but most people don't network their cameras. Municipal surveillance systems, like those at the port or beach, will likely connect to the police or another state agency. The OOC can access those."

"What about when we leave Belize? Can't they track us that way, then?"

Caleb nodded. "The issue is they have to network those systems. We'll find someplace where the government doesn't allow the United States unfettered access."

"I figured they could hack into any system," Khloe admitted.

"They can, but the last thing anyone wants is an international incident," he explained. "If we stay hidden and change our appearance, they will struggle to locate us."

However, as she stared at the dwindling supplies, she realized she had to go get something. Amanda was already experiencing cabin fever. The girl had grown accustomed to playing outside and visiting the beaches in Mexico. Now, she didn't understand that leaving the house might put them both in danger.

"Caleb, what do I do?" she asked the email provider on her screen.

Unfortunately but not unexpectedly, it failed to respond. To venture out, Khloe needed to ensure nobody recognized her. That meant not taking Amanda with her. But could she leave a three-year-old home alone?

The answer to that was no—in most cases. However, an American woman and a toddler were the sort of combo the OOC and maybe even the mafia were looking for.

The last time Caleb contacted her, he was trying to get out of Colombia. He hadn't given her the details, but said he'd been double-crossed. He'd urged her to stay out of sight.

"An old enemy tracked me to Belize," he explained. "They have resources as good or better than the OOC."

"Who is it?" she asked.

"It doesn't matter. Just trust no one," he replied.

That had been their last interaction. Caleb never gave her details about how he was escaping. She didn't ask. After only a few months with the man, she had developed a strong sense of operational awareness. The best way to avoid leaking plans to the enemy was to ensure nobody knew what they were. Caleb gave her enough information to protect Amanda and assure the girl her father remained safe. Khloe only let his daughter know he was okay and still traveling.

One thing nagged at Khloe. Was this life the best for Amanda? She was young and impressionable. While she might only barely remember her mother and brother, as she grew older, the constant running and fear would wear on the child. Or she could be totally fine. Kids bounced back from adversity with amazing tenacity.

For the present, though, she needed a solid plan. How had her situation changed so that just a trip to buy groceries required counter-surveillance and escape routes? It didn't matter. She was where she was. If it hadn't been for Caleb, she'd be dead. And to save her, he'd sacrificed his and Amanda's safety.

Khloe closed the Nomail.com site and opened Google Maps. The nearest market was a small mom-and-pop shop five blocks away. A straight path from the rental house they lived in to the store took only fifteen minutes, according to

Google. However, that was fifteen minutes on the street, coming and going. She needed a less direct route that kept her off the roads as much as possible.

She traced the streets from her front step to the shop. As she zoomed in on the area, Khloe noted a few alleys between homes. Each property had about a six-foot easement. Her fingernail trailed through lanes and streets, drawing an imaginary line to the store. It would take her twice as long with the double-backs, but she'd only be on the street for half a block each way. The roads here didn't have traffic cameras, but a lot of the homes had security systems. Khloe thought those would count as the cameras Caleb considered offline.

Amanda played in her room. She possessed only a few toys. Caleb had found her some blocks and old Matchbox cars at a church sale after they arrived in Belize.

If Khloe left when Amanda went down for a nap, she'd have about an hour before the girl woke up. It wouldn't give her much time at the shop, but it should do.

Khloe walked into the back, where she heard Amanda making car noises. Those had become the most prominent sound effects, and while Khloe appreciated the child's imagination, the constant *vroom-vroom-crash* noises were tiresome. If the store had a baby doll or other toy, she might bring it home to the girl.

"Hey, girl," Khloe called from the doorway.

"Hi, Khlo," the child replied, dropping the last syllable in her name.

"You need to clean up, sweetie," Khloe informed the child.

"But I wanna play more," Amanda complained.

"Sweetie, that's all you do," she informed her. "If you take a nap, we can play when you wake up."

Amanda wrinkled her nose in disgust. "I'm not sleepy. I can be a big girl."

"You know the rules," Khloe reminded her.

"Hmph!" the child threw the miniature sports car on the ground. "I don't wanna."

"You want to be in time-out?" Khloe asked her.

Amanda Harrod's face sank. "No, Khlo."

"Good. Then clean up. If you do a good job, I'll put *Moana* on for you."

The rental house's movie choices for kids were limited to *Moana, The Little Mermaid,* and *Tangled.* Since Caleb had left, they'd watched *Moana* at least twenty times. *The Little Mermaid* and *Tangled* tied for second, with about fifteen rewatches.

"'Kay," the girl answered. Her mouth turned up from a frown to a smile.

Khloe returned to the small galley-style kitchen. She had a piece of paper with a list she'd been making. Without knowing how stocked this market was, she made a broad list of groceries. With any luck, she would return with enough food to make meals for the next week. In the back of the freezer, she found a carton of chocolate mint ice cream. Khloe opened the container and flipped it upside down over a large mixing bowl before returning to Amanda's room.

"Okay, kiddo, hop in bed," she ordered.

"'Kay," she replied.

"You know the rules," she said to the girl.

Amanda nodded. "Stay in the bed until *Moana* ends."

"Are you going to cry out for me?" Khloe asked.

Amanda shook her head.

"Good girl. I might be outside, so if you don't hear me, that's okay."

Amanda gave a nod, and Khloe turned on the small flat-screen television mounted on the corner of the ceiling. The DVD player sat beneath it on a shelf. Khloe thought that was a smart place for it since it kept the device out of Amanda's reach. She'd already learned how independent the kid could be. Left to her own devices, Amanda would be staring at the screen all day.

The famous Disney logo popped up on the screen, and Khloe bent over to kiss Amanda's forehead. When she turned off the light and closed the door, she returned to the kitchen. It wouldn't take Amanda long to fall asleep. It rarely did. Keeping the child asleep was another matter. The girl didn't seem to need as much rest as Khloe thought she did. Sure, she'd get grumpy, but she was always manageable.

Khloe decided Amanda had gotten that from her father. Even when Caleb was here, he never seemed to sleep more than an hour or two.

In the kitchen, she picked up the ice cream container. The frozen green goo slid out of its package, plopping into the stainless-steel mixing bowl. A plastic zipped bag tumbled out from under the ice cream, leaving an impression in the minty mess. Khloe removed the sticky pouch, dropping it in the sink before putting the bowl with the softening ice cream in the freezer. After turning on the faucet, she rinsed melted ice cream off the plastic before unrolling it on the counter.

Stacks of cash came out of the bag. She sorted it, setting the packets of American hundred-dollar bills apart. In total, there was about fifty thousand USD. Another bundle contained Belize dollars. It held the equivalent of five thousand USD already converted into Belizean bills.

She peeled a thousand Belize dollars from the stack. It was far more than she expected to need. Once she put that money aside, she wrapped all the remaining funds in a dish rag and set out the bag to dry. Khloe pushed the rag containing the rest of the money into the back of the linen drawer, where it would stay until she returned.

With cash in her pocket, she cracked the door to Amanda's room. The girl, as predicted, was sleeping with her mouth open while Moana sang about her island. Khloe slipped inside and restarted the movie. It didn't buy her a lot of time, but if Amanda obeyed, she should still be in bed when Khloe returned.

The woman locked the house up and walked out the front door. She looked up and down the lane. It was mid-afternoon. Most locals were working, while tourists were out enjoying the day on the water or sightseeing.

With the mental map in her head, Khloe crossed the street toward the easement behind the residence on the corner. As she traversed the invisible trail she'd drawn in her mind, she repeated a mantra to herself.

Be casual. Look normal.

The hike took twenty-five minutes, and Khloe breathed easier when she stepped into the shop. The inside of the market looked more like someone's house than a grocery store. In fact, she was certain it had been a home in the not-so-distant past. Handmade wooden shelves lined the walls with an old Häagen-Dazs ice cream freezer and another labeled Choco-Taco. Time had peeled away the "taco" part of the name.

Behind the counter, a pair of women sat talking. They gave her a smile, and she returned the gesture as they continued their conversation. The older of the two was stitching a garment, and Khloe paused to examine it. The woman was repairing a tear, not sewing a new piece of clothing.

She picked up a handbasket and started around the

store. If she hurried, she should make it just in time for the *Moana* credits.

Halfway through her list, she found several things the store didn't have. Instead, she made do with cans of ravioli that bore a Latino substitute for Chef Boyardee. The shop had a nice supply of eggs, milk, and meat—although the type of meat was uncertain. While her Spanish had improved over the six months she lived in Puerto Vallarta, Khloe admitted how grateful she was that the official language in Belize was English. Had she tried to pass herself off as fluent in Spanish, she worried that would pin a brighter target on her.

The door opened, and a pair of clean-cut men walked inside. Khloe saw them from the other room, and a warning flashed in her mind. She stepped closer to the small coffee section, crouching down to examine the bottom shelf.

"Pardon me," one of the gentlemen said to the women at the counter.

"Yes?" the older woman asked.

"We are looking for a mother and her daughter," he announced.

Khloe's ears pricked up.

"Why?" the older shopkeeper wondered with a wariness in her tone.

"Their family is searching for them. They believe they are living near here."

"American?" she inquired.

"Yes. They may be with a male in his late thirties. The lady would be in her twenties."

"Lots of Americans down here," the seamstress pointed out.

"This is a toddler with her."

"Is her daughter?" she inquired.

"Uh, yeah," the man stammered.

Khloe closed her eyes and sucked in a breath.

"I've not seen anyone," she told them.

"If you do, would you contact me? There's a reward."

"How much?" the younger one wondered. Her voice sounded hungry.

"Two thousand American dollars."

"I'll look around," the second shopkeeper assured him, and the older woman scoffed.

"We thank you for your time," the man said.

Almost as quickly as they entered the shop, the pair left. Khloe grabbed a package of coffee, tossing it in her basket. She hastened through the store, grabbing more items while searching for products that didn't give away that she might have children. She stopped at a rack of stuffed bears in "Belize" shirts. With a sigh, she walked past them to the counter.

"That's a lot of money they are offering," she remarked to the two women.

"They liars," the older woman noted.

"Why do you say that?"

"Police," she explained.

Khloe nodded.

"I don't care. If I find them, I'll turn them in," the younger clerk announced.

"Can't blame you," Khloe admitted, trying to fight the tremor in her throat. "May I see his name?"

The girl snatched the paper. "If you know where they are, come back. I will call."

"You want to split the money?"

"I have his phone number," the woman countered.

Khloe shrugged. "I bet it's an American wife running from her husband."

Both women nodded in agreement.

"Might be bad for her," Khloe suggested.

The older lady nodded again, though the younger one didn't respond. Khloe lifted the bags before turning to the door. She wanted to wait and check that no one was waiting outside, but then she remembered her mantra: *Act Natural.*

"Goodbye," she told the ladies, exiting the store.

The street was empty, and she tried not to break into a run. Even controlling her walk to a slow stroll took all her effort. When she entered the front door of her rental house, she snapped the deadbolt in place and pressed her back against the wooden frame.

"Khlo, *Moana*'s over!" Amanda called from the bedroom.

"Just a second," Khloe replied, her heart still pounding as she carried the bags of groceries to the kitchen.

8

Caleb opened his eyes. The rumble of the outboard vibrated through the vessel. Above him, he saw trails of wispy clouds scattered across the blue expanse.

"Deke, get him some water!" Danny called over the engine.

Something pressed against Caleb's lips, wetting his dry mouth. He licked at the droplets.

He shut his eyelids again, hiding from the glare of the sun. When he blinked them open, the sound of the motor was gone.

"Watch out for that log!" Danny shouted.

Caleb lifted his head to see Deke on the boat's bow, holding an oar. He jabbed the paddle into the water. Caleb noticed he wasn't rowing.

"Danny, you gotta stroke the other way!" Deke bellowed.

The clouds overhead rotated as if Caleb's world was on a carousel. He closed his eyes, opening them as the hull scraped across the ground.

"Get it up on shore," Deke ordered.

"I'm trying!" Danny retorted.

Caleb woke up again. Darkness enshrouded the earth, and stars gleamed down. Was it still the same day? Caleb wasn't sure.

He rolled his head to the side to see the flames from a small fire burning. The two boys knelt over the fire, and Caleb smelled something cooking.

"Is it almost ready?" Danny asked.

"We have to catch some bigger fish tomorrow," Deke commented.

Caleb coughed.

"Shit, he's awake," Deke said, retreating from the blaze. "Rick, you with me?"

Caleb hacked again. "Yeah," he moaned.

"How are you feeling?" Danny questioned, placing a bottle of water to his lips.

Caleb struggled to swallow the water. His throat felt like it had swollen shut.

"Dead," he croaked.

"Not yet," Deke promised. "His fever might be down, Danny."

A hand pressed against his forehead. "Maybe, but it's still too high."

"Should we put him in the river again?" Deke queried.

"Not at night," Danny replied. "I'd prefer to see what was out there before we go wading around again."

"Yeah, me too," Deke agreed.

"Where are we?" Caleb choked out.

Deke shook his head. "We don't know. The boat ran out of gas."

"The current was too much," Danny remarked. "We had to reach shore before we all flipped."

"You've been out of it all day," Deke added.

"Can't move," the former assassin moaned.

"Don't," Deke warned. "You need more sleep. We're working on a plan in the morning."

"Plan?" Caleb questioned.

"We need to make it to Santarém, but we don't know how far it is," Danny explained to him. "I'm going to head there on foot and find some help."

Caleb shook his head.

"Man, you need a doctor," Danny informed him.

"Don't split up," Caleb groaned.

"We'll talk about it later," Danny said.

"Rick, you should rest," Deke advised as he dripped a wet cloth over Caleb's face.

Caleb imagined he could almost hear the drops sizzle against his skin. He believed he was thinking clearer, but some part of him questioned his sanity when he caught himself searching for Audrey again.

"Sleep, man," Danny told him in a soothing voice.

Caleb awoke later in the middle of the night. The embers from the fire glowed, and a small tree branch held a single tongue of flame that danced along the bark. Caleb saw the silhouette of one of his traveling companions seated next to the flame. The other form stretched out on the bare earth.

Portions of Caleb's subconscious seemed more alert to him. His muscles begged him not to move, but he turned his head. The ground was moist beneath his skin. Was it cold? Caleb couldn't tell.

Inside him, Corsair demanded information. He reached out to his senses. The scent of smoldering wood carried in the air. A rush of water somewhere echoed, and Caleb imagined the river's current flowing in rapids around a stump on the riverbank.

His effort to draw in details about his surroundings soon wore on him. Caleb closed his eyes again.

When he opened them, the sun shone down. Deke and Danny had constructed a shade for him out of branches and clothes. He rolled sideways, feeling better, although still not good.

On his side, he pulled his knees up, curling into a fetal position. Neither Deke nor Danny were in sight, and without making any actual choice, he went back to sleep.

Footfalls woke him as boots crunched down the vegetation.

"Do we douse the fire?" Deke asked, sounding panicked.

"I don't know," Danny replied. "Where's Rick's gun?"

Caleb opened his eyes. "What?" he stammered, trying to sit up.

"Rick, we have company," Deke warned. "A couple of men with guns down the river."

"Help me up," Caleb urged.

"You're too weak," Danny argued.

In response, Caleb lifted his arm for the young man to lift him to his feet. Danny sighed, exasperated, but hooked his forearm under Caleb's elbow.

Caleb Saunders struggled to get up. Sweat poured off his forehead, and he knew he shouldn't stay up for long. His clothes were damp, soaked with perspiration. And, Caleb just realized, urine.

"How many of them?" he asked.

"Two, but they have a boy with them."

"Local villagers?" Caleb queried. If there was a settlement close by, it could offer them sanctuary. Perhaps even some medications.

"I don't think so," Deke explained. "They look like they caught the kid."

"They have guns," Danny stated.

"What kind?" Caleb asked.

"Of men?" Deke questioned.

"Guns," Caleb replied with a grunt. He leaned against Danny.

"Machine guns," his companion told him.

"Where's my Glock?" he asked.

"I have it here," Danny said. "It's in the bag, Deke."

The other man bent over to retrieve the handgun while Danny supported Caleb's weight. Corsair stuck his palm out, requesting the Glock. Deke stared at Caleb's ashen countenance for a second before putting the grip of the nine-millimeter in Caleb's hand. Caleb fumbled to put the gun in his waistband.

"Without a boat, we can't outrun them," Caleb warned.

"What should we do?" Deke asked.

"I need to see them when they arrive," Caleb suggested.

"Man, you don't have the strength to even stand up," Danny pointed out.

This might have been the worst condition Corsair had ever been in. His brain fog lingered, and he fought through it to hold a clear thought. For the first time he could recall, he'd almost prefer to curl up and sleep instead of fighting. Still, he considered that even in this state, he should still be a better shot than Deke or Danny. Especially if they were facing armed combatants.

"Fine, we wait here for them to show up," Caleb relented. "Although, I'd like to sit down if I can."

"We have a log over here," Deke told him, pointing to the smoking embers. A large tree trunk stretched across the ground.

"Which direction were they coming?" Caleb asked.

"Over there," Deke answered, gesturing toward the brush.

"Sit me so I'm facing that way," Caleb suggested.

They did, and Caleb rocked gently on the log. His head pounded as if his brain was trying to break through his skull with a sledgehammer.

"Give me some space," Caleb advised, panting. "If they come in, you two need to do the talking."

"Should we spread out?" Danny asked.

Caleb nodded once, unable to gather sufficiently clear-headed thoughts to give a reason. He knew it was true, though. So, it appeared, did Danny. If the three of them were clustered together, they made an easy target. By dividing up, it would take the gunmen a second to fire on each of their positions.

Danny motioned for Deke to move toward the riverbank while he sidestepped away from the fire. Then they waited.

For Caleb, time trickled past. He blinked more than normal as he tried to focus through the sludge in his brain. His training guided him as he narrowed his senses to the brush he suspected the men would come through.

When they did, he didn't move. Two soldiers in tan fatigues that had seen better days stepped into the clearing. The man on the right had his left hand gripping a young, dark-skinned boy wearing a tank top and shorts without shoes. Both men carried FN FAL submachine guns that hung from the strap around their necks.

The three Americans surprised the two gunmen. The right one released the child, grabbing the stock of his FN FAL as the other raised his barrel at the group. He swept it across the clearing, aiming it at each of them for a second.

"Who are you?" the man on the left asked in Portuguese.

Caleb didn't respond, though Deke answered in Spanish, "We are Americans."

"*Gringos,* eh?" he replied with a chuckle. "The Revolutionary Alliance of Tapajós governs this land. If you are staying here, there is a fee."

Deke struggled with the Portuguese. Danny, however, asked, "How much?"

"Five hundred dollars," the man answered, narrowing his eyes.

"We don't have that," Danny explained.

The two men glanced at each other with a half-smile. Behind them, the boy started to bolt, and the one who'd been holding him rotated. His FN FAL came up, aiming for the young kid.

Caleb pulled the Glock and fired. The first shot hit the man on the left in the shoulder. Caleb's round whipped him around. He squeezed the trigger again, hitting the man in the back before he turned his Glock to the one targeting the youth, who registered his partner falling. He twisted toward the three Americans as Caleb squeezed off two more shots. He fell into the thicket, and Caleb slumped forward.

"Damn!" Deke cursed.

"Get the boy," Caleb rasped.

"Why?" Danny questioned.

"Hurry!" Caleb barked, allowing the Glock to slip into the dirt as he slid down the trunk, landing on his butt.

Deke complied, dashing into the undergrowth. It took Danny a few seconds longer, but he ran off after his buddy. Caleb leaned his back against the fallen tree, letting it hold him upright.

That took you four shots? You must be really sick.

He thought he'd drifted to sleep, but it could have just

been the fog of fever. When the two young Americans returned, they had the child with them.

"Rick, you okay?" Danny questioned.

Caleb nodded. Or, at least, he believed he nodded. He wasn't sure.

"Where's he from?" Caleb inquired.

The boy pulled at Deke's grip.

"Not enemy," Caleb mustered in Portuguese. He could barely keep his head up anymore.

"Rick, what do we do?" Danny asked, squatting in front of the man.

"Hide the bodies. We need to move," he said. What came out, though, was, "Hide the bodies. We need to mo—"

Caleb drifted over to his side as he passed out.

9

———

"Y ou're with us," a woman's voice broke through the blackness.

Caleb lifted his head, which weighed the same as a bowling ball. It hurt, but not like it had before. The constant thudding pressure had eased up. He dropped his head back on the pillow.

A pillow?

"Where am I?" he stammered.

"A village called São Miguel do Tapajós," the woman explained. "Don't move. I'll get you some water. How are you feeling?"

"Better than dead," he muttered.

"That's an improvement," she remarked. "I'm Bella."

"Caleb," he whispered.

"Caleb?" the woman questioned. "I thought your friends told me your name was Rick."

He groaned at his mistake. "Yeah, it is," he amended, but not before the woman lifted an eyebrow.

"Here, Caleb," Bella said, offering him a cup of water. "Let me help you."

Bella placed the mug against his mouth and tilted it. He drank it down, capturing every drop. When he finished, his tongue traced over his lips, rubbing the cracked surface.

"I'm hungry," he admitted.

"I bet you are," she replied. "Your friends said they got you to eat a bite of fish, but that's been all they could get in you."

Caleb shook his head. "I don't remember."

"You were running a dangerously high fever."

"I've never been sicker," he confessed.

"Malaria can do that. Although you managed it very well."

"Are you American?" he asked.

"Partly. Mexican-American. My dad was American. My mom is from Mexico City."

"And you're in Brazil?"

"I'm working with the village to create sustainable farming."

He nodded once as Bella moved away. Caleb pushed up on his elbow and examined the room for the first time. It looked like a small rustic cabin. Plain wood walls with a screened window allowed air to flow through the one-room home. A table with a water basin and some fresh fruit sat in the corner. On the opposite side was a cot with mosquito netting draped over it.

"You saved my friend, Domingo," Bella told him as she brought a plate to him. Halved guava sat on the dish with a spoon.

"Who's Domingo?" he questioned.

"The young boy the guerrillas captured. He said they were going to shoot him when you killed them."

Caleb didn't respond. The incident felt like a week earlier. As if it was only a dream he'd had once.

"Can you sit up?" Bella asked.

"Yeah, I think so," he answered, struggling into a seated position.

"Here," she offered him the plate. "Use the spoon to scoop out the flesh."

Caleb nodded, lifting the utensil. He devoured the two halves, leaving only the skin behind.

"Let's see how that settles you before we eat anything else," she suggested.

"Thank you," he told her.

"Who are you, Caleb-Rick?"

"We were just boating down the Amazon when we got into trouble."

"That's not the story your friends gave us," she pointed out.

Caleb cursed Deke and Danny. What had they said?

"Where are my friends?" he questioned.

"I think they were resting last night."

"What time is it?" Caleb wondered.

"About seven in the morning," she explained. "You've slept for two full days."

"Here?" he asked.

Bella nodded. "From what they said, you've been out twice as long."

"Four days?" Caleb couldn't recall ever losing that much time. "The men in the jungle?" he asked. "You mentioned guerrillas."

"Yes," Bella said. "They call themselves the *Aliança Revolucionária do Tapajós.*"

"The Revolutionary Alliance of Tapajós?"

"They are not revolutionary at all. More like criminal."

Caleb shrugged. "How many are there?" he questioned his caretaker.

"I don't know. Their leader is a man named Mateo. The guy is a real piece of work."

"Does anyone else know what happened in the jungle?" Caleb asked.

"Just Domingo and your friends."

"Will the boy talk?" he pressed.

Bella exhaled a breath through pursed lips. "He's a child. It's hard to say. I told him to keep it quiet so the guerrillas didn't come back for him."

"Scare tactic?"

She shook her head. "I wish. They want boys Domingo's age to fill their ranks."

"How old is he?"

"Eleven."

"Damn," Caleb muttered. "Glad I killed them."

Bella frowned. "I'm not sure about that. All life is precious."

"They were going to take your friend," he pointed out.

"I understand," Bella replied. "That doesn't mean I have to like that men died in such a violent way."

"They would have shot the boy," he reminded her.

"Look, I don't disagree with your actions. In fact, I'm grateful you saved Domingo. But either I treat all people as if they deserve life, or I am a hypocrite."

Caleb shrugged.

"You are some kind of soldier, right?" she asked.

"Something like that, I guess," he said cautiously. "Best if I leave out the details of it."

"You have no guilt about killing those two men?"

"Nope," he responded. "They put themselves in a violent life. Then, they took it another step and tried to kill an inno-cent kid. I only imagine the others they have killed along the way. If I stopped them from hurting anyone else, then why should I feel guilty?"

"They can never change now," Bella said, shaking her head. "You cut off any chance they had to turn their lives around."

"And saved them from doing the same thing to Domingo."

"I believe, Mr. Caleb-Rick, that we will have to agree to disagree."

"Call me Rick, okay?" he asked. "Especially with Deke and Danny."

"Your secret is safe with me," she promised him.

"How long have you been here, Bella?"

"Two years now."

"Teaching sustainability?"

"And about Jesus," Bella added. "It's not just the agriculture. The goal of Zion's Garden is sowing people, too."

Caleb nodded. Spirituality was a struggle for him. During his years in the field, Caleb witnessed the worst of humanity. He saw unbelievable pain that made no sense to him. Even when he and Audrey attended church, he never had the type of faith others had. As a child, he recalled that lack of faith was denigrated. His grandfather once asked if he had "questions," as if doubting his faith was the same as butchering a kitten on the kitchen counter. As if faith was something you're born with.

Caleb questioned everything and trusted virtually no one. Why should he put his beliefs in an unseen anything?

Still, he didn't argue with others who held devout faith. In fact, he wished he could emulate that blind trust. Though, the only thing he really trusted intrinsically was himself.

And Audrey, though she wasn't around anymore. A fact that only seemed to validate his position.

"Will this Mateo be looking for his men?" Caleb asked, wondering what Deke and Danny did with the corpses.

"I don't know," she admitted. "His group isn't large, so I imagine he'll notice them missing. Whether he cares or not is anyone's guess. However, you were ten kilometers west of São Miguel, so he will be looking for them elsewhere."

Caleb swung his legs off the cot, planting them on the wooden floor.

"You might want to be careful," Bella warned. "You might not have your footing yet."

"I need to move," he insisted.

"Let me help you, then," she suggested, reaching out to offer her arm to counterbalance his weight as he stood up. It surprised Caleb that he took her arm without a thought.

On his feet, he admitted to himself that his legs were a bit wobbly. He took a couple of steps, letting his body adjust to being up after several days.

"You're doing pretty well," Bella acknowledged.

"I'm a fast learner," Caleb stated. "Wait until I've had my coffee."

Bella laughed. "What we have here will make your Starbucks espresso taste like water."

"Oh, don't tempt me. I'll eat the coffee beans themselves if you have them."

She smiled. "We're cultivating a small grove," she explained. "You could eat them off the trees, but it's an intense amount of caffeine. You'll be buzzing around like you've just done coke."

"I'll just take the processed stuff," he assured her. "My heart might explode."

"You wouldn't be the first," she joked. "I tried it my first week here. It was like waves of pure energy broken by intense nausea. It's best to take it slow when you do that. Don't eat three in a row, thinking you can't feel it yet."

"That sounds remarkably like the voice of experience speaking."

"I did plow a whole field by myself that day, but the crash was worse."

He nodded, recalling a similar experience with adrenaline. However, those circumstances had been life and death.

"Do you have internet?" Caleb asked.

"Oh, sure. You should be able to log onto the Wi-Fi near the pool," Bella quipped.

"Ah," Caleb remarked. "Sarcasm, huh?"

She shrugged. "We don't even have power."

"It's the twenty-first century. There are options."

"Not here," she explained. "The villagers have a boat with an outboard to ferry some supplies, but it's cost- and space-prohibitive to bring the fuel back with you."

"I get it. We were heading downriver but missed our boat. Any chance we can get on another around here?"

"It's twenty miles to Santarém," she explained. "That's the closest port to catch a riverboat."

"That's not too far," he pointed out.

"Not normally," she agreed. "However, your friends with the Revolutionary Alliance are camped between us and the river."

Caleb noted the sound of trickling water, and he moved to a window overlooking a waterway.

"That looks like a river," he said.

"It is," Bella confirmed. "That's the Arapuins River. It connects at the intersection of the Amazon and the Tapajós."

"Will the guerrillas bother us?" he asked.

"Right now they might," Bella replied. "We got a visit from them a few days before you arrived. They demand we leave this area."

Caleb furrowed his brow. "Why?" he asked,

She shook her head. "I don't know. They killed one of our workers."

"A villager?"

"No, Bernie was a volunteer from America," she explained, her face falling with sadness. "He was a friend."

"I'm sorry," Caleb muttered. "What did they say?"

"That we had two weeks to move."

"What do they want here?"

"Could be anything," she remarked.

"This is a prime location," Caleb noted. "Maybe they want to build a resort here."

Bella lifted an eyebrow.

"I'm sorry, Bella," Caleb said again. "Are you moving?"

"We'd lose everything we built here," she told him. "We sent word to the Brazilian government, seeking some assistance."

Caleb clicked his tongue.

She frowned. "What?" she pressed.

"I wouldn't expect a strong response from them," he advised.

"That's what everyone thinks," she commented with a sigh. "What else can we do?"

"Move," he answered. "It's not the answer you wanted, but it's the truth."

"This village has been here for decades," she argued. "If we had a year to rebuild it, maybe. With two weeks, we don't have enough time to do anything but move."

"These men already killed someone," Caleb pointed out. "Men like that don't bend."

"It's not my call," she said. "The elders want to come to an arrangement with Mateo."

"Hmm," Caleb mused. "It might depend on what they want."

"What do you mean?"

"I joked about the location, but it's valid. What is their reasoning?"

"They're killers," Bella said. "What reason do they need?"

"While they might be killers, it's unlikely a group like that makes demands unless it is beneficial to them." He paused, considering the efforts Mahmoud Abbas had gone to capture him in Cartagena. "Or revenge," he added. "That's a motive, too."

She gave him a quizzical look.

"They grabbed Domingo," he said. "Why?"

"Recruitment," she answered.

"Figured as much," he replied. "The Taliban did the same thing in Afghanistan."

"That's how they build their ranks, forcing young boys to join."

"It's a common tactic. Get them while they are young and foster a false sense of loyalty."

"They're animals," she growled.

Caleb didn't argue with her. However, he disagreed. While some animals employed pack politics, most didn't forcefully recruit members to the pack. Even in a pack, following an alpha was based on which animal was the strongest protector.

Without meeting Mateo, Caleb suspected he was like many warlords he'd already met. The guise of protection preached from his own mouth, but in truth, it was about power. There must be something in this village that Mateo wanted enough to kill for. Caleb doubted it was the view.

"Bella! Bella!" a boy called breathlessly as he charged into the hut. Caleb recognized the boy from the jungle.

"What is it?" Bella asked.

"Those men are back," he wheezed.

Bella looked at Caleb with a downtrodden face. "You better stay here," she warned. "Who knows how Mateo will react."

Caleb nodded, but he wondered where his Glock was now.

10

From the other room, Ariel sang about how she wanted to be part of Prince Eric's world. Khloe sat at the kitchen counter. She heard the words coming from the mermaid's mouth, and they brought her out of the trance she'd been in for the last few days.

Part of his world.

She'd thought the same thing when she first met Dominic. He was this elusive tough guy. That was the persona he'd put on, at least. The allure of that life had pulled at her. This man had thrown money around like beach sand, treating Khloe like a princess.

Certainly, it was all a deception. Dominic was nothing more than a petty runner for the Cincinnati mafia. He was as low-level as they came, but at the time, Khloe thought Dominic would be the boss someday. Instead, he started cheating them and snitching on them. Her princess castle had already shown cracks in its foundation, but the day Sonny Departi had Dominic killed, the spires crumbled.

What was she part of now, though? Was she in a situation any different than her life before Dominic died?

Caleb was good to her, but he brought his own issues. She trusted the man completely. He loved his daughter, but she realized that love wasn't always enough. He had entities after him that made Sonny Departi seem like an irate bill collector.

She had warned him that the agent from the OOC had found her. Khloe should have run when that happened, but something about the Hubbard woman had comforted her. Now, she wondered if that was only desperation on her part. Desperation for a sense of security. Throughout her life, she had been told the government would protect her.

In her heart, Khloe understood she'd misplaced that faith. During her brief foray into the underworld, she'd encountered dirty cops and feds. People out to get whatever they could for themselves. Even the Hubbard woman wanted Caleb to help her take down her boss. Those agents at the Office of Compliance would kill Khloe and Amanda if they thought it would ensnare Caleb.

Lee Hubbard had assured her they were safe and she'd redirect the OOC's attention, but those two men in the shop had looked and smelled like agents.

She stared at the email message in her draft. Caleb hadn't answered in almost a week. His last note had promised he would be in contact by now. By long before now, he'd assured her.

But so far, a new message hadn't arrived.

Before he left for Colombia, Caleb had warned her that if he didn't contact her, she would be on her own. There was a safe house in Belgium he'd told her about. She'd have to risk booking a flight out of Belize.

She had enough cash to live on for a while, but that assumed no one came knocking. After seeing the men in the shop the other day, she knew they were now on her doorstep.

If Caleb didn't answer soon, she had to presume something had happened to him and start her escape. Given his proclivity for detail, Caleb had mapped out his suggestion for her and Amanda. Since Khloe only had her real identity, that made it trickier.

She opened up the flight tracker app on her computer. As she scrolled through the destinations with direct flights from Belize, she panicked. It was too soon. Caleb might still show up at any minute.

Khloe slammed the laptop closed. Her eyes failed to focus. In the last four days, she'd slept a total of ten hours. Most of those were unintentional dozes. Her nerves remained on edge, and she paced the front room, pausing occasionally to peek outside.

Every car that drove past jerked her to attention, and she hurried to the window to inspect the passersby.

How long should she wait, though? If anyone found the house, it would be too late to run.

She hadn't spoken to a single adult except the two women in the shop. The loneliness was wearing on her. Khloe had never been a social butterfly, but she enjoyed being around people. She liked random conversations about what everyone watched last night on Netflix or listening to a group of men chat about the latest football game.

Now her conversations revolved around how some seagull used a fork to brush its hair. Never mind that birds didn't have hair.

It dawned on her that she might be overreacting, thanks to her nerves.

Wait until the end of the day.

She made her decision. If Caleb didn't contact her by

tonight, she and Amanda would leave. It shouldn't be a direct route, she realized. Caleb had said the OOC would be watching for her to book travel. Since they seemed to know she was in Belize, they would track her as soon as she bought a ticket.

That meant waiting until the last minute to do it. Or she could drive out of the country, just like how they'd gotten in the first time. Mexico would be out, but she could cross the border into Guatemala or Honduras.

"Khlo!" Amanda called from the bedroom.

Khloe straightened up and marched to the back room. "What is it, sweetie?" she asked, realizing her demeanor had shifted before she addressed the girl. Khloe considered that this must be what being a parent was like. Always pushing aside the daily worries to take care of the little ones. There was no reason to give Amanda anything to frighten her. She'd lost enough in her brief life.

"I'm hungry," she announced when Khloe appeared in her doorway.

"I'll make you a sandwich," she told the child.

"Cheese sand'ich?"

"Of course," Khloe replied in a jovial tone. "You want it hot or cold?"

"Hot!" Amanda squealed and started laughing for no reason. She threw herself back on the mattress, cackling at herself. Khloe shook her head with a half-smile.

"Alright, goofball," Khloe stated. "I'll make your sandwich while you go wash your hands."

"My hands are clean," Amanda argued.

"Wash them again, anyway," Khloe urged.

"I promise there are no bactreea."

"Bacteria," Khloe corrected.

"Yeah, that."

"Wash them, Amanda," Khloe demanded, her tone shifting from convivial to parental.

"'Kay."

As she returned to the kitchen, Khloe decided tonight might be too late. She'd start planning their escape after she fed Amanda.

11

———

Caleb sat on the stool as Bella departed the one-room house. "Stay here," she warned Domingo in Portuguese.

Corsair assumed she wanted to keep Domingo out of sight and avoid giving the guerrillas another attempt to forcibly enlist the boy in their ranks. The woman left the hut, leaving Caleb and Domingo inside.

"You shot those men," Domingo told Caleb.

"Yes, but we don't want to tell everyone," he warned.

"Bella said not to talk about it to anyone," the child explained.

"I'm sorry you had to be there," Caleb said.

"You helped me," Domingo replied.

Caleb nodded, knowing that was only half true. Despite his fevered state, Corsair killed those two men to protect himself and his companions. Not that he wouldn't have saved the boy in a clear-headed moment, but he was barely functioning at the time. His actions were driven by survival at that moment.

"How did those men get you?" Caleb asked.

"I went to find where they told us to go," Domingo explained. "When they found me, the men wanted to know why I was there. Then, they decided to take me back to their camp. They didn't say why. The one soldier told me to do what they said, or they'd shoot me."

"You might be better off running next time," Caleb suggested.

"They were going to shoot me," Domingo countered.

Caleb nodded. "Probably. If you go with them, though, you'll end up dying, too."

Domingo curled his lip. "I hate them."

"I don't blame you," Caleb agreed.

A gunshot outside snapped his head up.

"Oh no," Domingo muttered, leaping from the chair and running to the door.

Caleb spun around the hut until he saw the pack under the cot he'd woken up on. He dropped, pulling it out and dumping its contents onto the floor. The Glock tumbled out, and he picked it up.

"Are you going to kill them?" Domingo asked.

"I'm going to investigate," Corsair answered. "You stay here. Do you understand?"

Domingo nodded.

"Stay," Caleb repeated as he moved to the door.

This was the first moment he stepped into the village. At least, the first time he remembered stepping into it. A steep staircase led down from the stilted hut. Crafted from a couple of felled trees with steps made from split logs, the stairs seemed like solid craftsmanship.

Caleb slipped the gun under his clammy shirt. When he was outside, the stench rising from his clothes hit his nose, embarrassing him. He'd been sitting with Bella for some time, smelling like a homeless guy who'd cooked in the sun.

He moved beneath the neighboring cottage, using its pylons as cover. Across the courtyard, he saw Bella, standing with several people he assumed were villagers. Three men with guns stood opposite Bella. The woman stared at them with angry defiance. That expression had resulted in the deaths of countless. Righteous indignation could be righteous while still getting one killed.

"Mateo warned you," the oldest of the guerrillas growled.

"They can't just move," Bella argued.

"Then they will all die," the same guerrilla replied in Portuguese.

"What does he want?" Bella asked.

"We are protecting you," the soldier answered.

Caleb moved to the next hut. He moved at a brisk pace from post to post. The three gunmen focused their attention on Bella and the community's leaders. He spotted Deke on the landing of a hut across the center of the village. The American locked eyes with Caleb, who motioned for him to get back inside.

Deke nodded and backed into the building as Caleb moved closer to the trio of armed men.

"You are the only thing we need protection from!" Bella shouted.

The one just behind the speaker whispered something to the group's leader. The man at the front grinned a wicked smile before facing Bella.

"You should come with us to talk to Mateo?" he offered.

Bella realized she was pushing too much and stepped back. "No, I don't want to meet him."

"No, I'm sorry," the insurgent corrected, "I didn't mean that as a question. You are coming with us."

"I'm not," Bella insisted, but the guerrilla behind the leader advanced toward her, grabbing her arm.

"Let go!" Bella yelled.

The guerrilla yanked the woman against him. He sneered down his nose at the missionary.

"Let her go!" a voice screamed.

Caleb turned his head to watch Danny charging out of a nearby house. The guerrilla holding Bella leered at him. The man who had been talking laughed and pointed at the kid.

"Brave American," he joked. "What do you plan to do?"

"Just let her go," Danny demanded, but less threatening.

Corsair cursed under his breath. He admired the kid's courage, but that tenacity would get him killed.

"Back off!" Deke shouted from his perch across the village.

Caleb looked in his direction and noticed his other traveling companion shouldering an FN FAL aimed at the group.

"Oh, shit," Corsair muttered. The FN FAL wasn't a precision weapon at that distance. Not for a kid like Deke.

The man with Bella jerked her around like a human shield as the other two snapped both their own submachine guns up toward Deke.

"Where did you get that gun?" the leader queried in Portuguese.

"I gave it to him," Corsair announced, stepping into the center of the village. His Glock hung at his side.

"Who are you?" he asked.

"A question you don't want the answer to," Corsair noted as he crossed the dirt clearing. His legs no longer wobbled, but he still had that tingling soreness one has after a hangover. Or five days of fever.

The guerrilla twisted to train his gun on Caleb. Thirty yards stretched between the two men. It was enough distance that either's aim needed to be dead-on to hit their target.

"I'm going to ask you again," the point man demanded. "Who are you?"

Caleb cocked his head. "Tell you what," he offered. "Release her, and we will let you return to your little friends."

"Or what?"

"You think there are only two of us here?" he questioned. "My team will close on you."

The leader looked from Danny to Deke and then to Caleb. He assessed the situation before he shook his head. "You are a liar," he stated. "It's just you and these two... boys."

With that, the guerrilla aimed his FN FAL at Danny, who only stood fifteen feet from the three gunmen. At that distance, a blind man with one arm could hit Danny with a submachine gun.

Corsair's hand came up, leveling the barrel of his Glock at the gunman.

The guerrilla saw him and chuckled. "Put down your guns, or your friend and the girl die first."

Corsair didn't break his stance. Instead, the assassin inhaled between his teeth, creating a high-pitched whistle. When his lungs filled, he held his breath, concentrating on the form on the other end of his Glock. He reached out with his senses. The breeze from the river hit his back at only a slight angle. The sun hung over his left shoulder almost directly overhead. Enough to create some glare for someone aiming at him.

"I will not say it again," the guerrilla warned.

With a long exhale, Corsair released all the air he had in his chest as he squeezed the trigger. The round left the Glock at just under 780 miles per hour. A gust of wind blew against Caleb's back, kicking up dust from the clearing. The bullet sliced through the air before the gunshot registered with anyone but Corsair. While he corrected for what he could, the distance between Corsair and the guerrilla, combined with the sudden rush of breeze and his own weakened condition, altered the bullet's heading a fraction of an inch. Instead of hitting the guerrilla in the center of his chest, it slammed into his right torso. The nine-millimeter slug tore through the soldier's pectoral muscles and shredded his lungs before shattering his clavicle. The result was the same as a sledgehammer striking the armed man. His body jerked around as he fired the gun. The FN FAL fell off his target, peppering the air and ground with bullets.

The guerrilla holding Bella let go of her, instinctively pulling his barrel up. Bella sprang away, running as the rest of the gathered villagers scattered. Danny sprinted for the hut where Deke stood with his gun drawn.

Don't fire.

Caleb willed Deke not to fire. He didn't trust the boy's aim in a situation like this. Caleb fired twice at the gunman, who released Bella. Neither shot found their target, but they sent him scurrying for cover. As the crowd dispersed, Caleb glanced toward Deke.

"Deke, shoot!" he shouted. It was irrelevant whether he hit the men as long as he distracted them for a second.

Deke obeyed, squeezing the trigger and letting out a burst of automatic fire that peppered the ground. Both guerrillas turned their weapons on the boy in the hut. Corsair sprinted across the opening with his Glock extended. He fired a single shot that struck the closest soldier in the side of his head.

The soldier's comrade-in-arms twirled, facing his now-dead companion as the man's skull exploded, spraying him with blood and brains. The final guerrilla released a burst of bullets toward Caleb without aiming before he bolted for the trees.

Don't let him get away.

Corsair dug deep, searching for a burst of energy to propel him faster. His legs ached, though. Hell, everything ached. He pushed forward as the guerrilla slammed through the branches of a palm and vanished into the dense foliage.

"Rick!" someone, maybe Deke, shouted.

Corsair ignored him as he ran through the brush into the undergrowth. The jungle canopy almost blotted out the sun. The other man's footfalls crunched in front of him, and Caleb lowered his head to run through a mesh of inter-twined vines and branches. Several offshoots caught his arm, trying to hold him back.

With a jerk forward, Corsair ripped free of the botanical grip. He stumbled ahead to see the guerrilla retreating through the brush. He slid into a shooting stance, peered down his barrel, and pulled the trigger. The gunshot echoed through the trees a split second after the gunman pitched forward.

The bullet struck him dead center of the back. In an instant, the man's spine shattered, and he fell to the ground, paralyzed and bleeding out.

Caleb retreated as the exhaustion hit him. He bent over, heaving his chest for air. The bushes behind him parted, and the assassin rotated on one heel with his Glock raised as Danny appeared in the vines.

"You killed him?" Danny questioned.

Caleb nodded once and stepped toward Danny, who seemed to understand. He looped his arm around Caleb's back to support him.

The leader wheezed on the dirt, but the villagers spread out from him, still frightened of the soldier despite his depleting life.

Caleb caught his breath and released Danny. He kept the Glock aimed at the man on the ground as he kicked the guerrilla's FN FAL away. He knelt beside him.

"What does Mateo want here?" he demanded.

"I'm dying," the gunman groaned.

"Do you want to live?" Corsair asked.

The guerrilla nodded, his face filled with pain.

"What does Mateo want?"

The soldier coughed, spewing droplets of blood. "I need help."

"Get some water," Caleb told Danny, and the boy hurried away.

"Talk to me," Caleb continued in Portuguese. "What does he want here?"

"Gold."

"Gold? Here?"

The guerrilla coughed up more blood. "There's a deposit near here."

"And the river might offer him the treasure he wants?"

Again, the guerrilla nodded.

Caleb straightened up to see Danny emerge from a hut with a pitcher. He waved his companion to stay there. Then he turned the Glock to the man on the ground and squeezed the trigger.

12

"What just happened?" Bella shouted in English.

"I think we saved you," Danny answered.

"You killed three people!" Bella yelled angrily.

"Bella, those men planned to take you," one of the villagers told her in Portuguese.

"Leandro," she responded, "what are they going to do when his soldiers never return?"

"I'm not sure what you wanted to happen," Caleb stated. "They intended to drag you back to their camp with them."

"You don't believe I can handle myself?" she demanded.

Caleb cocked his head. "Against three armed guerrillas?"

"It won't matter now!" Bella shouted. "I could speak to Mateo one-on-one."

"Bella, they were never taking you to him," Caleb explained.

Her brow furrowed.

"Why would a guerrilla leader give a shit what some

missionary says?" Caleb asked. "We'd end up finding you a kilometer or two in the wilderness."

She shook her head in defiance, but the vigor left her.

Leandro, the eldest male Caleb had seen in the village, spoke up. "What do we do now?"

"Danny, take someone and retrieve the body in the jungle," Caleb told his companion. "Be sure to get his gun."

"We don't need more guns here," Bella argued.

"Looks like you need a lot more," Danny pointed out.

She turned to glare at him, but Danny lifted his hands in surrender before waving at Deke to follow him.

Domingo appeared at the edge of the group. "You saved us," the child announced. Another villager next to Leandro hushed the boy.

"This isn't saving anyone," Bella protested. "Now they'll be back for vengeance."

"Mateo will return no matter what," Caleb told her. "There's something here he wants."

"We have nothing," Leandro stated.

"Gold," Caleb declared.

"What?" Bella stammered.

"These revolutionaries are out for a deposit of gold. I bet Mateo plans to pan the river for some easy cash," Caleb explained. "The soldier told me so."

"What?" Bella blurted out. "Was that right before you shot him in cold blood?"

"He was dying," Caleb retorted. "That was a mercy killing."

"Appeared to be an execution," she stated.

"Both can be true," he shot back.

"This is crazy," Bella snapped. "You can't kill people like that."

"You prefer the guerrillas do the killing?" Caleb demanded.

"Jesus said to turn the other cheek," Bella suggested.

"I'm not sure he meant it that way," Caleb told her. "Besides, your conscience should be clear. And since you are still alive and not being tortured by them, mine is, too."

"No one is asking you to protect us!" Bella cried.

"Bella, we need protection," Leandro urged.

She turned to the villager. "This is going to end up in bloodshed," she informed the village leader.

"They murdered Bernie," Leandro pointed out. "Bloodshed already occurred. If we plan to stay here, those men will be back."

"Do you want to leave?" Bella questioned. "Everything you built is here."

Caleb shook his head. The woman was rife with righteous indignation.

"What good does it do us if we are all killed?" the other villager beside Leandro asked.

"Davi, there has to be a peaceful way," Bella emphasized. "If the government intervenes."

Davi gestured with his head. "There are too many of them," he replied.

"Too many?" Bella repeated.

"Too many guerrillas. Or groups of them," Caleb told her. "The Brazilian government is underwater just trying to keep a handle on the drug trade in the jungle. Illegal mining has run amok here."

"They still can help," Bella argued.

"To what end?" Caleb wondered. "You think if they show up, this will resolve itself peacefully?"

She just stared at the former assassin.

Caleb added, "We're talking gold here. It's the main

reason all of South America speaks Spanish. People won't stop when it comes to gold. It might be responsible for more deaths than Christianity."

She gave him a big scowl at that comment.

"We don't have to take part," she argued.

Caleb waved his hands at the handful of villagers gathered around them. "It is their home."

"And their decision," Bella remarked.

Caleb nodded. "We can all leave," he declared. "Deke, Danny, and I. When Mateo returns, you may tell him we were the ones who killed his men. Explain to them we were after the gold, too."

"Where does that stand for them?" Bella queried.

"Right here," he said. "If you choose to withdraw, the guerrillas will let you be—for now. Heck, maybe after they strip the land clean and pollute the river, you can come back."

She sneered at him.

"Sir, will you help us?" Leandro inquired.

"Leandro, he doesn't need to," Bella answered.

Caleb shook his head. "I can't stay forever," he said. "In fact, I am already behind schedule."

"So you arrive and disrupt our peace before leaving?" Bella demanded.

"Geez, woman, I didn't say that," he snapped, rolling his eyes. "I simply said I can't stay here forever."

"Have to get back to soldiering, huh?" she accused.

He ignored her as Deke and Danny carried the third guerrilla into the village. "Got him, Rick," Deke commented between pants.

"Rick," Bella scoffed under her breath, and Caleb shot her a glare.

"Strip the bodies," he told his two companions. "Weapons, bullets, gear."

"Clothes?" Deke asked, wrinkling his nose in disgust.

"No," Caleb answered.

"What does that do?" Bella asked.

"We need to get rid of the corpses," Caleb explained. "If Mateo comes back and finds his dead soldiers here, we can't deny that they were here. If the corpses are all gone, there's no evidence they didn't leave here alive."

"He's going to wonder where all his men disappear to," Bella noted.

"He might," Caleb agreed. "Gangs lose members all the time. He may think they escaped him."

"We could stage it," Danny suggested.

"What do you mean?" Caleb inquired.

"Like, leave two bodies a long way from here," Danny explained. "Make it look like the third guy killed his friends and ran away."

The suggestion wasn't bad, but it would require moving the corpses. And taking them far from the village. A trip like that risked encountering more of the guerrillas patrolling the wilderness.

"Not a bad idea," Caleb acknowledged, "but we could face more of his group in the jungle. Hard to deny we killed his people if we're carrying their bodies."

Danny shrugged.

Leandro stepped forward. "We will dispose of the bodies," he assured Caleb.

"You can't be serious," Bella complained.

"What more should we do?" Leandro demanded.

The female missionary stared at them with no answer.

"Bella, let's talk while they handle this," Caleb suggested.

"Fine," she groaned, turning and marching back to her stilted hut.

Caleb followed her up the steep wooden steps. "I don't suppose you have anything else to eat?" he asked. "I think I burned that guava off."

Bella scowled at him again, but she pulled a bundle of clothes from a container. "Yeah, there's some bread over here," she replied. She unfolded the towels and produced a hunk of bread that she broke into two pieces. "It's a few days old, so it might be crusty."

"Thank you," Caleb said, taking the bread. He tore a hunk off and popped it into his mouth. The texture was tough and chewy, but he enjoyed the flavor. Besides, after only eating a piece of fruit over the last few days, anything would hit the spot right now.

"Eat it slowly," she warned.

"Look, Bella, I'm sorry about what happened out there," he told her.

"Caleb, Rick, whoever you are, I get it," she said. "These men are ruthless killers, but how can I teach the Word of God if I condone killing them?"

"The Bible is full of killing," Caleb pointed out. "In fact, God ordered Jacob to slaughter everyone before he took the Israelites into the promised land."

"I'm not sure we can compare," she argued.

"Well, we have to disagree. We don't have to enjoy it, but when Mateo returns with his men, he won't hesitate to kill you or your people."

"That doesn't justify us killing people," she replied.

"We could argue about this for days," he pointed out. "I'm serious. If you want us to leave, we will."

"You almost died," she reminded him. "If your friends hadn't gotten you here, then you probably would have."

"I can handle it," he stated.

"Who are you?" she asked, narrowing her eyes at him. "A soldier?"

"No," he responded. "I'm someone who is capable of certain things."

"Like Liam Neeson?"

Caleb smiled. "Sure, exactly like that."

"The people here can't fight," Bella told him. "Mateo's men have guns and no problem killing."

"True," he agreed. "That doesn't mean your people can't fight. Nor am I implying they should."

"What is your point?"

"I don't know how big this Revolutionary Alliance is," he replied. "If they have a hundred soldiers, then it's pointless to fight. Let them take the village and start over."

"But we'd lose everything," she moaned.

"If you try to fight a hundred men, they'll kill you all," Caleb surmised. "That's losing everything."

"You don't think the Brazilians will help?"

He shook his head. "The Brazilian government is, like most, notoriously corrupt. If word leaks you have gold here, then it won't just be Mateo and his troops trying to move you out. It will be untold forces bent on taking this village."

"How do we stop them, then?" she asked.

"You won't like it," he pointed out.

"Fine," she sighed. "Try me."

"If there really is a deposit, then you can buy protection."

"What do you mean?"

"Find the gold and hire soldiers to protect your village."

"Why wouldn't they do the same thing and attempt to take our gold?"

"Because you are already paying them enough," he

answered. "And mining gold is a lot of work. Mercenaries don't mind fighting for money, but back-breaking labor is a massive effort. If you are smart in who you bring in, pay them well."

"But there isn't any gold yet," she pointed out.

"Yeah. So find some first."

She stared off for a second. "We could start panning for it."

"But you still have the Revolutionary Alliance assholes out there," he added.

"Look, it's not my call. I'll talk to Leandro and the others," she said. "I don't like the idea of violence, though."

"Violence is coming whether you want it to or not," Caleb told her.

"How do we protect the village?" she asked.

"Shield the women and children first. Plan an evacuation in case it gets to that point."

Bella let her head drop. "I only wanted to make a difference," she whispered.

"Just because something doesn't work out doesn't mean you didn't affect the people," he told her gently.

"That's nice of you," she admitted.

"Don't go spreading it around," he joked.

"Who would I tell?" she wondered with a grin. "Even your friends don't know who you are."

"It's a long story," he stated.

"Don't tell me," she replied. There was a pause, and she added, "Thank you for saving me, though."

Caleb raised his eyebrows. "Of course," he answered.

"I didn't mean to sound ungrateful," she continued. "It was... a lot, I guess."

He nodded. "Understandable."

She settled across from him and reached for the loaf.

After tearing another hunk off the stale bread, she asked, "What do we do next?"

"We ditch the bodies and stockpile our weapons," Caleb answered. "While you talk to the others, I'm going to run recon on Mateo's group."

"Recon?" she echoed.

"Reconnaissance," he explained.

"No, I knew what it meant," she responded. "That sounds like a soldier talking."

Caleb offered her a half-smile. "If it makes you feel better, I'm a lot more than any soldier."

Bella furrowed her brow, staring at the man as he ate another bite of bread.

13

———

He tightened the muscle in his forearm as he watched the mosquito drive its proboscis into his skin. Mateo snapped his wrist, striking the insect with a *slap* and smearing a droplet of blood across his brown arm. That sucker had been full, likely feasting on the other men in camp.

Mateo Vargas leaned against the log as Alejandro tossed two more newly cut logs into the blaze. The wood, recently cut down, retained much of its moisture. The flames licked at the bark for several minutes until bubbles formed on the outside as the sap in the grain oozed to the surface to evaporate under the increased heat of the fire. His grandfather had taught him years ago to burn fresh wood in the fire to prevent mosquitoes from swarming the camp. People often debated its effectiveness, but his grandfather would have stated that the mosquitoes would be a lot worse if they weren't burning the moist wood.

He held a warm bottle of Cachaça by the neck. Alejandro settled beside the leader, who passed him the bottle of liquor. The man placed the rim of the spout to his lips and poured some into his mouth.

"No one has seen Carlo and Caio," Mateo informed his second-in-command. "'Jandro, you hear anything?"

"No, they probably ran off," Alejandro suggested.

Mateo clucked his tongue against his cheek. "Carlo, maybe. Not Caio. He's been with us for several seasons."

Alejandro nodded. He didn't suggest that the last few months had been leaner, and many of their ranks were getting unsettled. Mateo already understood that. It was part of his move to chase off the villagers. Still, he agreed with Mateo. Caio was one of Mateo's trusted lieutenants. Would he just leave?

Alejandro recognized the possibility. *La Aliança Revolucionária do Tapajós* didn't offer a retirement plan. Joining meant a lifetime commitment. Often, death and escape were the only viable options for quitting. The few who ran were often ones who surprised the leaders. They were intelligent enough to understand that Mateo would kill them for leaving, so they just ran, praying that the others never found them.

If they were unlucky enough to get discovered, the punishment was severe and always deadly. The issue was how fast the end came. Mateo enjoyed watching the deserters suffer. He would find new ways to torture them until they begged him for death.

"Should we send out a party?" Alejandro asked.

Mateo shook his head. "We can't spare the men," he replied.

Alejandro nodded, knowing Mateo was correct. The once-thriving alliance had over a hundred soldiers. Last year, a fever killed thirty men. During the aftermath, another twenty or so disappeared, deserting while they had the opportunity. In recent weeks, a few skirmishes and desertions had dwindled their ranks to twenty-seven.

Mateo demanded the remaining members find additional recruits. Where the fresh blood came from didn't matter to him. It was growing more difficult to find able-bodied men to enlist. Recruiting young boys from local villages was an easy method to increase their numbers, but those children wouldn't be battle-ready for some time. *La Aliança Revolucionária do Tapajós* required adult males capable of fighting, but the best way to obtain them was with money, something Mateo lacked.

The village of São Miguel do Tapajós offered the answer to that problem. Not so much the village as the land adjacent to it. It had been a trader a few months back who had clued Mateo into the precious vein. The man had brought a two-pound nugget of gold to a trading post upriver. Word trickled to Mateo Vargas, who sought the source of the gold. He discovered the dealer had swapped an inverter generator for the gold in São Miguel do Tapajós, of all places.

The gold deposit itself was still elusive, but if the nugget found in the creeks around the village was a sign, there must be a healthy deposit. Mateo needed to gain access to it before word spread.

Illegal mining in Brazil was a billion-dollar business, and other factions would step in to steal the gold with more manpower and firepower than *La Aliança Revolucionária do Tapajós*. With only twenty-five men, the villagers outnumbered his people by about four to one. More than that now, if Caio and Carlo were gone. That was where the threats against the community came from. If Mateo Vargas scared the residents away from the village, he would claim the land without a fight. Although, even if a battle occurred, it wouldn't be much of one. He would incur some casualties for sure. There was no way around it. His troops would fare better than the townsfolk, but with morale at an all-time low, he needed to manage this with less effort.

Time remained the greatest factor. The longer he waited to establish his claim, the greater the chance someone else claimed it. Even once he took control of the village, his men had to find the gold. That might take months or even years.

Still, that nugget had been huge. That implied a big lode.

"Mateo!" a voice shouted across the camp. "Mateo!"

The leader handed the half-empty bottle of Cachaça to his second. He pushed off the log, rising to his feet as Bento ran through the small encampment filled with canvas tents. João followed on his heels.

"What is it, Bento?" Matteo asked.

His lieutenant doubled over, breathless. Between gasps, he said, "They killed them."

Mateo stepped toward his man and rested a hand on Bento's shoulder. "What are you saying?"

"São Miguel. They have people with guns," Bento told him. "João and I heard the gunshots. We went to investigate. Two Americans carried Pedro's body back to the village."

"What?" Mateo spouted. "Who was Pedro with?"

"Gabriel and Luca," Alejandro stated. "They were supposed to check on the village and see their progress."

"What happened?" Mateo demanded of Bento.

The younger man shook his head. "I don't know, Mateo. We tried to get closer, but there were several Americans there with guns. I think they killed them all."

"Where did these men come from?" Mateo asked Alejandro.

"I don't know," his second admitted.

Mateo grabbed the bottle of liquor from his friend's hand and hurled it at the burning log. The glass exploded, spraying the flames with alcohol. Blue fire chased the splashes along the fiery wood.

"'Jandro, how did they get word out?"

Alejandro shook his head. "I don't know. Even if they had called in help, they would have had to fly in to arrive so fast."

Mateo crinkled his nose. "It's a fucking mining corporation," he snapped. "Those types are ruthless. News of the gold nugget must have reached them. I knew we should have leveled that trading post."

Alejandro nodded, but not enthusiastically. Mateo had threatened to kill the trader and his family, but it was Alejandro who'd urged discretion. He argued that killing the family might bring in Brazilian authorities. After all, most traders paid duties and taxes to the government. But he preferred not to remind his boss of that fact right now.

"How many men did you see?" Alejandro asked Bento.

"At least three," he answered. "But most of the villagers still hid in their homes. We didn't stick around and find out."

Mateo grabbed Bento by the front of his shirt and threw him to the ground. "You didn't want to find out?" he shouted as he came down on the man, throwing punches into his face. He continued hitting Bento until blood covered his knuckles.

Alejandro motioned for João to stay back. There was nothing they could do for Bento. Any interference might shift Mateo's anger toward one of them.

When the leader slowed down, Bento's head lolled to the side. Blood spread over his mangled face, but he was still breathing.

"Mateo," Alejandro interjected. "Are you okay?"

Mateo Vargas looked down at the man under him as if he'd just realized he was there. He pushed himself to his feet and stared at his bloody hands. Mateo turned to Alejandro, giving him a slight nod as he walked off. The leader of the guerrillas wiped his blood-soaked knuckles on his shirt as Alejandro signaled for João to carry Bento away.

"Mateo," Alejandro said, approaching his leader.

"I might have gone too far," the guerrilla admitted.

Alejandro didn't answer, though he wanted to emphasize how correct Mateo was. Every body they had was vital at this point.

João hoisted Bento to his feet. Alejandro glanced over his shoulder as João dragged his friend to a tent. The beaten man stumbled along, mostly dragging his toes but at least trying to walk. That was a good sign.

"Mateo, this could be bad," Alejandro remarked. "If the villagers have help, what are we going to do?"

Mateo Vargas stalked around the fire, his stringy hair flopping as he marched. He turned and pointed at Alejandro. "We kill them," he announced. "Take a group and kill them."

"Mateo, we don't know how many there are," he reminded the leader.

"He said three."

Alejandro shook his head. "He only saw three," he corrected.

"Go in at night," Mateo recommended. "If these villagers don't want to leave, you can kill them all."

"How many men?" Alejandro questioned.

"Take ten," Matteo suggested.

"We're getting pretty thin around here," Alejandro

reminded him. "If they have more than we think, this could go badly for us."

Mateo nodded. His demeanor had calmed, and he took a deep breath. "Scout the village first. If it is more than the three, get some real numbers. We can go at them with everyone if we need to."

Alejandro agreed. At least he had some room to adjust. "We'll go in tonight," the second-in-command assured his leader.

Mateo nodded. "I would prefer you kill them all, 'Jandro," Mateo informed the other.

"We'll make that call," Alejandro promised. "We may take two nights. Watch them the first night and count their forces before taking them the next."

"'Jandro, that gold is our chance," Mateo said, almost to himself as much as his commander.

Alejandro nodded.

"I shouldn't have broken our bottle," Mateo mused. "How will we toast your victory when you return?"

"There is bound to be another bottle in camp," his second replied. "Probably several."

"Will you check on Bento?" Mateo asked. "I shouldn't have beat him like that. I'll make it up to him."

"Of course, *Jefe*."

Alejandro left Mateo, who squatted next to the fire and pulled a burning stick from the pyre. He stared at the red and orange flames licking their tongues into the air like dogs tasting the morning. He struggled to focus, and his heart raced in his chest. Three men killed. Two missing. And he'd just removed another with his senseless anger.

Time was running out for Mateo Vargas. *La Aliança Revolucionária do Tapajós* would wither and die if he didn't find new recruits. But now he could barely feed the men he had. If the gold was a bust, his time would run out.

The best-case scenario involved the dissolution of the alliance. Worst case entailed a full-fledged mutiny, leaving Mateo Vargas at the mercy of his own mercenaries.

14

———

The jungle had an eerie aura about it. Moonlight filtered through openings in the canopy. Screams from insects echoed through the trees.

Caleb traversed through the undergrowth. He spotted the footpath but moved about fifty feet off it. He walked without a light, but he wished for a pair of NVGs. Although with enough ambient light, he thought he preferred using his natural vision. NVGs worked great in many situations, but at times, they constricted one's peripheral vision.

From what he'd learned by speaking with several villagers, the guerrillas' base was ten miles to the south. According to Davi, it had moved a few months earlier. It turned out that Domingo had the most accurate information. The boy had wandered the jungle in all directions, and based on Bella's praise, he was adept at stalking almost any prey. He'd explained to Caleb that he saw the camp before he ran across the two men who tried to capture him. If what he told Caleb was accurate, the boy traversed close to forty miles that day. It also gave him a smaller area to search for the camp.

Caleb moved quickly, despite the unknown terrain. His Glock hung on his side. It had nine rounds in the magazine, and once he finished those off, Caleb was out of ammo. The FN FAL he'd taken off the guerrilla dangled from his shoulder on a strap. The metal slapped against his thigh as he ran. On the other hip, a Chinese KBAR knock-off knife dangled in the sheath he'd taken off one of the guerrillas. The blade held a sharp edge, but it wouldn't last. The cheap steel wouldn't hold its sharpness for long, but it was better than nothing, Caleb supposed.

Caleb wore new clothes. At least they were new for him. He tossed what he'd been wearing into the fire. After a week of sweat and urine, he deemed them no longer usable. He had enjoyed half an hour rinsing off in the river, and when he emerged, he felt fresh.

Thankfully, a few of the villagers had scrounged up enough clothes that fit him, so he didn't have to run naked through the trees. Though, even that would have been an improvement on his condition before his river bath.

The first sounds of humans came an hour and a half into the hike. The voices traveled through the growth, and Corsair dropped to the dirt. Lights flashed in the distance, and once he established the direction, he closed on the source.

It was a unit of ten men dressed similarly to the guerrillas he'd killed in the village. All of them carried FN FALs; some had sidearms as well. All of them were younger than thirty, except the one Caleb pinned as the leader. He was at least ten years older than the rest.

They did not try to be quiet as they stomped through the underbrush. Flashlight beams bounced around. No NVGs for this group. Not a lot of training, either. That didn't surprise him. Not after encountering the three in the village.

Men like this thrived more on fear and intimidation than anything else. He'd seen that with street gangs and such. There might be some leadership with military expertise, but most of the recruits were simple kids roped in by force or seeking to escape something.

Caleb trailed behind the group for half an hour. He was worried. The unit's heading seemed to be back the way he'd just come—back to the village. Ten armed soldiers could do a lot of damage. This was a squad readying for battle. Caleb heard it in the snippets of conversation. None of the speech was clear enough for him to make it all out, but he surmised a sufficient amount of it. This group was on a revenge mission.

How was that possible? Caleb had missed someone. The three men in the village were alone, and when the shooting started, the witnesses returned to Mateo and the rest to report on the attack. Was there another guerrilla still lurking in the jungle? Caleb cursed himself for missing him.

He had the element of surprise. If he circled around and got ahead of them, an ambush would thin the ranks quickly. However, it was unlikely he could take out all ten men.

If the troops marched into the village in the dead of night, though, they could slay half the population before the rest woke up. Deke and Danny had gathered three more submachine guns to match the pair they'd taken off the men in the jungle earlier. Since Caleb had one, that left four weapons to fight ten armed men. Winning that battle wasn't unlikely if the villagers were familiar with the FN FAL and prepared to defend their home.

Caleb wouldn't let them get to the village, though. But he needed to get nearer to do any damage, and Corsair had already formulated a plan. The group marched in two sloppy lines. There wasn't much formation to the unit—

dead man's head. After donning it, he started toward the group as they gathered together.

He lingered on the path with his light off as the others wandered back. The leader had put no one on patrol or watch. Foolish. Yet another sign of this group's inexperience.

Caleb considered letting the unit line up and start shooting from behind. The FN FAL could unload one of its fifty-round magazines in a few seconds. He steadied himself as he joined the group at the back.

"Form up!" the leader shouted from the front. "We must be quiet from here on."

A few affirmatives acknowledged the command, and the other soldiers took their position. The rear-most line glanced back at Caleb, who had his head down and his finger resting on the trigger in case they recognized him as an imposter. Cloaked as he was in the dark, Caleb's ruse seemed to work as the two men turned back to face forward.

However, that proved a short-lived reprieve as one of the men frowned and asked, "Where's Anka?"

Caleb replied in mumbled Portuguese, "I don't know."

The guerrilla turned back to examine him. With a closer inspection, the soldier's eyes widened when it dawned on him that Caleb wasn't his comrade.

Corsair raised the FN FAL, squeezing the trigger. With a firing speed of 600 rounds per minute, it took less than fifteen seconds for Caleb to empty the fifty-round barrel magazine. The first few bullets ripped through the pair of soldiers at the rear. The next pair spun around, killed before they made the 180-degree turn. After that, chaos took over, sending panic through the ranks. Men scattered, running away without trying to fight back. Corsair's gun sliced through two more before they got off the path.

Almost as soon as he started, Caleb dodged off the trail,

dropping the empty barrel mag in the jungle as he slapped a twenty-round magazine into the FN FAL. Survivors opened fire on him now that they'd sought cover in the darkness. However, their delay had given Caleb ample time to distance himself from his shooting location. As bullets flew through the jungle and muzzles flashed in the dark, Caleb found cover behind a fallen tree. None of the rounds reached him.

"Stop firing!" the leader shouted.

It took a few seconds before all the gunfire ceased. More than likely, the soldiers had depleted their magazines, forcing them to hold their fire long enough to reload. Quiet returned to the jungle, though Caleb's ears rang from the cacophony. A tree branch fell with a crash, and another volley of shots erupted as the troops on the edge fired at any sound.

Caleb scanned the area over the sights of the submachine gun. The rainforest looked empty. Moonlight continued to filter down, but here the canopy grew thicker, blotting out much of the light.

"Regroup!" the leader ordered, but no response came.

Caleb watched the shadowy jungle, waiting.

"We need to move!" the voice called out, and Caleb pinpointed his approximate location.

Now came the problem. Who moved first?

Caleb counted in his head. Two at the back—the next pair. And he thought he'd dropped two more. He couldn't be certain whether he had killed the final two or only wounded them. However, that still left at least four soldiers, including the leader. If the two he'd shot were out of the fight, then there were only three left.

A manageable number.

15

The man known as Ifrit stared at the images on the screen. He focused on the wedding photo of Tom and Audrey Harrod that showed a smiling couple. Ifrit maneuvered the mouse pointer over the face that belonged to the fictional Tom Harrod and zoomed in. His eyes betrayed him. This wasn't some insurance salesman or dentist, no matter what he purported to be. Those eyes had watched people die. Often.

Ifrit, whose given name was Ibrahim, sat in the internet café in SoHo. He leaned back on his stool and sipped his espresso—his third in the last hour. After this one, he would switch to an herbal tea.

Corsair. Born Caleb Saunders in the state of Georgia in the southeastern United States. He'd joined the Marines, proceeding on to boot camp—or whatever the Americans called it. The US depended on division to the point even its military organizations had to have rivalries, albeit friendly ones. Ifrit knew of the Marines, having faced a few during his days in Afghanistan working for the Taliban and Al Qaeda. They thought they were tougher than everyone else, though Ifrit found the assumption humorous. After all, he'd killed plenty of them on his own.

He never tallied his kills, but Ifrit imagined if he logged the deaths he caused, his number would be higher than most Marine Corps units. During the war, it wasn't only about the money, although Ifrit's skills had cost even his Islamic brothers a hefty fee. Now, the expense to have Ifrit solve one's problems breached the millions.

He'd informed Al-Farouqi his fee for Corsair was a flat million USD. Al-Farouqi hadn't batted an eye. Not that Ifrit would work for less. Not for a target of Corsair's caliber.

The assassin codenamed Corsair had become legendary. Ifrit had only been a boy during Corsair's reign, but tales of him spread through the ranks, often whispered at night. A few times, Ifrit encountered someone who claimed to have firsthand experience with the American assassin. He did not believe any of them. The only way one survived an encounter with Corsair was to side with him. Those who worked with the Americans wouldn't speak of the operation, much less brag about surviving Corsair.

He flipped to the next image, showing a young lady wearing a cap and gown. More pictures appeared with the same girl and an older couple. Khloe Evans from Cincinnati, Ohio. He studied the documents that came next, a detailed dossier on the Evanses and their daughter.

Ifrit had gathered that Khloe Evans was now a traveling companion of Caleb Saunders, though Al-Farouqi had assured Ifrit that as of two weeks ago, the pair weren't together right now. Corsair was last seen in Colombia, South America. Prior to that, he was in Belize City, Belize. A separate agent had sent Corsair to Colombia. For what reason, Ifrit neither knew nor cared. The intent had been to trap the assassin, though that plan had failed, and Corsair killed Al-Farouqi's predecessor.

Ifrit assumed that person was Salar Tolazar, given that Al-Farouqi worked for Mahmoud Abbas. Anyone in Ifrit's line of work knew that Abbas had placed a bounty on Corsair for personal reasons. Ifrit guessed it traced back to Corsair's involvement in the death of Abbas's son years earlier. It was an easy enough deduction, as few things could draw the million-dollar ire of a weapons dealer. A child's death was one.

Ifrit stared at the Evans family photo. This was a happy family. He suspected that even if the daughter were on the run, she'd have a way to communicate with her parents. Ifrit guessed it was the same method Khloe would use to contact Corsair, too. After all, she wouldn't be an expert in subterfuge, so anything she learned would be through Corsair.

However, that same reason made hacking Khloe or Corsair much more difficult. They'd have measures to protect them. Khloe Evans's parents, however, looked more like a pair of blue-collar workers who were lucky to sign into their own email.

A week ago, Ifrit initiated a phishing program in an email to Haley Evans from a spoofed Facebook friend. The subject read, "Is this Khloe?" When Haley Evans opened the message, there was a hyperlink. It surprised him that it took her three days to click the link. He'd waited, noticing on his tracker that she hadn't opened the email.

As soon as Haley Evans clicked on the link, a backdoor virus landed on her computer while the browser took her to Khloe's Instagram. Ms. Evans answered the message with, "It is. Why do you ask?" Of course, Ifrit never replied.

He'd gained unfettered access to Haley Evans's

computer. He spent the next few days combing through her files and internet history until he found his objective: a Yahoo mail account left open on her Firefox browser. A ridiculous mistake.

Now in the café, Ifrit saw the mailbox had one new document in the draft folder. Nothing was in the inbox, outbox, or sent box. Ifrit opened the draft to read the message.

"Khloe, I've been worried about you. Your Granny Lena has been sick. The cancer is back. I know you can't tell me where you are, but this doesn't look good for her. I spoke with Janet Stovall. She said that some new guy is taking over Sonny's businesses. It might be okay for you to come home. I wish you would. Your dad and I miss you so much. I hope you'll call when you can. I love you, Mom."

Ifrit read the email without emotion. He had no feelings for the girl on the run from the mob. It wouldn't matter if someone new took over the mafia. Khloe Evans would never feel safe in Cincinnati again. Ifrit guaranteed that.

He moved his mouse over the message and dropped the cursor in. Embedding a hidden link was easy enough, and if Khloe opened the draft, he should get her IP address. That would take him directly to her.

Since he assumed the girl was in Belize, he'd already purchased a ticket from Heathrow Airport to Belize. His flight left in seven hours, and Ifrit intended to be in Central America by tomorrow morning. When Khloe's IP address came through, he would be ready to swoop in on her exact location.

He closed out of Haley Evans's computer, leaving the Firefox browser up with the Yahoo email opened. It was only a matter of time, and he could wait. Allah had given Ifrit the gift of patience. Most jobs required an excessive amount of waiting and planning, and he understood that well. Whether his current benefactor agreed was another issue, but Mahmoud Abbas couldn't hurry the task if he wanted it done right.

Despite that, time was of the essence. Corsair would eventually rendezvous with Khloe Evans and his daughter. That window would narrow with each passing day. Once that happened, Ifrit could still track Khloe. He would just have to deal with Corsair.

That proved inevitable, though. Ifrit had now set himself on a collision course with the former American assassin. For a million dollars, he only had to capture or kill Caleb Saunders and deliver him, alive or dead, to Al-Farouqi. Or, more accurately, to Mahmoud Abbas.

Ifrit lifted his espresso and slugged the remaining liquid down his throat. He checked the time. With a few hours left before he had to head to Heathrow, Ifrit rose from the café's computer, shouldered his bag, and exited the establishment.

16

The jungle came back to life with the screeching of insects. The remaining guerrillas hadn't moved, but then neither had Corsair. Caleb assumed that whoever remained on the other side was on high alert and searching the shadows for any movement. They had taken cover and extinguished all their lights.

That made it a waiting game. How long the other side would wait to move was in question.

The answer came quickly, though, as Caleb saw a shadow move about thirty feet from him. The figure moved between two trees. Caleb's gaze followed the shape as it merged with the tree. He peered down the barrel of the FN FAL. The blackness around the trunk swelled as the soldier took cover. Had Caleb not seen him move into position, he might have missed the shifting shade. Now, he inhaled, exhaled, inhaled again, squeezed the trigger, and fired one round. The crack of the gunshot silenced the calls of the bugs. Even from this distance, he heard the body fall and a loud moan.

Gunshots rang out, but the remaining guerrillas weren't

able to pinpoint Caleb's location. He rolled to the dirt and crawled along the jungle floor on his belly. His figure stayed below the brush, and he took a slow path, hoping not to jostle any branches and give away his position.

Caleb's eyes focused on a large tucuma palm tree. Twisted thorns covered the trunk, and Caleb crawled toward it. As slow as possible, he raised himself up behind it. When a minute passed without anyone taking a shot at him, he trusted no one had witnessed his movements.

The assassin scanned the darkness, searching for the rest of the members of *La Aliança Revolucionária do Tapajós*. Everyone remained still, having learned from Corsair's last victim's mistake.

Corsair kept his eyes moving. With his head down, he had been unable to isolate the source of the rest of the gunfire.

It took five minutes for the remaining guerrillas to get anxious. Silence and inaction often spurred individuals to react, whether it was to start a conversation or a battle. People got unnerved by the quiet. Intrusive thoughts crept in. Fear screamed at them from their subconscious. Before long, panic took over.

"Where is he? Alejandro?" someone called.

"Shut up, you fool," the other hissed.

Caleb tracked the sounds, estimating where both came from. He stared into the darkness where he suspected the two remaining men were.

Alejandro must have been the leader, given how the other soldier had been trying to seek solace from his commander. However, Alejandro had none to give his man.

If Caleb had a sadistic streak, he might have smiled at that. The mental stress weighing on the lone soldier would only grow. His superior offered him no comforting words or assurances that help was coming. From Corsair's estimation, the pair were split up by at least thirty to forty feet—possibly more. From the strained shouting, there was some distance.

Again, this was good. The two soldiers couldn't come up with a defensive strategy, separated as they were, and anything offensive was made more difficult.

Caleb guessed that Alejandro had a little more patience than his inferior, even if he lacked proper training. However, Corsair trusted his preparation over that of the guerrilla's. In a few hours, the sun would rise, and if the two men hadn't moved by then, they'd be an easy target. As far as Corsair cared, Alejandro could remain paralyzed with doubts and fears until dawn. He knew he'd be just as alert.

Despite the silence of the rainforest, Caleb wasn't certain Alejandro hadn't reached out for assistance. He hadn't heard him speak, other than responding to his soldier, but a radio or even a sat phone could transmit a distress call without Caleb's knowledge. If reinforcements were en route, Caleb might find himself in a daunting battle. However, he wasn't going to let that concern permeate his mind.

That was something his mentor, an agent codenamed Hood, taught him. The mission was in front of him. Always in the present, never the past or the future. The immediate situation almost always took precedence.

"Solve the current problem," Hood had said. "If you do that, you'll be around to fix the next one coming down the line."

Corsair's current concern was only two men. That he could handle.

As if on cue, one of the areas Caleb was watching changed. It wasn't a significant movement, just a shift to get into a more comfortable position or to get a better view. It hadn't been much, but it was unnatural. Once the mind understood its surroundings, the out-of-the-ordinary became obvious.

Corsair sighted down the length of the FN FAL, lining up the front sight through the rear aperture. The blob of shadows hadn't changed. He breathed slow, rhythmic breaths, concentrating on his target area. Someone was in the shade of the underbrush. He knew that.

A branch moved above the shadow. Corsair lowered the barrel and tracked the sights leftward. He was about to give up his location, probably to Alejandro, but he'd chance it.

Corsair squeezed the trigger, firing on full-automatic mode. Six rounds shot through the night as he strafed the bullets from left to right. As the last round fired, Corsair rolled to the side. As expected, the tucuma palm erupted as Alejandro unleashed his FN FAL at the tree.

Caleb cowered on the ground less than ten feet from where he'd just fired from. Splinters of wood sprayed through the thick, humid air. He tracked the shots back to a clump of brush about twenty-five feet away. Much closer than he'd expected.

Corsair opened fire on the undergrowth where Alejandro had been. The FN FAL tore the ground and brush to bits as Caleb bounded to his feet and sprinted.

Alejandro returned fire, but Caleb's ploy worked. He'd intended to send the man for cover while he changed position. Alejandro's aim seemed directed at where Caleb had been, not where he ran.

Corsair dropped the now-empty magazine and slammed another into the machine gun.

"Alejandro!" Corsair taunted. "I think you're the last man standing."

The guerrilla leader didn't answer, but released a burst

of bullets into the night. Caleb stretched on the ground behind a Brazil nut tree. It didn't matter, though, because Alejandro's aim was off by about ten feet.

Corsair peered at the underbrush where he suspected Alejandro was taking cover.

"I can spare your life!" Caleb shouted. "If you tell me about Mateo and the rest of your men."

"Go to hell!" the guerrilla screamed, firing again. He'd corrected his aim, even hitting the Brazil nut tree. Luckily, it was too high. It also gave Caleb a tighter window to target as he evaluated the muzzle flashes coming from the shadows.

"If you aren't going to talk, I don't need you!" Corsair called out as he squeezed the trigger, releasing a volley of rounds into the darkness.

No one fired back.

Caleb remained motionless. He'd expected Alejandro to fire on again—if he could. A minute passed in silence. Then two. Three.

After ten minutes of silence, Caleb suspected he'd gotten the leader. Until he saw the body, though, he didn't trust it. Again, at almost a snail's pace, he climbed to his feet. No gunfire came.

Hood's advice came to him again: "Solve the problem." Corsair needed to confirm that all the guerrillas were dead. This time, he didn't have to gauge how many were out there. He just had to account for the bodies.

Another rule Hood taught him was: "Never assume." According to Hood, it was "the fastest way to an early grave."

Still, he had to move to check the bodies. He sprinted from the Brazil nut tree to yet another tall timber he couldn't recognize in the dark.

No one shot at him.

He moved again, staying crouched and low. Despite that,

his movements should have been easy to spot. He could feel some relief coming on that he'd neutralized the group.

Another dash took him to the underbrush where he suspected Alejandro was. He pushed through the foliage and found no one. Caleb dropped to the ground, expecting an ambush.

Nothing happened.

Caleb caught whiffs of blood in the air. His hand touched a pool of moisture on the dirt. When he sniffed his hand, he confirmed it was blood. Whatever happened to Alejandro, Caleb suspected he'd wounded the guerrilla.

Now he was venturing into the unknown. If the leader had sought cover, he could still target Caleb. But Corsair couldn't stay here. He vacated the brush in a crawl, his foot kicking something metal.

Caleb paused and reached back, retrieving an FN FAL from the ground. The magazine was empty. Caleb straightened up.

While that wasn't a guarantee that Alejandro was unarmed, it leveled the field. Several of the guerrillas had sidearms along with the submachine guns. It was smart to assume that as the leader, Alejandro had armed himself with a sidearm, too.

Caleb withdrew his Glock along with the flashlight in his left palm. He stretched his left forearm over his right, aiming the flashlight along the Glock's barrel as he moved through the trees. With the beam of light, he found a trail of blood. Alejandro had been hit, and was bleeding a lot.

He moved along the rainforest floor, following the droplets that looked brown in the artificial light.

A squishing sound caught his attention, causing him to swing his Glock ninety degrees to the left. He proceeded carefully, taking each step in slow motion.

Alejandro had a Beretta in his hand, although it wasn't aimed at anything. Blood soaked the guerrilla's once-tan shirt. One of Caleb's rounds had gone into his shoulder from above. He must have been prone when Caleb shot him. As Corsair swept the light over him, he saw another gunshot wound in his side.

The guerrilla locked eyes with the assassin. He waved his hand as he tried to aim the Beretta, but Corsair kicked it out of his loose grip.

"*Dios mio*," Alejandro muttered.

Caleb knelt down next to him. "You're dying," he told the man in Portuguese.

"No shit," the guerrilla mumbled back. "Was it just you?"

Caleb nodded.

"All my men?"

The American didn't respond.

"Mateo will bring more," Alejandro said.

"He won't like it," Corsair assured him.

Alejandro blinked twice as his eyes dilated. Then, he was gone.

Caleb leaned forward and closed the soldier's eyes.

17

―――――

"We haven't found her," Clay Dobbs told Lee in the conference room as she sipped her morning coffee.

"Nothing?" Pendleton asked, ignoring that Dobbs had directed his comment to the deputy director.

Dobbs shook his head. "We have teams covering the city. What we need is more surveillance coverage. Can we access any of the local security feeds?"

Lee replied, "We're working on it, but this isn't like tapping in the States. Most of the municipal cameras are outdated. Half don't work anymore. Even fewer cameras connect to a central location."

Pendleton curled his lip in disgust. "Damned third-world country."

"This isn't a third-world country," Lee corrected. "Don't refer to it as such outside of this meeting."

Pendleton didn't appreciate being reprimanded in general, but he immensely disliked Lee doing so.

"They don't have the resources we need," Pendleton complained.

"She might have fled," Dobbs suggested.

"How?" Pendleton queried. "We have the border control being monitored."

"You imagine an asset like Corsair wouldn't show Khloe Evans how to skirt that?" Lee pressed.

"So you think she's gone?" Pendleton inquired. "Why are we even here, then?"

"Pendleton, watch it," she warned.

"You know what, Lee? I'm over this shit," Pendleton cursed. "You lost Corsair—what?—three or four times now."

Lee cocked her head. "And how many times have you found him?" she asked pointedly.

Pendleton snorted. "If I found him, I wouldn't lose him again."

"Let's hope not," Lee agreed. "Of course, you need to find him first. Something that so far, you've failed at."

Dobbs snickered under his breath while the two junior agents, Sparr and Garrett, looked on like surprised deer.

Pendleton pushed to his feet. "I'm getting a smoke," he blurted out before storming out of the room.

Lee lifted an eyebrow after the other agent vacated the makeshift conference area. Dobbs turned his attention away from Lee to the paper in front of him.

"Sorry, guys," Lee offered. "Where were we?"

"We targeted these locations yesterday," Sparr explained, waving her hand over the map. The young female operative had some potential, and Lee appreciated her attention to detail.

"And we got nothing?" Lee questioned. From the corner of her eye, she reviewed the street layout on the map. They were within a short distance from the house where Khloe Evans was hiding. Too close, Lee thought. If they started a door-to-door search, it would only be a matter of time.

Luckily, that wasn't on the table yet. In a foreign country, such searches were harder to pull off without alerting the government. Not doing so, however, opened intelligence officers up to accusations of espionage.

For a nation like Belize, it wouldn't mean a lot. Perhaps a complaint to the ambassador, which, at best, might earn a slap on the wrist. In other countries, though, it resulted in getting the agents expelled. That assumed that the American personnel had committed no crimes.

Lee considered revisiting Khloe to check in on her. Her words to the girl had been simple. She'd wanted to speak with Corsair about clearing him and taking down Carl Winston. So far, the former OOC agent hadn't reached out to Lee, which could indicate he hadn't gotten the message or couldn't do so yet. But it was feasible that Caleb Saunders preferred to have nothing to do with Lee Hubbard and the Office of Compliance. She understood his trepidation about that, but if he didn't cooperate with her, she'd have to change her tactics. That would involve coming after him with the full force of the OOC.

Would that spook the girl if she reappeared again?

"We had one woman call and report an American woman had been in her store," Dobbs informed. "But there was no kid with her."

"Amanda Harrod is too young to be left alone," Lee considered.

"We don't know that the Evans girl doesn't have anyone else here. There's a community of ex-pats, and finding childcare might not be that difficult."

"Are we asking within the ex-pat population?" Lee asked.

"It's spread out, but yes, we're doing what we can," Dobbs detailed.

"Let's keep at it," Lee told the three agents. "Sparr, why

don't you take a couple of people? We need to check the off-shore islands. There are lots of Americans and tourists to get lost with."

"That will be like a needle in a haystack," Dobbs pointed out.

Lee agreed. "I agree. However, it's the perfect place to blend in, right? No doubt Corsair set them up somewhere the three of them wouldn't stand out."

Dobbs nodded. "That makes sense."

"Listen, I'm open to ideas," Le said. "We continue to monitor the airport, ports, and bus stations, but if Khloe Evans is hiding out, we will get nowhere until she emerges."

"How long can she stay below the radar?" Sparr wondered.

Lee shrugged. "Honestly, who knows? It is safe to assume they have adequate means to live on," she explained. "She could hide indefinitely in her house and only deal with food deliveries."

"Should we track those?" Garrett asked, breaking his silence.

"We can try, but that would be a monumental task," Lee noted. "Our world is driven by deliveries."

"Perhaps we get the word out to delivery drivers," Garrett suggested.

"We couldn't keep it contained," Lee advised. "We could post her picture and find her a lot quicker, too, but we'd tip our hand. If Corsair didn't know we were here, he would then."

"But Corsair is probably still in South America, right?" Dobbs asked.

"To the best of our knowledge," Lee responded. "That doesn't mean he isn't monitoring what's happening around here. He might have someone else, like Khloe Evans, watching social media. What do you think she'd do if she saw her face splashed across the internet?"

"Burrow deeper," Dobbs replied.

"Exactly," Lee confirmed.

"Okay, guys," Dobbs addressed Sparr and Garrett. "You heard what Director Hubbard said. Let's make it happen."

Both junior agents nodded as they gathered the papers in front of them. Dobbs lingered until Sparr and Garrett left.

"Lee, what about Pendleton?" he asked.

"What about him?"

"He doesn't like you," Dobbs pointed out.

"Your intuition is spot-on," Lee remarked.

"Look, I don't mean to push," Dobbs said. "Director Winston pulled him into his office. I think he might be grooming Pendleton to be his lackey."

"Pendleton is just smart enough to be Carl's shadow."

"I have nothing against you or Director Winston, but Pendleton thrives for all the attention. He will run you down if he thinks it'll get him your title."

Lee nodded. "I appreciate your looking out for me," she told Dobbs. "I'll be mindful of him."

"Technically, we're supposed to answer to him, and he answers to you," Dobbs reminded her.

As Lee knew too well, chain of command was a nefarious device. Pendleton could complain to Winston that his direct reports were ignoring him to follow Lee's orders. Never mind that she outranked Pendleton and he was directly under her. In bureaucracy, such things were fodder for the fire.

"Report to him and me," she suggested with a devious smile. "Just remember to listen to me only."

"Yes, ma'am."

Dobbs gathered his files and left Lee in the conference

room alone. She stared at the street map of Belize hanging on the wall. Sparr had marked off areas they had already canvassed. So far, they'd covered most of the city with no luck.

It was no surprise. A manhunt was like a game of Whack-A-Mole—only in this case, the moles weren't sticking their heads up to be whacked. No heads meant no target. Unless Khloe Evans and Amanda Harrod's heads jutted out of their burrow, the OOC's fugitive squad had nothing to hit.

She needed some air. Lee appreciated Dobbs's warning, but at the moment, she wasn't sure how to handle Pendleton. He was interfering, and if he was in direct contact with Carl Winston, that changed things.

Did Winston suspect that Lee was working behind his back? Other than Angie and her brief conversation with Khloe Evans, Lee had kept her agenda to herself. That didn't mean Winston was ignorant of it, however.

Lee narrowed her eyes. Her relationship with Angie was a secret in the office. A workplace romance was already challenging enough. Add in national security and a blatantly homophobic superior, and issues multiplied.

Why hadn't Corsair gotten back to Khloe? That bothered Lee. By now, he should have been out of South America. It wasn't like there weren't plenty of options. Hell, drug runners ran cocaine daily to the US and other nations.

No, something had happened. Either he'd found himself delayed—not detained, or the OOC would have been informed—or he'd made it back and already left the country with Khloe and Amanda. But Lee didn't believe it was the latter.

If she contacted Khloe again, she might warn her that the OOC was closing in. Perhaps that would garner enough goodwill with Caleb Saunders that he would contact her. It was a big gamble. Approaching Khloe again might send her and Amanda running, and they'd lose them altogether.

Lee decided the chance was worth it. She'd rather watch Khloe escape than have the OOC, who might use unscrupulous means to catch Corsair, rope her in. Truth be told, Lee preferred Caleb out in the world than captured by Carl Winston. Right now, he provided a potential failsafe against Winston.

That settled it for her. Lee gathered her things and exited the room. She saw Dobbs talking with Pendleton across the courtyard. Dobbs lifted his eyes to look at her, but Pendleton refused to glance her way. In fact, his rigid determination not to acknowledge her was visible from this distance.

Lee didn't care. Let him stew about her.

She headed for the parking lot and the rental Toyota waiting for her. There was no need to look back to see Pendleton watching her. Lee sensed his eyes burning a hole into her back.

A minute later, she was on the street. She would need an excuse for her trip, but she had time to create one.

18

"How many?" Danny asked, dumbfounded.

"Ten," Caleb explained to the two American travelers and Bella. They stood in a semicircle around a table in Bella's hut. Twelve machine guns, four handguns, and a pile of various ammunition and magazines were strewn on the table's surface.

"You killed them all?" Deke clarified.

Caleb didn't answer. "They were coming here. My guess is a late-night raid."

"Why would they do that?" Danny questioned.

Bella said, "Because they found out we killed their men."

"How?" Deke asked.

"We missed someone lurking in the rainforest," Caleb speculated.

Bella folded her arms. If she was trying to hide the disgust on her face, she failed. However, Caleb guessed she wanted that message delivered to all of them.

"Well, now that you've made it worse, what do you expect us to do?" Bella asked Caleb.

"These guys were untrained," Caleb explained. "I'd also wager they were the elite of the group."

"What makes you say that?" Danny asked.

"If it was a raid—and they know we killed their other men—they aren't going to send the weakest fighters out. If I were sending them to attack the village, I'd expect them to kill most of the people here. You don't deploy untested men to murder women and children."

"Unless it's a test," Deke suggested. "Like how gang members back home have to be initiated."

Caleb shook his head. "You might have a point, but these weren't fresh recruits. They could handle their weapons. At least adequately enough to suggest they'd had some practice."

"You said they were untrained," Danny pointed out.

"I meant that they lacked the same discipline as most military organizations," Caleb corrected.

"You think they planned to kill us all?" Bella questioned.

Caleb nodded. "These guys weren't coming to a barbecue," he stated. "They sent three—or four—men, and we took them out."

"You," Bella interjected. "*You* killed them."

Caleb ignored her. "This time, Mateo, or whoever's in charge, sent ten men, thinking that would do the job."

"But Rick," Deke said, his voice sounding almost awestruck. "You stopped all of them."

"I'm going to talk to my people," Bella announced. "We have to decide if we stay or not."

"Not is probably smarter," Caleb recommended.

Bella glared at him without another word and marched out of the hut.

"Seriously, Rick, who the hell are you?" Deke demanded. "Like a Navy SEAL?

He shook his head. "Listen, guys. This is going to get dangerous here. If Bella's people leave, you should go with them."

The two young men exchanged glances. Danny spoke first. "I want to stay."

"Are you certain?" Caleb asked. "This isn't your fight."

Deke nodded. "He's right, Rick. We'll stay."

"Yeah," Danny added. "Look, I've done nothing with my life. Not anything important. This feels like a thing I'll regret if I walk away from it."

"Guys, if you stick it out, this might not be something you will ever escape," Caleb warned. "I don't know how many more men they have. It might get worse."

"You had our backs," Danny reminded him. "Otherwise, Deke and I would be dead."

"I think we're here for a reason," Deke surmised. "Like, this is why you saved us."

Caleb chuckled. "It's possible I saved you so that you could save me. If you two hadn't been there, I'd have died on that river."

"That's the same thing," Danny countered. "We kept you hydrated and fed. You took on an entire gang for us."

"I think we just want to believe we did the best we could," Deke added.

"Hell, from now on, I'll be asking myself, 'What would Rick do?'" Danny remarked. "It's going to be my new mantra."

"Don't follow my example," Caleb said, shaking his head.

"Can you tell us what you are?" Deke asked. "Or is it top secret?"

Caleb nodded. "It's top secret. And the truth is, if you talk about me to people, it might put a target on your back."

"Great, so we fight off some army and never get to brag to anyone about it," Danny joked.

"Just don't mention me," Caleb said. "Take all the credit."

"What do we do now, Rick?" Deke asked.

"How well can you two shoot?" he asked the pair.

"Most of my target practice came from *Call of Duty*," Danny admitted.

"You seemed to handle the gun decently yesterday," Caleb said to Deke.

"I know enough about guns. My dad used to hunt with me as a kid. Gun safety was important."

Caleb gave Danny a questioning look.

"Same, but I never hunted," he said.

"Okay, quick firearm lesson," Caleb announced, picking up the submachine gun on top of the stack. "This is a FN FAL submachine gun. Most of them have twenty-round magazines." Caleb patted one of two drum magazines. "These hold fifty bullets, though."

"That's a lot," Deke remarked.

"Not really," Caleb countered. "When everyone is shooting, you're going to panic and fire more than you need to."

"Conserve ammo?" Deke questioned.

"Nah, but hit what you are shooting. Number-one rule: don't aim the gun at anything you don't want to shoot. Rule number two: don't put your finger on the trigger until you are prepared to shoot. Three: don't squeeze the trigger until you are certain you want to kill what you are aiming at. Roger?"

"Roger," both men replied.

Caleb dropped the magazine from the FN FAL and cleared the chamber before handing it to Deke. "Get the feel for it," he advised. "Dry-fire it a few times to test the trigger pressure. You need to know how much effort you need to apply. The last thing you want is to fire the weapon when you aren't ready. Danny might not appreciate you accidentally shooting him."

"It breaks the rules," Deke pointed out, and Caleb gave a nod. Deke raised the rifle up and peered down the barrel.

"Use the aperture to line up your shot," Caleb instructed, tapping his index finger on the rear eyepiece.

Deke obeyed him, seeming to take aim before firing.

"Stop," Caleb ordered. "When you pulled the trigger, you immediately jerked your eyes up to check your target. That causes the barrel to come up. You could miss your target completely."

"Right," Deke said. "Don't raise my head."

"Deke, remember that if you follow the rules, when you pull the trigger, you'll hit what you aimed at. So don't lift your head. Instead, assume you hit your target and move to the next one," Caleb instructed. "But don't move until you pull the trigger. It's all about the timing."

"Got it," the boy said, taking his position again and squeezing the trigger.

"Better," Caleb praised. He pulled the magazine off another gun, cleared the chamber, and handed it to Danny.

"Okay, both of you aim at that stain on the wall," he told the pair, pointing at a dark discoloration in the wood's grain. Both obeyed. "Fire."

Caleb heard the click as the hammer came down on an empty chamber. "Aim for the window and fire."

Two more clicks.

"Now, I want you to rotate from the stain to the window to the picture behind us."

The two boys turned back to see a watercolor painting of a flowering bush. Bella's name scrawled across the bottom claimed her as the artist. "Fire together and change targets. Keep doing it until you two are in sync."

They started. Click, rotate, click, rotate, click, rotate. Caleb studied them as they moved.

"Don't stop," he urged after Deke slowed down around the tenth rotation. "Stay together."

By the twenty-second time, Deke and Danny were moving in time with each other. They looked almost like some strange clock that continued ticking after the initial winding stopped.

"Can we fire some real ammo?" Deke asked after twenty minutes of drilling.

"We can't spare it," Caleb admitted. "We don't know how big a force is coming, and we will need all the ammo we can get."

Both men nodded in understanding.

"Here's the other thing," Caleb said. "This is our armory. It's the one thing we need to stop these guerrillas."

"We need to guard it?" Danny inquired.

"Yes," Caleb answered. "At least one of you up here with it. Armed, of course."

"What are you going to do?" Deke asked.

"First, I should speak with Bella and the villagers," Caleb said. "A lot depends on what the Zion's Garden team does. I don't think we can count on them to fight, but that might be okay. The community has to decide, too. They may decide to leave the village for Mateo and his people. If that's the case, we remain on defense."

"Will this Mateo follow them?" Danny asked. "We—I mean, you killed a lot of their men."

"If it comes to that, we'll see," Caleb replied, although he suspected the answer was yes. No matter what happened, Mateo would have the village of São Miguel do Tapajós in his sights. Once he established the gold deposit, he'd come after the settlement. If for no other reason than to force the villagers to mine his precious ore for him.

"Rick, this is the right thing to do?" Danny inquired.

Caleb cocked his head. That was something he had been struggling with himself. Not that protecting São Miguel do Tapajós was wrong. These people needed help, and it was important that men like Caleb or even Deke and Danny stepped up to support them.

No, Caleb's concern was elsewhere. In Belize. He missed Amanda. This had been the longest he'd ever been apart from her. Even before Audrey and Jackson died, he'd only spent one week with Audrey on a cruise while the kids stayed with his in-laws. That had been seven days. Now, he was pushing three and half weeks away from her, and almost two since he last contacted Khloe. She was probably worried sick, and if she'd done what Caleb instructed, she and Amanda should be on the move.

That scared him more than anything. Amanda's passport was perfect, but Khloe only had one in her given name. The whole point of the trip to Colombia had been to secure her a forgery. And that had gone so well that now Caleb was about to go to war with a small guerrilla army.

Was this little village worth it? Worth losing Amanda? Even if he didn't lose her, was this fair to both girls? While Amanda was young and would trust anything Khloe told her, the woman would be beside herself with worry. He'd gone over several means to leave the country, but it was a lot easier when one had some experience. Besides, Khloe and Amanda looked like easy targets for many bad people.

Thoughts of them twisted his stomach in knots, a new sensation while he was in the field. Corsair had never had entanglements. He had no real family, no loved ones, no friends. That, Caleb realized, was what had attracted Carl Winston to him. The perfect killing machine was someone who didn't have to come home because no one was going to miss him. Before he met Audrey, Caleb Saunders had fit that bill.

At present, he was extremely worried about a three-year-old girl over a thousand miles away. Somewhere inside him, that left him feeling empty yet hopeful. It wasn't a sensation he could have described before having children. Perhaps not even until he lost Jackson and Audrey.

The answer to Danny's question, though, was still the same. And it followed Hood's rule: it was the problem in front of Caleb right now.

"Yes, we're doing the right thing," Caleb said.

19

———

"What are the rest doing?" a blond girl in her twenties asked Bella as Caleb entered the hut where the Zion's Garden team had gathered.

"I'm not sure, Sophia," Bella replied. "I plan to talk with Leandro after I finish with you."

"They killed Bernie, though," another man declared. He was in his early thirties with a shaggy beard. If Caleb had to sketch a modern-day hippie, he would have drawn this guy, right down to his thin linen shirt with drawstrings around the neck. "I'm totally for helping our friends, but dying for them is completely different."

"I understand, Jason," Bella responded. Her tone remained diplomatic, and Caleb was reminded of a kindergarten teacher with a mellow but stern demeanor.

"Bella, they almost kidnapped you," Jason continued. "If it weren't for those other guys, who knows what they would have done to you?"

"It didn't happen, though," Bella argued.

"Yeah," another older man replied. "Because that guy

killed them." The older gentleman pointed to the rear of the hut where Caleb stood.

All eyes turned to train on Caleb, who gave a single nod of greeting.

"Rick, wasn't it?" the older man inquired.

"Yes," Caleb replied.

"Don," he introduced himself. "What are you going to do?"

"It will all depend," he told Don. "If the villagers decide to flee, then there's nothing to do."

"Do we go with them?" Sophia wondered. "If they move."

"I don't know yet," Bella said.

"That will matter, Bella," a twenty-something boy noted. "What's our incentive to stay?"

"The incentive is the same, Jason," Don declared. "We came here to help the people. If they stay here or go start over elsewhere, our goal should be the same."

"Amen," Sophia concurred.

"We have to consider the team's safety," Bella told them. "I would need to reach out to our leadership at Zion's Garden to see what they want us to do."

"They'll evacuate us," Don stated.

"Most likely," Bella agreed. "But there are logistical problems with our leaving right now."

Caleb leaned against the wall, listening.

"What are they?" Sophia asked.

"Probably the concern that these guerrillas may be waiting for us to leave and split off from the village," Don said.

"We don't know that," Bella amended.

"Why would they do that?" Jason asked.

Don replied, "They don't want us to report what they're doing. The Brazilian government might intercede."

"Again, we don't know that," Bella repeated. "We would need to arrange transport, and Felipe isn't supposed to return with the boat until Monday."

Caleb suddenly realized that after his fever and lost time, he had no idea what day it was. It took him a few seconds to narrow down that it was Thursday, although he might verify that with someone just to be sure.

"It's only twenty miles to Santarém," Jason said.

"We still have to cross the river," Don argued. "Then we're still running through the jungle where these thugs live. What if we run into some of them? Will they let us live?"

"What do you suggest, Don?" Sophia questioned.

Bella's face showed her frustration, but she allowed the others to speak.

"Well, what's Rick going to do?" Don asked.

"Like I said, it will depend," Caleb answered again. "However, if the village doesn't or can't leave, I'll stay and help them."

Bella stated, "I plan to stay as well."

"Are you going to fight?" Sophia wondered.

"I will," Jason volunteered.

"Bella's not going to fight," Donsaid, breaking her silence in the back of the crowd..

Bella shook her head. "No, I'm not fighting, but I can help."

"People like this won't just stop," Don remarked, his tone more aggressive. "If you stay—if we stay—we will have to fight."

"I don't," Bella shot back. "I can serve God without killing people."

"Probably get to see him quicker, then," Don mumbled.

"Don!" Sophia barked.

"Listen, I'm sorry," Don apologized. "I'm not wrong, though. Have you seen these people?"

"Didn't you hear what Rick did?" Jason blurted out. "He killed like ten of them."

Don rolled his eyes. "So he says."

Caleb smiled as Bella glanced back at him. For the first time since he'd arrived in the village, the woman appeared to connect with him on a deeper level.

"We all saw what he did with those three who tried to grab Bella," Sophiapointed out.

"Anyone could have done that," Don argued. "He surprised them."

Jason spat out a laugh. "Like to see you do it."

"You doubt my ability?" Don countered. "Four years in the army, man."

Caleb cocked his head. Perhaps he had misjudged Don as one of those burnouts who pulled a stint or two in the military before he couldn't take it anymore.

"Army?" Caleb questioned.

Don turned to regard Caleb. "Yeah, what of it?"

"If you decide to stay and fight, that might come in handy."

"What's your experience, Rick?" Don asked, though not out of curiosity. The older man wanted to establish a pecking order, though Caleb doubted Don could compare his time in the army's motor pool with being an assassin for the United States. Hell, Caleb had pulled the trigger more than once at the express command of POTUS, who had given the order from the White House Situation Room.

However, at least the army taught their soldiers to shoot. That was a leg-up on almost everyone else here.

"Well?" Don pressed.

"I was in the Marines," Caleb said. It wasn't a complete lie. He'd been in the Marine Corps for a few weeks before being plucked from Parris Island by Marcus David, AKA Hood.

"Good," Don said. "What about your buddies? They Marines, too?"

Caleb shook his head. "It doesn't matter."

"Are you going to stay and fight, then?" Sophia questioned. "How many are there?"

"We don't know," Caleb answered.

"Rick believes that the group he encountered last night planned to come into the village and kill everyone," Bella said.

"Really?" Jason exclaimed. "That's crazy. Why?"

"These are bad people, Jason," Sophia said in her high-pitched voice. Caleb suspected that either she and Jason were a couple or there was some chemistry between them.

"Sophia's right," Caleb replied. "I don't know why they're coming here."

Bella's stare connected with his, and she gave him a brief, satisfied nod. He'd gambled that she hadn't told her team about the gold yet. That might be smart. He'd told her already that people get strange when something like gold or anything that seemed like untold wealth came up. Even her Zion's Gardeners might just give up farming in favor of prospecting.

"We should all leave," Sophia suggested. "I don't want to die here."

"Sophia is right," Jason agreed, not seeming to surprise anyone.

Bella looked over at the one individual who hadn't

spoken since Caleb arrived. The woman was ten years older than Caleb, making her the eldest of the group.

"Joanne, what do you think?" Bella asked.

The older woman straightened up. She took several seconds to stare at each person in the room as if she were assessing their value.

"We don't have a lot of choices available," she acknowledged.

"That's not an answer," Don scolded.

"I'm not done, Don," Joanne snapped.

Don threw his hands up in a frustrated gesture.

Joanne went on, "I've been around a bit. Ten years in Africa with the Corps."

Caleb's ears pricked up, and the woman noticed his attention.

"Peace Corps," she added, giving him a grin. He smiled back at her.

She continued, "I've seen warlords and bad things come through. Often, everything we built got destroyed in the fights. I don't intend to pick up arms, but I'm here for the people of São Miguel. If they stay, I'll stay. If they go, I'll go."

"You might die," Jason warned.

"I could die flying out of Rio," Joanne countered.

"This seems more likely," he argued.

She shrugged. "Then so be it."

"I want to go," Sophia repeated.

Bella gave Caleb a dubious stare. "I'm not sure how we can do that," she told Sophia.

"Soph, there's no boat," Jason reminded her.

"What do we do, then?" Sophia asked anxiously.

"Evacuate," Caleb suggested.

Everyone turned to look at him, and he continued, "Whether or not the villagers want to stay and fight, we have to start evacuating some people. The best thing we can do is move the women, children, and elders out. It will protect them and reduce our liability."

"Liability?" Jason repeated. "You sound like an insurance guy."

Caleb ignored him. "If those of us putting up a defense have to worry about unarmed villagers, we lose some advantage. Because I can promise you that Mateo and his people won't care one bit whether our people are armed or not. Better to get them to safety in case we don't succeed."

"You don't think we can win?" Sophia asked.

"I never said that," he countered. "However, the possibility of failure always exists. Either we take it into account, or we leave ourselves open to destruction."

"You mean like a plan B?" Don pondered.

"Something like that," Caleb agreed.

"How do we do this?" Bella asked. "You seem to be our expert in warfare."

"He's not the only one," Don said quickly, envy lacing his voice.

Bella regarded the older man. "Right, of course," she said quickly.

"You know what, Don?" Caleb interjected. "I think you and I can discuss our strategy for holding the village after we decide where to safely move everyone else."

"How much time do we have?" Jason asked.

"Tomorrow would be my guess," Caleb offered. "At the earliest. If their plan was to come in last night, then late today is the soonest Mateo would expect word. However, that's aggressive. I didn't find any radios on the guerrillas I searched. They weren't in communication with the base camp, or they would have called in reinforcements."

"You're sure they didn't?" Don asked.

"No," Caleb admitted. "But if they had, I think we'd have seen signs of them by now."

"It's not like we're watching the jungle," Don pointed out. "How would we know?"

"Someone would've been shot," Caleb answered.

Don raised his eyebrows. "Great barometer there, Marine."

Caleb turned his attention back to Bella. "We need to get the villagers moved," he urged her.

"I'm heading there next," she said. "To talk with Leandro about this."

"Is he the leader?"

"De facto," Don commented.

"Yeah," Bella said. "Like Don said, it's not exactly hierarchal here, but he's one of the older villagers who takes charge."

"Makes sense," Caleb acknowledged.

"Why don't you come with me?" Bella asked.

Caleb nodded, turning to Don. "Why don't you take a look at the outskirts of the village? We need to start setting up defenses."

Don smiled. Being tasked with a command like that clearly pleased the former soldier. Caleb noticed a half-smirk cross Bella's face as she recognized Caleb's tactic. She motioned for Caleb to follow her. "I'd like to go with the villagers," Joanne said. "They'll need help getting set up where ever they go."

Bella nodded. "Good idea, we need someone to stay with them." There was an unspoken comment that everyone thought—"In case we don't survive here."

The pair left the hut, searching for the town leaders.

"Nice move there," she remarked.

"With Don?"

"Yeah, I figured he'd want to tag along to talk with Leandro. That seemed counterproductive to me."

Caleb shrugged. "If he has some experience we can use, I'll take it."

"Don's a lot of hot air," Bella commented.

"That may be," Caleb said. "Or he might come through in a clinch."

"I hope it doesn't come to that," Bella stated.

"Me too," Caleb agreed. "Don't count on it, though."

"That's what I'm afraid of," Bella replied sadly. "This won't end well."

Caleb glanced at the missionary, knowing her words were foreboding but likely accurate.

20

———

The house looked empty. Lee knew it before she got out of the rental car. A vacant aura surrounded the house. The other houses in the little neighborhood showed almost no life, either, but somehow this one looked more sterile.

She parked by the curb and proceeded toward the home. It was a bit after lunch, and the afternoon brought activity. Neighbors walked along the sidewalk. Most were women pushing strollers or walking with their toddlers in hand.

Lee stood at the front door and knocked. She turned slowly, examining the street. There were few vehicles visible. Most people had returned to work for the afternoon. Those who were at home stored their cars in garages.

Besides her car, she noticed one other vehicle, a blue Ford Escort. Much like the residence, it had a clean, unused appearance to it. Much like her own rental car.

No one answered the door. She reached down and checked the knob. The place seemed secure.

Lee looked back at the Ford Escort parked half a block away. Just far enough to be out of sight if someone peeked out the front window. That could be a coincidence, though. The car could simply belong to a person who lived in a house down the street, or to someone else with a vacation rental.

Lee didn't like it, though. She felt sure Khloe wasn't inside the house. Well, "sure" was an overstatement. Lee suspected Khloe was gone. Whether she'd just taken a quick trip with Amanda Harrod to the beach or the park was another question.

The deputy director of the Office of Compliance walked around the house to the rear. Lee opened a chain-link gate that led to a rocky backyard. Like the front of the house, the area behind it seemed unused. No toys left where the girl had played. Not a surprise. That could reflect a conscious effort to hide a child in the house. Lee expected as much from Corsair. And Khloe, his protégé.

That thought reminded Lee that Amanda Harrod was only three years old. This little girl had lived her life on the run. What kind of experience did that give her? Could Caleb Saunders keep her living like that?

No, Lee decided. That wasn't feasible for the long term. Caleb Saunders intended to settle down somewhere off the grid or with a new alias. Amanda Harrod was young enough to not remember anything that happened in the last year. Or if she did, it would be the vague recollections of a toddler.

That thought almost comforted Lee. Despite her duty to the OOC, she rooted for Caleb and Amanda. They had to escape this life. Since she didn't believe Corsair had committed treason as Carl Winston liked to claim, she didn't share his compulsion to bring him to justice. If anything, Lee Hubbard believed that Caleb Saunders deserved a nice retirement.

However, she still needed him. If she could convince

Corsair to aid her takedown of Winston, she could help the assassin clear his name and get him into a protection program.

But all of that mattered little if she didn't find him and Amanda. What if Caleb had already made it back? They might be gone for good.

The rear of the house had an enclosed patio with a sliding glass door. She placed her hands on the pane, peering inside. When she saw no one, she tested the sliding door. It slid open, and Lee stepped inside. Her skin prickled, and she reached for the Kel-Tec PF9 holstered under her shirt. In the heat of the Central American sun, she tried to hide the weapon as much as possible.

Lee shook off the anxiety and stepped toward another door. Her nerves fired off alerts throughout her body, and the Kel-Tec came out of its holster without her thinking. She stared at the entrance to the house. It hung ajar, but the imprint on the door jamb triggered Lee's alarm bells. Two flat impressions had crushed the wood and scraped the paint clean, revealing a couple of small stripes of bare wood.

The marks looked like they came from a thin crowbar or hammer claw. They were located in exactly the place she would have inserted such a tool if she intended to break into a house.

Her left hand pushed the door open. As it swung wide, she noticed the deadbolt still extended and the frame where it secured the lock shattered.

She stepped into the house with the Kel-Tec raised. When she entered, she found herself in a narrow galley-style kitchen with a small gas stove and half-sized refrigerator. Unlike the yard, someone had used the kitchen. Dishes lay on a towel where they had been washed and left to dry. The trash overflowed, and Lee wondered if Khloe Evans hadn't taken it out for fear of attracting attention. The garbage had brought the flies in, and several buzzed around the can.

Green goo filled the basin, and when Lee saw the over-turned container, she recognized the mixture as melted ice cream. A plastic zipper bag sat on the edge of the sink. It had some dried green ice cream on it, too.

Lee continued through the space. Her sharpened senses warned her she wasn't alone. Whether the other person in the house was Khloe or not remained a mystery. Lee hoped the girls had left, but the busted back door suggested otherwise.

She moved into the living room. A couple of old paper-backs lay beside the couch. From their covers, they looked like romances, but Lee passed them without further inspection.

Her feet locked in place when something shifted some-where in the house. Lee faced the short corridor with three doors, all of them closed. If Khloe had been here, she'd have left the doors open, wouldn't she? If Amanda played in the rear, Khloe would want to stay in earshot of her. Unless someone was in the bathroom, it made little sense to shut that door, either. At least that was Lee's assessment of people. They were too lazy to close all the doors.

She reached for the knob of the nearest door. Lee stood with her spine pressed to the plaster to the left of the door. As she turned the handle, the wall on the right side of the door popped as a bullet ripped through the thin walls.

Lee threw herself away from the room, stumbling as she did so. The agent landed on her back in the middle of the hall. A figure appeared in the door, and Lee fired. Her rounds struck the doorjamb, and the shape retreated into the room.

Something scraped loudly across the floor. The house shook as the door slammed shut, hitting the wall.

Lee rolled to her feet, keeping her Kel-Tec up as she charged at the door. Another gunshot blew a hole through the door near her head. Lee retreated before a third shot sprayed splinters across the hall.

Backing down the passageway, Lee yanked open the door to find a small windowless bathroom. Glass shattered in the adjacent room, and Lee raced down the passage, praying the intruder in the room didn't fire into the hallway now.

As she charged out the kitchen door, she saw a form leap over the gate.

"Dammit!" Lee cursed, spinning to dash toward the front entry. She barreled through the door to see the Ford Escort down the street race away.

The deputy director of the OOC stepped back in the vacation rental before the neighbors could report a crazed woman with a gun in their neighborhood. She turned to survey the home where Khloe Evans and Amanda Harrod had been. She closed her eyes, rewinding the last two minutes in her head.

When the image of the figure in the doorway appeared in her memory, she tried to freeze it. A fleeting glimpse of his face left his features undefined. He had dark skin, but not someone of Latino heritage. No, he looked Middle Eastern. The man wore a linen jacket and pants as if he'd purchased the welcome-to-the-tropics starter set. He only needed the straw hat.

Lee walked back to the bedroom where the intruder had barricaded himself. She threw her shoulder against the door, finding resistance. With more pressure, she rammed the door again. Another loud scraping came from inside. It took two more solid blows from Lee's shoulder to budge the door open enough to squeeze inside.

He'd shoved the twin bed against the door, slowing Lee's entry while he'd broken the window and escaped through it. Lee stopped to see the droplet of blood staining a jagged piece of glass. Lee went to the kitchen and found a piece of plastic wrap. She returned to the bedroom, where she wrapped the shard before breaking it off the window frame. Once it broke free, she wound more plastic film around it.

The room the intruder had barricaded himself in looked like Amanda's. The DVD cases from *Moana* and *The Little Mermaid* lay on the floor. He'd been searching the space when she entered the house. Had he stopped when she knocked on the door? Or had he not heard her? She doubted that. Perhaps he hadn't expected an armed agent? Or had he been in such a hurry that he didn't care?

That a faction from the Middle East wanted Corsair dead came as no surprise to Lee. She'd butted heads with a pair of assassins and her one-time partner in Florida. Those men had likely been employed by Mahmoud Abbas. While Abbas wasn't the only enemy of Corsair's willing to gun him down, the arms dealer had the money and power to send a small army after the former assassin.

Lee wondered if Abbas was involved in this situation as well. From all accounts, a second team in Cartagena had also hunted Corsair. She hadn't been able to trace the money behind that one, though, and the individuals Corsair had allegedly taken down weren't Middle Eastern. Most were mercenaries, like the pair she'd run into in Florida. Apparently, Abbas could spare no expense in his pursuit of Corsair.

Now it seemed someone else had found Khloe and Amanda. Lee circled the space, staring at what remained.

No clothes. Some toy cars and children's DVDs. Lee stalked to the other room. The only clothing she found was some men's shirts. Probably Caleb Saunders's size.

Lee sighed. Khloe had left already, and it didn't look like Caleb had returned. Had the intruder scared them off? She didn't think so. Not if they'd taken their clothes with them. Though they'd probably hurried, Khloe and Amanda had escaped with enough time to pack.

Lee returned to the kitchen. The refrigerator was full of groceries. Lee pulled a container of milk from the shelf, which was still within its expiration date. In fact, it was only missing about a glass's worth of milk. Lee lifted the garbage can and overturned it, spilling the contents all over the kitchen floor.

She pushed the trash around with her toe, sifting through the refuse for anything. She retrieved a receipt covered in what looked like mac and cheese. It was dated yesterday, at Hernandez Grocery. Khloe had spent over a hundred dollars on food.

Lee considered Sparr's report. They'd spoken to a woman there who had encountered an American woman. Lee pulled out her phone and opened the maps app. When she searched for Hernandez Grocery, the app declared it a fifteen-minute walk from her current location.

She dialed Sparr's number and waited.

"Agent Sparr," the female OOC agent said.

"Sparr, it's Hubbard. Do you recall where you had the eyewitness who saw an American?"

"It wasn't me; Dobbs and Garrett did it. Hang on, let me check with Garrett," Sparr replied. Lee heard her cover the speaker and ask, "Hey, Garrett, where did you find that witness yesterday?"

There was a muffled answer, and Sparr came back on

the line. "He says his notes are at the hotel. He thought it was a Hernando Grocery."

"Hernandez?" Lee asked.

She waited as Sparr clarified with Garrett.

"He said it was possible," Sparr replied. "He's not a hundred percent sure."

"Where was it?" Lee questioned.

Another muffled response from Garrett.

"He said it was over near Marage Road, but he doesn't know the actual address," Sparr said.

Lee thanked her and hung up before reopening the maps app to find the red pin on Hernandez Grocery. The nearest cross street was Marage Road.

"Bingo," Lee muttered to herself. Now she wondered if Khloe had spotted Garrett and Dobbs. The pair were excellent agents, but they both looked like how clean-cut government agents were supposed to look. Walking into a store as a pair had ruined any attempt at subtlety.

While Lee was now very worried about Khloe and Amanda, two other questions nagged at her. Who was after them? And had he found anything in this house that could lead him to their current whereabouts?

21

Ifrit cursed his foul luck. He'd thought the woman at the front door had left, and in his haste, he hadn't made sure the back door was secured. It was a foolish error, but thankfully, the mistake hadn't cost him much. He'd had a few minutes to search the house before she came barging in. His search had gained him nothing, except the knowledge that Khloe Evans and Amanda Harrod had bolted from their hideout.

The other woman looked American, although he'd only had a split second to see her. He should have killed her, but at the time, he assumed she hadn't come alone. After all, she looked like an American agent. Perhaps she was one of the Office of Compliance people who were supposedly after Corsair as well. He hadn't expected them to be in Belize, too. Or, he thought they wouldn't be as close as he was. Now, he knew otherwise. He wasn't any closer to capturing his prey, and he had some competition.

Ifrit pulled the car over. He didn't mind a bit of a challenge. Besides, besting the OOC was a feat in itself. It might even help him out. If he could tap into their investigation, he might get a head start. That would require a bit of work, though. Ifrit considered that. He would need to find an in with the OOC, but he knew the perfect person to help him.

For now, though, he needed to focus on Khloe Evans and Amanda Harrod. Had they just changed houses? Maybe they'd found another safe house? Or had they fled the country altogether?

He'd reach out to a contact who could connect him with immigration in Belize. Of course, that presumed that Khloe Evans had taken the time to check out of the country. If she'd driven, she could cross several borders in a matter of hours.

Whatever the case, he suspected that she'd left the house this morning. There were too many groceries.

Ifrit had expected to cross paths with the OOC, but he was surprised they'd found the house. Especially at the same time he had arrived. That was a coincidence he didn't like.

For the first time since escaping Khloe Evans's house, he considered the implications. If it wasn't a coincidence, was the OOC tracking him?

That didn't seem possible. Ifrit ran counter-surveillance on everything. His passports were double-stopped. All of his funds were either cash or on clean credit cards. If the Americans had been tracking him, he hadn't seen any sign of it.

He tapped the wheel of the rented Ford Escort. The car would be a problem now. That wasn't his biggest problem, though. His left hand reached over to his right shoulder. Dried blood crusted the fabric, and there was a jagged rip through the shirt. The slice itself was superficial. In fact, he hadn't noticed it until he was a mile down the road.

How had he been so stupid to get trapped in there with an American agent? At first, he thought he'd gotten away without giving the woman a good look at his face. Now, Ifrit worried that he'd left blood on the scene. That could prove a problem for him. He'd done a good job keeping himself off the grid and out of most systems. In most countries, he wouldn't even worry about them tracking his DNA. The Americans, though, had the resources to trace him with that blood.

It changed his perspective. Should the American find any blood, it could connect him to a few hits he'd performed over the last few years. He could return to the house, wipe the house of any blood, and forgo the pursuit of Khloe Evans, but that would also put him on the wrong side of Abbas. Something he didn't want to do, either.

No, he simply had to find Khloe Evans and Amanda Harrod before the OOC caught up.

That brought him back to the girls. They'd fled the house, but not long before he'd arrived. Ifrit needed to find an internet connection.

But that would have to wait until he got a new vehicle. Ifrit put the Ford into gear and drove toward the center of Belize City. If the agent reported the Ford right away, it would take half an hour for the OOC to trace it to the rental agency. However, that would be a dead end. The card and passport Ifrit had used were for a British man listed as a wholesaler. Even the picture on the passport had been altered. Not enough to throw them off completely, but they wouldn't have an accurate image of him.

However, it meant he couldn't rent another car down here. Ifrit couldn't risk the OOC putting an alert at all rental agencies. If he tried to lease another vehicle in Belize, even under a false identity, he couldn't hide his ethnicity. Not many Middle Eastern men visited Belize, and certainly not alone.

Ifrit found his answer four minutes later as he drove past a shopping center. He turned around and pulled into the lot, parking in the middle of it. Ifrit backed into the space, and when he got out, he walked swiftly away from the vehicle.

His new car, a Subaru Outback, pulled into an empty space. The older white woman exiting the vehicle was alone. American, he thought. All the better.

As the woman turned to pull a bag from the car, Ifrit came up behind her. A thin, porcelain-bladed stiletto knife came out of his pocket, palmed in his hand.

The woman turned as he approached. Shock washed over her face as the blade entered just under her right breast. Ifrit's hand covered her mouth before she could scream. The razor-sharp point punctured the woman's heart. In mere seconds, the life faded from her eyes, and she dropped the keys and her purse on the asphalt. Ifrit pushed her into the back seat of the Subaru.

The assassin scooped up the keys and slid into the front seat. He slid the car into reverse and backed out of the spot. A minute later, he pulled around to the back of the shopping center. Ifrit dragged the body from the rear of the car, depositing her under a pile of trash.

Ifrit pulled out of the shopping center, in search of an internet café.

22

Khloe waited in the restaurant, a tiny diner that looked smaller than the living room of their rental house. The place, called Señor Frogs, was a local restaurant, not the famed island chain of the same name.

She picked at her plate of rice and beans. Amanda sat across from her, rolling a toy Corvette and a small brown Ford pickup truck over the table like it was a road. The truck reminded Khloe of the one her grandfather had when she was a kid. It wasn't brown but hunter-green, but she thought about those summers when she was ten years old and riding in the back of the truck with a couple of bales of hay as Granddaddy carried the hay out to the fields.

The memory flooded through her, and her eyes welled up. Granddaddy had died in that same truck. He'd gone like he always had, carrying hay to the horses. A few hours passed, and he hadn't come back for dinner. Her father and grandmother found him an hour later. A massive heart attack had killed him as he drove through the fields, and the truck had rolled into a gulch.

She remembered her dad telling her the story. They hadn't seen the vehicle but heard the faint singing of Dolly Parton belting out "Jolene." The radio was still playing.

She wondered what discovering Granddaddy's body had been like for her father. Even after finding her boyfriend Nic murdered, she doubted it was the same. Her grandfather had been a kind man, while Nic had been nothing more than a thug. She'd already decided to break it off with him, but then everything changed. Khloe never had time to grieve, and as the months passed, any grief she might have felt for Nic turned to rage for getting himself killed in the first place.

She opened the laptop in front of her. She had checked all the flights out of Belize. Several options presented themselves, but she chose the one flying south to Buenos Aires. The closer she could get to Caleb seemed like the smartest move. That flight left in three hours. She estimated she'd need to buy the tickets only a couple of hours before the plane took off. Any sooner, and the Office of Compliance people would have ample opportunity to catch her at the airport. Waiting less than two hours didn't give them a lot of time, though.

She still had an hour before she could do anything, and the restaurant offered Wi-Fi. She composed an email to Caleb detailing her plan. So far, he hadn't responded to her last message. Khloe didn't want to mention it to Amanda yet, but she was worried. Something must have prevented Caleb from contacting them as he'd promised.

Khloe stared across the table at the three-year-old girl ramming the truck into the Corvette. Would she have to tell her that her father was dead? That terrified her.

Come on, she reassured herself. Caleb had proven himself the most capable man she'd ever met.

Still, she thought back on her grandfather. And her dad. She wanted to call him and her mother. Caleb had advised her to assume the OOC monitored them as well. He'd told her to teach her mom how to use the same type of email drop to communicate with her. She planned to wait to send a message to her family when they left Belize.

"You need to eat, Amanda," Khloe urged. "We have a long trip."

"Are we going to see Daddy?" she asked.

"I hope so, but I'm not sure yet," she admitted. One thing she'd told Caleb early on was that she didn't want to lie to the girl.

"She's too young to know everything," Caleb had warned Khloe.

"I agree," she had replied. "But I don't want to straight-out lie to her."

He'd agreed, but tempered it with the same warning that Amanda remained too young to know everything. According to him, anything that related to operational security shouldn't be explained to Amanda.

"We can explain more as she gets older, of course," Caleb had finished. "But for now, we still have to protect her."

For Khloe, telling Amanda they were going to see Caleb when she wasn't sure they would counted as one of those lies she couldn't utter.

"I hope he's there," Amanda commented.

"Me too," Khloe confessed.

The child scooped a bite of chicken and rice into her mouth. Half the grains fell off the spoon into the girl's lap.

"Good girl," Khloe praised.

The child continued to eat her meal, albeit taking breaks

to smash together her two Matchbox cars in a demolition derby-like manner.

Meanwhile, Khloe checked the flight times before comparing them to the map. The timing was crucial. She figured the OOC would know the second she booked the ticket, though Khloe had no idea how fast they could get agents to the airport. How willing would the Belize government be to help the OOC stop Khloe and Amanda from boarding? Would they then be waiting in Argentina for her to land?

Too many questions, and not a lot of choices. Why wouldn't Caleb respond to her?

She clicked over to the screen with the email draft. Despite knowing nothing had changed, some hopeful side of her prayed that he'd responded in the last five minutes.

No such luck.

She took a few more bites and watched Amanda play. The girl looked at her caretaker. Khloe smiled at the child, who let go of her toy cars to spoon another bite of rice into her mouth. With rice spilling from her lips, she grinned at Khloe.

Khloe closed out the email to Caleb and opened the one to her mom. She saw a new message from her mother. "Khloe, the doctors say Granny Lena's cancer is inoperable. Your dad thinks you shouldn't come back. I wish you could. I miss you so much. Please call me when you can. I'm worried. Love you, Mom."

Khloe typed the start of a response, but stopped after "Mom." She backspaced, erasing everything. It would be better for her to reply once they reached their destination. Khloe also needed some time to process the last two messages. She wasn't able to be there for her sick grandmother.

That gnawed at Khloe, but until she and Amanda found their next place of refuge, any contact with her mother might be dangerous. When they'd left Mexico City, Khloe had called her folks, knowing that by the time they could trace the call, she'd be gone. But she'd done that with Caleb's help and timing.

She still didn't trust herself without his guidance. If she gave anything away, the OOC might swoop in and snatch both her and Amanda.

That made for an untenable situation, and it would spell the end of Caleb. He'd tear through the OOC until he got to Amanda. Khloe wondered if he might do the same for her, too. They'd become close. He was the first man, other than her father, who treated her as if he had no interest in her physically. Caleb came across as more like an uncle than anything else.

In public, people assumed Khloe was his wife, and that was a safe thing to pretend. However, even if she was interested in Caleb, he wasn't in her. That man still only had room in his heart for Audrey Harrod.

She smiled to herself as she recalled hearing Caleb tell Amanda a story about her mother. The words had woven joy and sadness together in a way that Khloe had never felt. After Amanda went to bed, he talked to Khloe about her, too. Caleb credited Audrey as the only reason he was still alive. He still spoke with his late wife, but only when he thought he was alone, usually in the kitchen while he was cooking.

Khloe checked the time. Half an hour until she needed to purchase the tickets. When she clicked to complete the purchase, someone at the Office of Compliance would receive the flag on her name. Given the nature of Corsair's past, they'd call their supervisor, who would then report it to the director. If the OOC had people in Belize, which Khloe knew they did, the director would contact them. At the same time, she had to assume that someone in the OOC would attempt to stop the plane while also pinging the IP address where she'd bought the tickets.

In total, based on what Caleb had taught her, she and Amanda had half an hour before agents stormed the restaurant. That was plenty of time to reach the airport and clear through security.

Khloe tapped the table. "Hurry and eat, Amanda," she urged.

"I'm trying," the girl said with a mouthful of rice.

"Would you like another Coca-Cola?" the woman who operated Señor Frogs asked Khloe.

"Can you give me four bottles?" Khloe asked. "Without opening them?"

The woman nodded before vanishing into the kitchen. She returned less than a minute later with four unopened bottles of Coke.

"Thank you," Khloe said, stashing the glass bottles in her shoulder bag. She'd condensed everything they needed into a backpack and a satchel. Khloe had also stashed the cash from the ice cream container in her bag. Most of the money was stuffed inside various pockets, but the bulk of it was in a secret compartment in her hairbrush.

Caleb had found the brush for her. The handle unscrewed, revealing an empty cylinder. She'd squeezed several thousand dollars into it. Normally, having that much money on her made her nervous, but that was a minor concern compared to the US government breathing down her neck.

Khloe checked the time again. The last half hour had crept past, and now she had to purchase the tickets. She looked at her watch as she scrolled to the flight she needed. After backing out of the website, she clicked on a different flight leaving at the same time and purchased two seats on a United flight to Houston. She jumped to another browser, where a Miami-bound flight was already displayed. Khloe bought two tickets on it. Yet another browser showed a flight that departed an hour from now, heading to New Orleans— she bought two seats on it. Once she was done, she had tickets for six flights in her and Amanda's names, all departing from Belize in the next three hours.

"Let's go," Khloe announced, closing her laptop and grabbing Amanda by the hand. She dropped a hundred-dollar bill on the table. It was a lot more than their tab, but it made up for the US currency.

Khloe and Amanda reached the street as the Uber driver in a Honda Accord pulled up. The pair climbed into the back seat, and the car sped away from the restaurant.

23

Mateo watched his men mill around the encampment. He hadn't heard from Alejandro, and it worried him. Communication out here was difficult. The troops' radios were simple handheld ones with restricted range. On a clear landscape, the signal might travel up to ten miles, but with the canopy of the rainforest, those radio waves seemed to lose strength. The other issue was one of power. Over half the radios were rechargeable, and while the camp had some limited electricity, it wasn't enough to maintain the charges.

Batteries were even more difficult to acquire. The last supply shipment came a week ago, and it only had three packages of AA. It would be later this week before more arrived.

Normally, this was nothing more than an inconvenience. However, with the threat of a battle coming up, Mateo wanted more information.

He sent a pair of younger boys to bring back word from Alejandro. That had been early this morning. He knew Alejandro expected to wait until tonight to attack, but Mateo worried. His anxiety had ramped up since he heard about the men in São Miguel. They'd just killed three of his soldiers with no effort.

Not that Mateo was under the delusion that he had some unstoppable force. However, like most bullies, he'd bought into his own propaganda. Given how much the locals cowered to him and his men, it reinforced to Mateo how feared they were.

Only now, there were some who saw them as weak. That wouldn't do. Once Alejandro obliterated that village, word would spread to the surrounding settlements. *La Aliança Revolucionária do Tapajós* would drag the fear from these people once again.

It wasn't just the men in the village that concerned Mateo. His troops were restless and, even worse, hungry. The communities around the Tapajós River dried up, and with them, any food and money the guerrillas could scrounge.

But if he could find that gold vein, Mateo would print his own currency. Of course, that would come with troubles, but with gold, he could buy whatever he desired. Right now, that was men. He needed more people wanting to fight for him, and gold bought loyalty like nothing else.

By exterminating São Miguel, he wouldn't need to worry about the villagers bringing the government around. All of it depended on him getting into the village and finding the gold before someone else came along.

He crossed the camp. There was still no word from the other two men, Caio and Carlo. Mateo grew concerned for Caio. The pair had been friends for years, and Caio wouldn't run from the group. He doubted Carlo would, either. Although, he knew that the ones who surprised him were those he swore would never betray him.

Such was betrayal, though. No one expected it, which is why it was always so devastating.

Mateo worried for Caio. It hadn't crossed his mind until now, but if his friend had run into those men in the village, perhaps they'd killed them, too.

The guerrilla leader shook his head as he stalked through the sea of tents. Caio was supposed to be nowhere near São Miguel. Were these men doing more than just protecting their town? Could they be coming for Mateo's men? Hunting them?

Someone shouted his name, and Mateo turned around. Several guerrillas merged as some commotion came through camp.

Mateo saw Rian running through the area. He was one of the two boys Mateo had sent out to check on Alejandro.

"Rian?" Mateo asked, raising his hand to stop him.

"Sir, they are dead," the child gasped as he tried to catch his breath.

"Did you run the entire way?" Mateo wondered.

Rian nodded as he panted.

"Alejandro killed everyone in the village?" he asked.

Rian shook his head. "No, sir. He is dead. All our men are dead."

"What?" Mateo exclaimed. "Are you sure?"

Rian gave a nod. "I counted them. Ten."

"Alejandro?" Mateo pleaded.

His head bobbed.

"No!" Mateo shouted, raising his gaze to the trees. His cry echoed through the jungle, and many eyes turned on him. "What happened?"

"We found them on the path. Only a few kilometers from São Miguel."

"We? You went with Luan, yes?"

The boy's face looked down. "Yes, sir."

"Where is he?" Mateo inquired. His head craned to see the other boy coming behind Rian.

"He ran away," Rian admitted. "I tried to stop him."

Mateo stared at the boy with narrowing eyes.

"I'm sorry, sir," Rian replied, begging for mercy.

"He got scared?"

Rian nodded.

"But you weren't?" Mateo clarified.

The boy didn't respond. Instead, he nodded slowly again.

"You were afraid?" Mateo pressed.

"Yes, sir. They all died together," Rian explained. "Many appeared to still be lined up."

"Lined up?"

"Like someone shot them down while they marched."

Mateo wrinkled his brow. "You saw them all?"

Rian nodded. "Yes, sir."

Mateo lifted his eyes, scanning the men moving between tents. "Where is João?" he called.

Rian looked back. "Want me to find him?"

"No," Mateo snapped. He pointed at a nearby soldier. "Get me João," Mateo ordered.

The guerrilla acknowledged his command with a "yes, sir" before running through the camp.

Mateo focused on the young recruit. "Tell me what else you saw?"

"Their guns were gone," Rian explained. "All of them. Even the pistols."

"Ammo, too?"

"I think," Rian admitted.

"You did well, boy," Mateo told him. "Why didn't you run away, too?"

"I'm not a coward," Rian stated.

"I thought you said you were afraid," Mateo questioned.

"Yes, but I'm not a coward," he repeated.

"Good, my son. We need brave men like you."

"What about Luan?" Rian wondered.

Mateo straightened up. "What do you think we should do with him?" he asked the boy.

"He's a coward," Rian acknowledged. "He would make us weaker."

Mateo nodded in agreement and waited.

"But he should pay for his cowardice," Rian replied.

"Is he your friend?" Mateo asked.

"No, sir. I'm no friend with a coward."

"But you were?" Mateo pressed. "It's okay if you say yes."

Rian nodded. "I didn't know he had no courage, though."

"Of course not," Mateo agreed. "I want you to find him."

"Yes, sir," Rian acknowledged. "Do I bring him here to you?"

Mateo shook his head slowly.

Rian's eyes widened. "Don't bring him back?" he asked again.

"He doesn't deserve that," Mateo said. "Does he?"

"No, sir."

"Good job, Rian. Handle it for me."

The boy dropped his chin before running off

"Sir." João came through the camp with another man, Bento.

"Bento, you look better," Mateo stated. "I regret losing my temper with you."

The bruised and battered guerrilla replied through a swollen mouth, "I understand."

"Thank you for not holding it against me," Mateo said. "I'll make it up to you."

"What can we do?" João asked.

"Rian returned with distressing word," Mateo explained. "Alejandro is dead, along with all his men."

"All of them?" João asked, dumbfounded.

"From what the boy reported, yes," Mateo answered.

Bento kept his face down, staring at his feet. João repeated, "All ten of them?"

"Sounded like someone ambushed them," Mateo informed them.

"Those bastards," João mumbled.

"João, I want you to take the place of Alejandro."

"Sir?"

"You've been faithful. Alejandro was not just my friend, but my advisor, too. I expect the same from you."

"Of course, Mateo," João replied, beaming.

"Bento, you will help João. We are in a crisis."

The same man Mateo nearly beat to death nodded his affirmation.

"We also lost Caio and Carlo," Mateo told the pair. "Alejandro didn't believe Caio would run. Do you two agree?"

Both Bento and João voiced their confirmation. "No, Caio proved faithful," João declared.

Bento added, "I don't think Carlo would leave, either, if it matters."

"We have to assume the people who are helping the villagers are doing more than just lending defense. They are coming for us."

"How dare they?" João demanded.

"I'm going to share with you why we want São Miguel," Mateo said.

Both men gave their leader undivided attention.

"Gold," Mateo replied. "That village sits on or, at least, very near a large deposit of gold."

The two men's faces lit up. Gold had that effect on people. It also made them willing to do things they normally wouldn't.

Mateo continued, "I suspect the men in the village are aware of the deposit, and they intend to destroy us so they can keep it for themselves."

"We can't allow them," João insisted.

"No, the alliance will succeed," Mateo agreed. "But I need to deliver a message."

Bento raised his head. "Sir, let me take a group and attack them."

Mateo's head shook. "Not a direct one," he explained. "That didn't work for Alejandro. We must remember that this rainforest is our home. These newcomers don't understand it like we do. Our men must be jaguars, able to slip in and infiltrate the village undetected."

"What do you want us to do?" João asked.

"We need more men," Mateo stated. "But we can't wait. Bento, you take a small group to some of the villages south of here. No mention of the gold, but find me some strong bodies."

"Yes, sir."

"What about me?" João questioned.

"You are going to put together our best fighters. No more than five. I want them to be quiet and stealthy."

"I know just the men," João responded.

"Good," Mateo replied. "We don't have a lot of time. Bento, move fast. I need you back no later than tomorrow with at least twenty men. I don't care if they are boys as long as they can pull a trigger."

"Yes, sir."

"João, we're going to focus on pulling those fighters out of the village," Mateo said. "I suspect they have organized patrols around there. They will expect our attack."

João smiled. "Good. I want to shed some blood."

Mateo returned his grin. "Oh, there will be blood. It will flood the jungle."

24

Caleb walked through the village. Most of the residents were sleeping. It had taken most of the afternoon for Leandro and the other leaders to commit. After much discussion, they decided the children and women would evacuate to a clearing on the opposite bank. It would take several hours to move most of them across the river with a contingent of men to guard them.

With only the small boats the locals used to fish the waterway, evacuating these villagers would be a task. Nevertheless, to Caleb, the river provided the protection those people required. Unfortunately, the time constraints meant they would start the crossings at dawn.

Corsair calculated the risk that the guerrillas would attack tonight. His options to stop it remained limited. However, he told Don to set up a perimeter guard a half-click outside the settlement. Don, along with four male villagers in their twenties, stationed themselves around the community. While Caleb pilfered several handheld radios from the men he killed the night before, the plan was to maintain radio silence. At that distance, Caleb would hear any gunfire. Even that only provided a few minutes to prepare for attack.

In São Miguel, Danny and Deke assumed watch duty. Both took positions in two of the raised huts on either end of the village. Each location offered the best view of the settlement. If they saw anyone breach the edge of the forest, they would raise the alarm.

Caleb instructed the pair to rest during the late afternoon, knowing that the overnight watch would be the most important. He had only gotten a few hours of sleep before dusk. It had been a fitful slumber at best. When he wasn't dozing, his thoughts were with Amanda. He wanted to reach the coast soon. Right now, he felt as if he was failing his daughter for strangers.

"I'm worried about her, Audrey," he whispered to his wife.

Of course, there was no response. Although he imagined what she would have said. "Khloe will care for her."

"Like I was supposed to watch over you and Jackson?" he questioned.

"That wasn't your fault," Audrey reminded him.

"But it was," he countered. No amount of assurances to the contrary would ever change Caleb's assessment. He knew he should have seen the pair of carjackers staking out the gas station. He should have been alert. After all, Caleb Saunders lived a life immersed in threats, and he'd survived the worst of them. Yet, on some random road in South Florida, his guard had been down.

No, it would always be Caleb's fault. He'd let someone shoot his son in the head and then his wife. All while he was buying a couple of sodas.

The night air buzzed as insects swarmed the former assassin. He endured the bites. Davi offered him a salve the locals used as an insect repellent. It probably worked the same way the spray stuff in the states did—some, but not a hundred percent.

Caleb lifted his head to the stars. Millions of glittering lights spanned across the sky. It was a sight only available so far from the light pollution of the cities. He'd seen the view on plenty of continents. Even out west, when he and Audrey once took a camping trip through Utah. He remembered being stretched out in that tent with her. She'd insisted on getting a tent that had a mesh roof so they could lie on their backs, gazing up at the galaxy.

It was quiet moments like this that wore on Caleb. He couldn't get Audrey out of his mind, and he didn't want to. Caleb worried that one day, he would forget what Audrey looked like. Or he might not remember his son's voice. He had lost anything depicting them, whether videos or photos. He assumed the OOC had raided their home in Atlanta, which meant they'd confiscated any pictures or videos.

Neither he nor Audrey used social media, so there were few photos of them. He'd instilled in her the need to stay off the grid that way. When he was still active, facial recognition was a somewhat recent development. Now, with the advances in AI, it was fast and effective. He tried to keep current on the latest advancements, but even the forums and subreddits that assumed they knew what capabilities existed underestimated the technology's efficacy, meaning anything the trolls on the internet considered possible had long been so.

The only pictures he had were in his mind. Audrey's parents likely still had some, but he figured the OOC had permanent surveillance on them. And her parents would be justified in blaming him for her death, too, especially if an OOC agent hinted to them what kind of man he'd been.

"I guessed you would be out here," Bella's voice cut through the dark.

"Why aren't you asleep?" he questioned.

"I doubt anyone is," she admitted. "The children might be, but the adults are all scared."

"They should be," Caleb concurred.

"What happens after all this?" she wondered.

"With any luck, the village rebuilds, and you get to plant more crops."

Bella let her gaze drift into the darkness. "And you go on your way?"

"I have to," he confessed.

"Who are you really, Caleb?" Bella asked.

Caleb turned to study the missionary. The dark-haired woman stared back at him.

"Someone who shouldn't exist," Caleb revealed.

"You're full of secrets," she said. "Why don't you unburden yourself?"

"It would endanger you," he explained.

"More than waiting for an army to annihilate this community with me in it?"

He shrugged.

"Be honest, Caleb," she insisted. "What keeps you from letting anyone close to you?"

"I used to work for the government," he confided.

"The US?"

He nodded.

"The CIA or something?"

"Something."

"Are you a spy?" she inquired. "Like James Bond?"

"Well, I'm not British, and I was married."

"So was Bond," Bella pointed out. "Only for part of a movie, though."

"You're a Bond fan?" Caleb asked.

Bella shook her head. "Not really. My dad was, though. We watched them all when they came on at Christmas. Personally, I find him to be a two-dimensional character with some misogynistic qualities."

"Fair assessment," Caleb agreed.

"So, you were a married spy?"

"No. I escaped the life and then got married."

"She changed you?" Bella inquired.

"Audrey wasn't the reason I quit," he confessed. "But she changed me. She's still the voice of sanity in my head."

Bella stared at him, studying his expression. "Audrey's gone?"

He nodded.

"I'm sorry, Caleb." Bella paused for a moment. "Why are you using the alias Rick?"

"The organization I used to work for doesn't just let you retire," he said.

"Oh," Bella replied. "So they're after you?"

"Yeah."

"Do they have people down here?"

He pursed his lips. "Yes, I would bet they do. If not them, there are others out there looking for me, too."

"You make a lot of friends, do you?" she asked wryly.

"Well, I suppose I leave an impression."

Bella laughed. "I'd say. Why are you in a rush to go? The Amazon makes the perfect place to vanish."

"I have a daughter," he admitted. "If my enemies find her, they'll try to use her against me."

Bella's eyes widened. "Oh! I didn't realize."

"She's all I have left now," he said, grimacing a bit.

"What is it?"

"I haven't talked about her to anyone before," he said.

"You know, most dads brag about their kids, but I don't think I ever do." He couldn't resist smiling. "She is great, though."

"How old is she?" Bella asked.

"Three, and quite precocious."

"Aren't they all at that age?"

"Probably."

"It's hard to raise her alone?" Bella inquired.

He shook his head. "Not just that," he said. "What kind of childhood am I giving her? This has been the longest I've been away from her since she was born. When I get back to her, we have to go on the run again. I don't know if I can ever give her a normal life."

"Psh, what's normal, anyway?" Bella asked.

"A mom, dad, two-and-three-quarters kids?"

"Don't buy into that," Bella argued. "Look at Domingo. He's ten, and normal to him is running through the jungle with a group of guerrilla fighters threatening his home."

"I suppose," Caleb considered. "But as a father, you want to give them more."

"That's true. But you seem to worry about it, and that says a lot."

"What do you mean?"

"In my experience, the parents who tell themselves that they are failing are never the ones who are actually failing."

"I doubt that," Caleb remarked.

"Don't get me wrong," Bella said. "Could you do better? Of course. We could all do better, right? But doing what you are means you are trying."

"It doesn't seem that way," Caleb replied.

"I'm not a parent, but I've seen plenty. My parents weren't perfect, but they tried. A far cry from many who would just as soon let someone else raise their kid."

Caleb gave her an ironic smirk. "You say that as another woman is watching my kid."

"Why did you leave her?" Bella wondered. The question wasn't pointed, and he noticed the genuine empathy in her voice.

"It's complicated," Caleb said. "I thought it would help us disappear."

"Will it?" Bella questioned.

"No, it was a trap," Caleb admitted.

Bella raised an eyebrow. "So someone really is after you down here?"

"I don't think they followed me into the jungle, but yes."

"What did you do to get the United States government after you?"

"It's still complicated," he answered again.

She shrugged. "Keep your secrets, Caleb. But I've seen you in action. While I disagree with your methods, I can tell you're a decent person."

"Not in the least," he argued.

"There's no way someone who wasn't a good man would stay here and fight for a group of strangers he just met," Bella debated. "I know good people who wouldn't—couldn't —do that. No. Men like this Mateo aren't good."

Caleb shrugged. "He might think he's doing the best he can for his people."

Bella shook her head. "There are some in his group who follow him out of loyalty. Most are there for what they hope to gain, or because Mateo forced them to fight for him. It's not some noble cause. You said it—they only want the gold."

"That's why—"

Caleb stopped talking as gunshots echoed from the distance.

"Was that shooting?" Bella demanded.

Caleb spun toward the hut, where Deke stood at the railing. The other man looked at Caleb, who shouted, "Which way?"

"East, I think," Deke called, pointing at the forest.

"Get everyone up!" Corsair ordered Bella. "We're out of time."

Before she could respond, Corsair broke into a sprint into the jungle. He threw his hand up in a signal to Deke to stay put.

Palm fronds struck his face as he vanished into the foliage. He gripped the FN FAL, slowing his run into the trees. More gunfire sounded, and Corsair slowed his advance. Nothing made a better target than someone blindly charging through the dark. He needed his senses alert. If Mateo's men breached the small perimeter Don and his team had created, he had to see them in the shadows.

He spotted the first figure. Running. Corsair raised the FN FAL, tracking the person as they ran. They weren't one of their boundary guards. He squeezed the trigger. A crack tore through the night as the enemy dropped.

Corsair went on the move again the second the rifle fired. He trusted his aim, and if he stayed put, he would only make himself an easy target.

He found the body two minutes later. Don's chest rose and fell as he struggled to pull himself up on a thin tree. Caleb slid beside the retired Army veteran.

"The others?" he gasped when he saw Caleb's face.

"I'm getting there next," he told the dying man.

"He surprised me," Don rasped.

"I got him," Caleb assured the old soldier.

"Good," he wheezed.

Caleb helped him sit up. The man's shoulders and back had blood all over them. The enemy's bullet had entered through his back. With no exit wound, Caleb assumed the round was still in him.

"You need to go," Don urged. "There are more."

As soon as he said that, more gunfire sounded about a quarter of a mile west of them.

"It's fine," Don informed Caleb.

"You're lying," Caleb responded.

"Marine, you have others to save," Don told him.

Caleb nodded to him.

"Tell Bella I'm sorry," Don begged as he leaned against the tree.

"You did your duty," Caleb assured him.

"I tried," he coughed.

With all his effort, Don raised his hand to his temple in a half-salute. Caleb stood up and saluted the old soldier before he turned to leave the dying man on the jungle floor.

25

Bella didn't have to wake anyone. Like she'd told Caleb, no one was sleeping. She ran toward Leandro's hut to find the elder stumbling out of the entrance.

"Is that gunfire?" Leandro asked.

"Yes," Bella answered. "we need to get as many people out of the village now as we can."

"We can't cross at night," Leandro argued.

"Then we need to head somewhere," Bella countered. "The shooting is to the east, so we go southwest along the riverside."

"Won't they find us there?" Leandro suggested.

"I don't know," Bella admitted. "We have to get across the river."

Davi ran up to them. "Where is Rick?"

"He went to Don and the others," Bella explained.

Two more villagers, Raul and Calvo, came up. The younger pair had practiced with Caleb and Danny on the submachine guns, and now both carried the weapons on their shoulders.

"Raul, Calvo, you need to stop them if they come through," Davi ordered, pointing toward the tree line where Caleb had vanished a few seconds earlier.

Leandro declared, "We take everyone along the river. Davi, what if we drag some boats down the bank? We can cross at light."

"Too heavy," Davi stated. "I'll float one down. Maybe Tomas can bring another."

"Good idea," Bella announced.

Leandro nodded. "Do it," he agreed.

Davi ran off to find Tomas as Bella and Leandro split up to rouse everyone from their huts. In five minutes, most of the village was marching along the riverbank, with Leandro leading the pack.

"Are you coming, Bella?" Domingo asked.

"I'm staying in case they need me," she told the boy.

"Can I help?"

"No, Domingo. You need to protect the rest."

"I can fight, though," the child argued.

Bella knelt in front of him. "I'm not fighting," she explained. "I don't want you to fight, either. Please, just take care of the others."

"Bella, I don't want to leave you," he said regretfully.

She smiled. "Me either, but there are children in that group. Watch over them. This will frighten them."

"Won't you be scared?" Domingo asked.

She nodded, saying, "But if I know you are helping the little ones, I won't have to worry about them."

He looked up at her. "Don't let them kill you," he demanded.

Bella couldn't stop her smile. "Never. If it comes to it, I plan to run."

"Good."

She ruffled the boy's head, and Domingo pressed against her, hugging her. She wrapped her arms around the child, squeezing him against her.

"Go!" she ordered, pushing him away from her. "Hurry!"

Domingo pivoted and ran after the crowd that was already moving out of the center of the village. Bella straightened up and turned. Deke signaled for her to seek cover. She shook her head, marching toward his hut.

"You need to get somewhere safe," Deke warned her when she joined him on the railing.

"I'll hide when the shooting starts," she promised.

"Bella, they'll be firing at me," he reminded her. "This isn't safe."

"I want to be ready to help," she insisted.

"Rick will kill me if you die," Deke remarked.

"If it helps, I won't appreciate it much, either."

Deke chuckled. "Who would have thought?"

"What?"

"Danny and I figured biking through South America was going to be the be-all-and-end-all of adventures."

"Well, I guess it is," she joked.

"Never imagined I would sign up for this."

"Scared?"

"Shitless," he replied, then he winced. "Sorry."

She shrugged. "Don't blame you."

"Are you?"

"Scared?" Bella questioned. "Very."

"Is it worth it?"

She smiled at the young man. "I'd like to hope so."

"Me too," he muttered.

More gunfire echoed through the trees. Deke tensed, sweeping the barrel of the rifle across his field of vision. Rick had told him that if anything moved, shoot at it. That was a vague instruction, and Deke knew it. He couldn't just open fire on anyone. Rick just wanted to remove any lingering hesitation Deke felt to pull the trigger.

"Hey, Bella, why did you come here?" Deke asked in a shaky voice. His eyes remained trained down the sights of the FN FAL.

"I wanted to help people."

"Yeah. But here we are in the same place, though we came for different reasons. I was just looking for an adventure I could post about on Instagram."

"Deke, it doesn't matter why you are here," she assured him. "You're here. Nothing kept you from leaving except yourself."

"Not quite the same," he countered as more shots rang out. "Those are closer," he commented. "Are those our guys or theirs?"

"I don't want to think about it," she replied.

A flash caught Deke's attention as the shooting began. Bullets struck the structure, and Bella screamed as she dove for cover. Deke fired the submachine gun, realizing he hadn't aimed it at anything. More rounds sprayed the hut, sending the two young Americans for cover.

"Deke!" Bella cried, grabbing the man's arm and pulling him into the hut's door as wood splintered around them.

Deke scrambled after the woman as more gunfire showered the small structure in gunfire. The pair retreated deeper into the hut as chunks of timber shredded from the front of the building. Deke covered Bella with his body while holding the FN FAL with his left arm outstretched at the doorway.

"I've got you," he swore in Bella's ear, but he knew the gunmen had outgunned him. If the guerrillas charged the hut, the two of them were dead. He stared down his gun at the entrance.

The shooting stopped, and Deke assumed they were reloading.

"Bastards!" someone shouted from below them.

More gunfire filled the empty night. The din of battle masked any other sound. Deke covered Bella. Her every breath pressed her back against his chest, and in between bursts of gunfire, he heard her sobbing.

His eyes barely blinked as he waited.

Below them, the roar of fighting raged on. It felt like an eternity as the starlit air rang out with barrages of bullets. Cordite permeated the space, burning Deke's nostrils.

Then, the screaming of machine guns stopped. Deke continued to hold his arm out with the FN FAL directed at the doorway. Bella panted underneath him.

Below them, voices called, and Deke struggled to understand them. The words were in Portuguese, and with his ears ringing, he struggled to focus.

"Is it over?" Bella whispered.

"I don't know," he replied.

She stirred under him, and he pushed up off her, still aiming the gun at the door in case the enemy stormed the building. "Stay down," he urged Bella as he rose to his feet.

"Deke!" Rick's voice shouted. "Status!"

"Rick!" Deke called from above. "We're clear."

"Who's up there?"

"Bella and me," Deke answered.

"You better come down," Rick bellowed.

Deke stepped out of the hut onto the landing. Rounds had torn the front of the shack to shreds. The steps leading down were equally dismantled. Deke took them carefully, distrusting their sturdiness.

Two bodies splayed out on the ground beneath the dwelling. Their matching machine guns were still gripped in their palms.

Deke turned, noticing several villagers crowded under the structure. He watched Rick lean over something, and as Deke got closer, he realized it was a body.

"We need some towels!" Rick called out.

Sophia, who had been standing back, ran across the courtyard to get them.

"What is it?" Deke questioned, stepping forward to see Danny stretched out on the dirt. Blood covered his front, and Deke gasped when he saw the bubbles of blood coming from his mouth. "No!" he shrieked. "Danny!"

Rick shouted something in Portuguese, and the three villagers spread apart to let Deke get closer.

"Is it okay?" Deke asked before he kicked himself. His friend was far from okay.

"It's bad," Rick told him. "We need to stop the bleeding, but there is a lot."

"It was him!" Deke shouted, kneeling beside his companion. "You saved us, didn't you?" he asked Danny.

The man on the ground blinked at him.

Deke shook his head. "You stupid son of a bitch." Danny's hand flexed toward him, and Deke grabbed it. "Don't you die."

His friend didn't reply. He just blinked back at Deke.

"Why did you do that?" Deke asked.

Danny's mouth formed an O as he tried to say something.

"Don't talk, Danny," Rick urged the young man.

Sophia appeared, handing Rick a towel. He pressed the rag against the hole in Danny's chest.

"No, no, no," Deke mumbled as he watched his friend struggle to breathe.

"His lungs collapsed," Rick announced.

Bella knelt behind Deke, her palm resting on the young man's shoulder.

Rick pulled a knife from his belt and cut Danny's shirt down the middle. When he bared Danny's torso, Deke gasped. The bullet wound in his breast looked like a wad of bloody flesh.

Deke squeezed his friend's hand as Rick called for another towel. The blood-drenched one flew behind Rick as Sophia passed a fresh one to him.

"Can you help him?" Sophia asked Rick in a pleading voice.

Rick didn't respond. He pressed hard against the wound. "Breathe slowly," Rick urged Danny.

Deke felt his body shake. Bella was now sitting on the ground next to him. She wrapped her arms around him and rested her right palm on the arm, still holding Danny's hand.

Danny coughed, and Deke realized he was trying to speak.

"Don't talk," Rick admonished Danny. "Save your breath."

The dying man shook his head, although the movement was almost imperceptible. "Sorry," he gurgled.

"No, Danny," Deke said. "It's on me, man."

Bella squeezed Deke's bicep as Rick threw another blood-soaked rag to the ground.

"The bleeding won't stop," Sophia declared, sounding desperate.

Rick placed another towel on his chest. "Someone get Danny some water," he called out.

"I'm on it," Sophia replied, vanishing again.

Rick's eyes met Deke's. He shook his head, and he watched Deke's eyes well up with tears.

"No, no, no," Deke repeated.

"Can we get him help?" Jason asked.

Rick didn't respond. Danny choked on blood, and Rick jammed an index finger into Danny's mouth, clearing the airways.

"Danny, I'm here," Deke told his friend. "Next time, we'll just go to Fort Lauderdale, okay?"

Danny's eyes brightened for a second. He coughed again as he mumbled, "Next year."

"Right, next year," Deke said. "Fort Lauderdale, all the way."

Danny blinked.

"Shit," Rick cursed.

Sophia ran up, carrying a bottle of water. She passed the container to Deke, who put it to Danny's lips. His friend took a sip and choked. He tried to smile at Deke.

"I'll tell your folks you love them," Deke assured him.

Danny tried to nod, but his strength left him. His eyes fluttered before they stared up at the expanse stretching out above them.

Then he was gone.

His grip loosened in Deke's hand, and Deke started crying. He lifted Danny's palm to his chest.

"I'm so sorry, man," he said. "Don't die."

Bella wrapped her arms around the grieving man as Rick leaned forward and closed Danny's eyes. Deke continued to hold Danny's hand as Rick straightened up, then Deke let go and rocked backward. Bella caught him in her arms, hugging him. He buried his face in Bella's chest as he cried.

He sensed Rick standing up, and Deke sucked in a breath of air as he tried to calm himself. As he pulled away from Bella, she reached up and wiped his face.

"Danny saved us," Deke stated.

"That's right, dude," Jason declared. "Man ran at those two like a bat out of hell."

Deke looked at the pair of corpses. "Fuck them," he spat before turning his eyes up to Rick. "I want to kill them all."

"Do you mean to tell me we lost her?" Carl Winston asked on the other line.

"It appears so," Lee admitted. "At least that's my assessment. She baited us at the airport."

"Baited *you*," Winston corrected.

"That information came from Washington," Lee informed him. "The boys in the Basement flagged the first flight."

"Is it confirmed whether she left on a flight?" he questioned.

"No, Carl," Lee replied, using her boss's first name. It was her little jab at him. He hated lack of decorum, but he was too proud to ask for respect. Lee enjoyed prodding him like that. "It was a distraction. My guess is she was already out of the city. Probably out of the country before she bought the tickets."

"What was the point?" Winston demanded.

"We're guessing it was her who did it," she reminded him. "There's still no sign of Corsair. He may be the one behind this."

"Of course he is," Winston remarked. "Did he arrange it to pull our resources?"

"It's Corsair," Lee insisted. "He might be observing us. By sending everyone to the airport, he depleted the people we had in-country."

"What about the other borders?" Winston asked. "If she didn't fly out, she had to leave somehow."

"Without some local cooperation, we're limited in manpower to monitor every crossing. Hell, this isn't the US. There aren't exactly fences between Belize and Guatemala. Someone could hike across the jungle and make the crossing."

"She's got a three-year-old with her," Winston advised. "Corsair won't drag her through the wilderness."

"I don't know about that," she said. Lee suspected Winston was right, though. It was unlikely that Corsair would further endanger Amanda, but she also trusted that if he chose to do something, it would be with her safety top of mind. If going off-road was the best way to protect her, he'd do that.

"I want people at the borders," Winston demanded.

"We don't have the resources, and if they're already gone, as it appears they are, we're only wasting time."

"What other leads do you have?"

"Driver," Lee suggested, referring to the forger who tipped the OOC that Corsair had been in Belize. "I suspect Corsair might come for him."

"Do you have any idea where he is?" Winston asked.

"Not yet," Lee admitted. "We're still sifting through the house he had here. It took some time just to identify him."

"You didn't actually identify him," Winston reminded her.

"No, but we know who it is. 'Driver' is the pseudonym of

a suspected forger and information broker. We need to track his movements. If we find him and put him under surveillance, I bet Corsair shows up."

"But when?"

It was, unfortunately, an intelligent question, especially since the play with Driver was a feint on Lee's part. She doubted they'd nail down Driver in a million years. He had been the one to report to the OOC that Corsair had been in Belize, of course, but that was nothing more than self-preservation. Once he learned that his betrayal of Corsair had gone awry, he knew he'd crossed what was likely the most dangerous individual in the world. She suspected Driver would have burrowed himself deep in a hole.

Further, Lee believed Winston was pursuing Corsair the wrong way. He had all his teams hunting for Saunders like he was still the same assassin who worked for him so many years ago. However, Lee's perspective differed. They weren't chasing Corsair now so much as Caleb Saunders. Or, even more accurately, an amalgamation of Tom Harrod, Caleb Saunders, and Corsair. They were all the same person, of course, but time had integrated the family man of Harrod with Saunders and Corsair.

"I can't say," Lee answered. "He will protect his daughter at all costs. This might be a debt he leaves open for a while."

"Corsair never left loose ends," Winston noted.

Lee detected a note of unease in his tone. He, no doubt, was worried. If Corsair didn't leave unfinished business, Carl Winston had to assume he was on the killer's list somewhere.

She considered reminding him Corsair wasn't the same man for what had to be the umpteenth time. But she'd learned that Carl Winston thought no one capable of change. After all, he resisted it with every effort.

"Where should we direct our people, then, Lee?" he demanded. "Because so far, we've struck out on all fronts."

"Carl, we trained him," she reminded him. "They don't get better than him."

"We did, didn't we?" Winston replied thoughtfully. "Fine. We have to at least keep a line on him."

"I doubt he'll be moving with traditional means," Lee suggested. "He isn't about to catch the next flight out. He'll cross a few borders before he contemplates a commercial airline."

"Private plane, perhaps," Winston speculated.

"Or freighter," Lee added.

"Makes sense. The daughter will slow him down," Winston considered. "He could take a position as a deckhand on any number of freighters and catch a ride across the ocean."

"There are too many vessels on the water to track that," she pointed out. "Even if we isolate the port he sailed from, he could be on hundreds of ships in a short span. We'd need the exact day he set sail to get close."

"Almost none are US-flagged," Winston added. "I doubt he'd try to return to the US."

You better hope not, Lee thought.

"Doesn't matter," Lee interjected. "If he has his daughter, he won't travel on a commercial freighter."

"Private vessel?"

"That's even harder to chase down," Lee said. "A small yacht can come and go a lot from the various coastlines. If he travels under a false name, which we know is the case, we'll never find him. By the time we trace the names that potentially match Corsair, he'd be gone again."

"We might get lucky," Winston suggested.

"Yes. That would be the only way it would work," Lee countered.

"If you don't have any other ideas, I'd recommend getting your team on it."

"We will," Lee agreed. It wouldn't be the entire group, but she'd spare Pendleton, who was already worthless, and Garrett to search for private yachts that had left port in the last few days.

"Good. We need to bring this chapter to a close," Winston remarked in his tidy, bureaucratic voice.

"This is going to be a marathon, not a sprint," Lee reminded him.

"Every minute Corsair is out there, he places the United States at risk," Winston said heatedly. "Corsair is one of the few men capable of eliminating whatever target he chooses. He's already committed treason. What stops him from assassinating the president or some other dignitary? The world press would eat us alive if they discovered we trained the man responsible for killing a major political figure."

"I don't think he's looking to do that, sir."

"Look, Caleb Saunders has very few resources. Assassin is his number-one job, and there are groups out there willing to pay him a fortune."

"You might be right," Lee agreed, although she doubted it. Caleb Saunders was over a decade away from his wet work. Their research on his life as Tom Harrod offered no sign that he was selling his services.

Nevertheless, Winston was correct. People would seek out Caleb now that the world was aware of his continued existence. Soon, investigators would credit him with unsolved murders due to lack of other leads.

"If you find nothing today, I want a full update on your

strategies tomorrow," Winston said. "If he's gone from Belize, there's no reason for you to stay there."

That surprised Lee. She hadn't expected her boss to want her back in D.C. There was another motive there. Perhaps this was to bring her into the office while Winston's new golden boy Pendleton spearheaded the Corsair search.

That would be a waste of time. Pendleton couldn't find his asshole with a wall-sized mirror.

"We'll talk tomorrow," Lee assured Winston.

"I want a lead," he informed her. "Better yet, wrap Corsair up with a ribbon and bring him home."

"Yes, sir," she replied half-heartedly.

27

"This is very bad," Jason muttered as he stared at the bodies stretched out in the center of the huts.

Don, Danny, and the four villagers who'd held the perimeter lay lifeless. Other members of the village were preparing graves outside of the settlement. Rick sat on a stool on the landing of the same hut where Deke and Bella had survived the raid.

"What's his next move?" Sophia asked, jerking her head toward Rick.

"Raul thinks he plans to lead an assault," Jason replied.

"On the army?"

"It's not an army, Sophia," he corrected. "They're more like a gang."

"They seem pretty well-armed for just a gang," Sophia argued. "How's he going to do that? Just walk in shooting like John Wick or something?"

"Deke said he was some kind of special forces, so he might. Did you see him take down those three guys the other day?"

Sophia shook her head. "It isn't the same thing. He surprised them."

"What about the men in the jungle? He killed ten of them." Jason sounded like he was praising a three-point shot.

"We can't stay here, Jason," Sophia stated. "They're going to be back, and this time I don't think they'll just send four or five guys."

"Yes," Jason agreed. "But no one will go with us."

"You and I can leave," she explained. "It's a day's hike to Santarém. We can catch a boat out."

"What if we run into these guerrillas out there?"

"Everyone says they are south of us," Sophia stated. "We cross the river and walk. I'm leaving one way or the other. What happened to Danny was—I don't know—too much."

Jason nodded. The newcomer's death had struck all of them hard. Don's death in the attack had also frightened the Zion's Garden missionaries.

"We need some supplies," Jason suggested. "In case we get lost or slowed down."

"I'll get some water and food," Sophia agreed. "Can you grab one of those guns?"

"Do you think we should be caught running around the rainforest with an automatic rifle?" Jason inquired.

"I'd rather you had a gun if we were to run into anyone," she pointed out.

"I'll see what I can do," Jason conceded. "Do we want to stay for the funerals?"

From the stilted hut they were in, Sophia peered down at the bodies. Bella and Lita, one of the older village women, had slowly wrapped the corpses in linen. They didn't have coffins or embalmers down here, and most deaths would be reported to the government when the next mail boat arrived. That could be weeks later, so locals managed their own burials.

Jason had heard Bella explain to Deke that they'd mark Danny's grave if his family wanted to bring him back to the States. Hours had passed since anyone had seen Deke, who'd disappeared after Danny's death.

"I don't think I can handle it," Sophia said after a minute. "It's Don. He was constantly around. I still liked him, even if he was a lot to deal with."

"I understand. Bernie. Then Don and Danny."

"And Timon, Pierre, and Antonio, too," Sophia added. "Who was the other one?"

"Yago."

"Right," Sophia said. "Yago was always quiet."

Jason nodded. "Fine, we need to leave soon. Even now, we won't make it before dark."

"Better than being here tonight," Sophia told him. "It's going to be bad when those guerrillas come back."

"I agree," Jason acknowledged. "You find food and water while I get a gun."

Jason left Sophia and walked toward Bella's hut, where they were storing all the weapons they'd taken off the dead soldiers. He wondered what they did with the bodies of the soldiers who raided the camp. Danny killed two of them, but from what Jason had heard, Rick eliminated the rest. Just not before they took out their men on the perimeter patrol.

The young American missionary had to admit his awe of Rick. Sophia had pegged him as John Wick, and while Jason had only seen a couple of those movies, he remembered the main character was like some invulnerable beast. Rick struck Jason the same way.

Jason had watched him charge back into the camp last

night. Reddish-brown stains covered Rick's clothes, and at first glance, Jason thought Rick was injured. It turned out that a lot of the blood had been Don's.

It saddened him that Don had died alone in the jungle. He'd often found the older man annoying, but he was still a friendly fellow. They'd often chatted about football and *Star Wars*, two things none of the villagers were familiar with.

This hadn't been what he'd signed up for when he joined Zion's Garden. He was supposed to be a year down here working, and he'd planned to spend some time traveling around South America after finishing his stint here. He'd developed a crush on Sophia almost immediately, and when she'd expressed similar feelings, the pair had started spending all their extra time together.

A month ago, it would have thrilled Jason to while away a day in the jungle with Sophia. But then it would have been more of a romantic escapade instead of an escape for their lives. But he didn't want her to run off by herself. Jason wondered if she'd do that without him, anyway. Sophia could be a lot of talk, but he wanted to continue their relationship outside the Amazon. That wouldn't happen if Jason didn't man up and get her out of here safely.

He wanted to leave, too, but with everyone dying, he worried that others would see him as a coward. Jason had no desire to linger here, even to lend aid like Bella. He needed to be somewhere safe where no one would shoot at him.

As Jason climbed the steps to Bella's hut, Deke appeared at the doorway. "What are you doing here?" Deke demanded. Jason saw his face. His eyes were red, and his cheeks flushed.

"I'm getting one of those guns," Jason told him.

"Did Rick send you?"

Jason shook his head. "Sophia plans to leave for Santarém. I'm going to escort her there."

"Can't let you have them," Deke stated. "Not unless Rick says it's okay."

Jason wrinkled his forehead. "Man, come on. We need to get out of here."

Deke shook his head. "I can't do it."

"Deke, dude, I'm sorry about Danny. But we don't want to end up like him and Don."

"Ask Rick," Deke insisted.

Jason huffed. "Fine. I'll be back."

He stormed out of the hut. Jason figured Rick would discourage them from leaving. Could he take Sophia unarmed? He thought that might be for the best, but Sophia obviously disagreed.

The young man stalked across the village toward the shack where Rick stood watch.

"Rick," he said as he climbed the steps. "How are you?"

The man had an intense glare on his face, and the forbidding expression scared Jason a bit. He'd seen that same fierce aura on his dad, usually before he let loose on Jason or his sister.

"Jason. Everything okay?" Rick asked, his demeanor softening.

"Rick, I'm taking Sophia to Santarém," he confessed. "We're leaving soon."

The man nodded. "That's probably for the safest. You should see if Bella or the others want to go, too."

"I will," Jason agreed. "Deke said I needed your permission to take one of the machine guns, though."

Rick gave him an appraising look. "Are you familiar with guns?"

"I've shot some, yes," he told Rick.

"What are you going to do if you run across someone out there?"

"Uh, I don't know," Jason replied. "I guess it depends."

"On?"

"On if they try to shoot at us or not."

"Why would they shoot at you?"

"They've been shooting at everyone," Jason pointed out.

Rick nodded. "Are you comfortable killing a person?"

Jason didn't reply. After a minute, he shook his head. "No, I'm not. But I'm less comfortable letting them shoot at me or Sophia."

"We can't spare a lot of ammo," Rick told him. "You can have one gun and a mag full of ammo. If you make it to Santarém, you can send the authorities."

"Of course," Jason agreed, then he paused. "Does this make me a coward?"

Rick cocked his head. "What makes you say that?"

"I'm running away. Danny and Don are dead. Who will protect the village?"

"You have nothing to worry about," Rick said. "Escorting people to safety is almost as dangerous as waiting for them to attack."

"Doesn't seem that way," Jason admitted.

"Wait until you are alone in the jungle," Rick informed him.

"Oh," Jason replied. "What are you planning to do?"

"I don't know," Rick said.

"The villagers need to just leave. Don't you agree?"

Rick shrugged. "It's their home."

"Is it worth dying for?"

"To them, it might be," Rick considered. "Is it worth letting someone stronger take something that isn't theirs?"

"Doesn't America do that?" Jason asked, raising an eyebrow.

"I wouldn't use that as a justification," Rick stated. "We've done a lot of things we shouldn't have."

"Why don't you leave?"

Rick offered a half-smile. "It's probably penance," he said. "Whoever Mateo and his guerrillas are, they shouldn't get free range to rape and pillage an area because they want something that's not theirs."

"Was it worth Danny's life?" Jason asked.

Rick shook his head. "It wasn't worth the guerrillas' lives, either. I don't want to see anyone else die over this."

"Unless we all leave, that's inevitable."

"Even if we all leave," Rick countered. "Once Mateo settles in here, he'll feel he deserves more. Men like that have no off button—until someone comes along and finds it, that is."

"Someone claimed you were part of Marine special forces," Jason said tentatively. "Is that true?"

"I was never really a Marine. Started out as one, but I went beyond that."

"My grandfather was a Marine, and he told me nothing was tougher than them."

Rick smiled. "All Marines say that. Then again, so do the Navy and Army."

"But you're not any of that?"

Rick's expression darkened. "No, I'm not."

"That sounds scary," Jason commented.

"Only for those guys in the jungle," Rick said.

28

The bus jostled over the country roads, tossing the sleeping Amanda against Khloe's side. To minimize the girl's bouncing, the woman wrapped her arms around her and pulled her close. The child had been sleeping for over an hour, allowing Khloe to relish the quiet after their long, uncomfortable journey from Belize City.

Neither Khloe nor Amanda had gotten much sleep last night. Amanda had given in to her fatigue on the bus and curled up in Khloe's lap. Nerves prevented Khloe from finding any rest. She watched the faces of the people around her.

There were almost no empty seats left, and the passengers filled the bus's interior like cords of wood stacked on each other. Khloe had ridden a Greyhound bus a few times back in the States, and at the time, she'd considered the trip an ordeal of discomfort. Now, she reminisced fondly about the comfortable seats, power plugs, and Wi-Fi.

This bus looked like it had been top of the line in 1947. There were holes in the seats big enough for Khloe to insert a fist. None of the upholstery was intact; most had rips and tears that exposed the foam cushioning. Several windows were down, allowing the outside air to be the only climate control in the cabin.

The entire time they'd waited for the bus to depart, Khloe's head had swiveled, searching for signs of the Office of Compliance. The ruse with booking the various flights worked. She'd considered taking the one flight to Buenos Aires, but Khloe had decided to use it to mislead the OOC.

Over eight hours had ticked by since she and Amanda boarded the bus. So far, she'd only been approached by two men, who eyed her suspiciously. Khloe carried a Karambit knife on her forearm. Caleb had helped her pick it out. With the blade hidden up her sleeve, she knew if either of the two men attempted to grab her or Amanda, she could fight them.

Dawn was approaching, and Khloe stared out the window at the eastern sky. Shades of purple spread over the expanse as the horizon grew lighter. Exhaustion crept in on the woman, and right now she wanted to get them off the bus and find a safe hotel to curl up and sleep in. That was still almost twenty hours away.

Their final destination was La Ceiba, Honduras. She'd picked it based on the travel time. While the idea of being on a bus for over twenty-four hours sounded horrific, it seemed the most anonymous way to travel. The border control on this route wasn't strong, and she hoped the small crossings didn't even have internet. Meaning, her crossing might not be recorded for a day or so. By then, she hoped to be on the move still.

Her last message to Caleb detailed her plans, although she grew more concerned with each passing day that Caleb wasn't answering for a reason. She didn't want to find out he was dead. What would she do if he died? Would it be too dangerous to take Amanda to the States? Perhaps her grand-parents would take her in. Caleb had mentioned that Audrey's parents were still alive. She didn't know how he communicated with them, but she knew he left them messages, ensuring them that Amanda was okay.

Once in Honduras, she hoped Caleb would get in touch with her. She would give him a few days before she and Amanda moved again. Caleb ultimately wanted to get them all to Europe, thinking they could blend in better over there. But with only her real passport as ID, Khloe would have trouble getting there.

That clinched it for her. She needed to research how to get a new passport. Surely somewhere on the internet, someone knew how to do it. Caleb had walked her through accessing the Dark Web, but he had stressed that she had a lot more to learn.

Right now, she needed to use the bathroom. This bus didn't have the luxury of a water closet, and the next stop was an hour and a half down the road. Even that was an ordeal. Khloe couldn't leave Amanda unprotected on the bus. That meant she'd have to rouse Amanda and carry her off the bus to the closest restroom to the next stop. And she'd have to accomplish all of that in the ten minutes the driver remained at that location. Hopefully, the girl would fall asleep again when they got back onboard.

Khloe reached into her shoulder bag and retrieved a paperback copy of *Twilight*. She'd read that book in junior high school, but it was one that someone had left on the shelf at their rental cottage. It seemed better than nothing to pass the time, but while she recalled enjoying the story as a teen, she struggled to get into it now. It impressed her that what she'd viewed as so romantic as a teen now came across as creepy.

Amanda shifted out of Khloe's lap and balled herself into a tight wad on the seat. When Khloe glanced down at the girl, the tiny figure reminded her of a cat curled in a box half its size. Once the child was off her, Khloe straightened up, stretching her knees out and arching her back until a few vertebrae cracked.

She eyed the man seated ahead, his presence causing her apprehension. He turned to lock eyes with the American, and Khloe returned the stare. In the last few months, she'd realized how tired she'd become from men seeking to control her. She expressed this one day to Caleb, who told her it was up to her to handle the situation. During Amanda's naps or after she'd gone to bed, Caleb had worked with Khloe to learn some self-defense moves. She still lacked proficiency, but holding the Karambit, she felt more confident than the previous year.

Without breaking her gaze with the individual, she lowered herself back into her seat. It took Amanda less than five minutes to reposition herself in Khloe's lap again. The older woman stroked the girl's hair as she read her book about Bella and the sparkling vampires.

Three rows behind her, she didn't see the figure watching her. His dark, beady eyes appeared closed as if he was sleeping, and he hadn't moved in over three hours. But his stare leaked through his narrowed eyelids and trained on the two American females.

29

Once he knew how Khloe communicated with her mother, Ifrit had guessed that the woman would use the same technique to message Corsair. It took longer to access that account. Khloe was far more careful than Haley Evans. No doubt, Corsair had instructed her on certain spyware applications. Yet, she'd clicked on an airline ad that continued to pop up when she checked her email. Even when she clicked on it, Ifrit realized it had been on accident. The pointer hit the flashing graphic and opened the webpage instantly, but Khloe Evans reacted fast, closing it.

Nonetheless, she hadn't been fast enough to prevent the Trojan virus from slipping in. Her mistake was not powering down and taking the computer offline. Instead, she'd closed out the window and gone about her business.

She'd left a message for Corsair. Based on the diary-style letter she wrote the assassin, he hadn't communicated with her in weeks. Just the tone of her writing displayed the immense stress the woman must be feeling. But more to it existed than just that. Khloe Evans was worried, and given the span of time that Corsair had been incommunicado, Ifrit understood the girl's concern.

It highlighted something that Ifrit hadn't considered before. Could Corsair already be dead?

From what he'd gleaned from Al-Farouqi, the man's arms dealer boss still believed the American assassin had survived his conflict in Cartagena and remained alive. Without the previous messages from Corsair, Ifrit did not know what he'd told his protégé about his ordeal in Colombia. However, he surmised Corsair had made contact after leaving Colombia.

But where was he now? That question bothered Ifrit. Without Corsair, he would receive no million-dollar bounty. Mahmoud Abbas wouldn't pay to have the assassin's child, would he?

Perhaps. For Abbas, this had become a mission of vengeance. If Ifrit's assessment was correct, Corsair had killed Abbas's son. Even if the American agent was dead, Abbas might take pleasure in killing the man's only daughter. Men like Abbas reveled in such pomp and circumstance. Ifrit never comprehended such concepts, but that lack of comprehension didn't mean he wouldn't take money from Abbas.

Ifrit was a Muslim, albeit not a devout one. Still, Ifrit believed those not of the Muslim faith to be lesser. The complex contradiction wasn't a topic he ever contemplated sharing with anyone. Most traditionalists would decry his sacrilege, and Ifrit made a substantial amount of money working for extremists. If it leaked that he lacked conviction, those contracts would dry up. He might find himself on the wrong side of the war, too.

Some might suggest that justice prevailed in such an instance, but that was a concept Ifrit didn't believe in, either.

The idea implied there was a certain equality among those who wronged one another. Only, it never equated. If Abbas killed Corsair or just his daughter as retribution for his son, the scales of justice remained uneven. After all, Corsair had spent over a decade living his life after killing the young Abbas. That was ten years Corsair had with his new family that Abbas missed with his son. There was no equality there.

That didn't consider the men Corsair had eliminated in the last few weeks, including Abbas's trusted security chief. If a scorecard existed, Corsair would have a higher count.

Ifrit was reminded of a boxing match. The mercenary enjoyed the American sport, despite not fully comprehending it. Even if one fighter railed hits on the other, racking up points, the other needed only to knock the first out with one punch to win the match.

Ifrit hoped to deliver the knock-out punch to Corsair. Corsair had landed blow after blow, killing every individual Abbas sent after him. If Ifrit destroyed Corsair, it wouldn't matter how many men Corsair had killed before. Ifrit planned to land the winning—killing—blow.

The bus trip was uncomfortable, but nothing Ifrit hadn't already faced. He imagined what a payday like this would do for him. Working under a pseudonym allowed Ifrit a separate life. In fact, it was one he enjoyed. As the vehicle shook and rocked along the narrow highway, Ifrit watched the two Americans a few rows in front of him.

The woman remained alert while the child slept, and Ifrit saw her notice the man several rows forward. Her instincts proved accurate. Ifrit recognized him as a dangerous type. At least, dangerous to a pair of young girls. Human trafficking was one of the growing threats prevalent in both Central and South America in the last few years.

After all, it was a business that required nobody to make a product, only to steal it. Two healthy females fetched a few thousand dollars each if one knew where to off-load them.

Ifrit shifted his gaze between the two women and the man. No, wait. There were two men. Their occasional eye contact, despite not sitting together, betrayed their collaboration.

Ifrit would maintain vigilance. If Ifrit spotted two cooperating, he needed to assume others had slipped past his notice.

The next stop was in half an hour or so. The last sign they passed said they were still eighty-five kilometers from Chacte in Guatemala. Khloe Evans squirmed and shifted in her seat. When the bus stopped, she'd get off and use the facilities present. The woman would either rouse the child or carry her off the bus. The smart move would be to wake her. Khloe Evans would have far more trouble fighting off an attack while cradling the child. At least if the girl were walking, the woman would have both hands free, making it much easier to pull the Karambit she carried in her sleeve if she remained unencumbered.

He settled back as the bus rambled along in the early morning hours. They'd reach Chacte in time for breakfast, although Ifrit didn't concern himself with food. He thought he might use the two men to his advantage.

For now, he waited, his eyes barely open.

30

Caleb stretched out under the brush, watching. The edge of the camp was a hundred feet from his location, and he peered through a pair of binoculars. Since the FN FALs lacked scopes, he considered it lucky that one of the Zion's Gardeners had something he could use to spy on the camp. When Caleb had mentioned needing a scope, Bella headed off to retrieve Don's binoculars, telling Caleb how Don had been an avid birder.

"I'm pretty sure it was the main reason he volunteered to work here," she stated. "All of his free time went to tracking down birds."

Caleb wasn't using it for birds, though. He had a different prey in mind.

Both Bella and Deke argued that striking out for the camp in the middle of the day was foolish, but Caleb replied that the guerrillas seemed to prefer to attack at night. He assumed they thought the village would have its guard down then, and as one who'd entered many compounds in the dead of night, he understood that logic. Caleb preferred to infiltrate between three and four in the morning. At that hour, the guards often had been on duty for several hours and had grown bored. Everyone else would be asleep. It made for the perfect time.

However, with two night attacks already, Caleb suspected Mateo thought the same way he did. If he'd gotten word from scouts that the villagers killed the raiding party, he would have to mount a third—or rather, a fourth attack. It meant the middle of the day was the opportune time to gauge the guerrillas' strength.

From his cover, Caleb watched the encampment, tallying soldiers as he saw them. So far, he'd only counted fifteen, and those men didn't look as formidable as the ones he crossed the other night. Corsair was depleting Mateo's troops, and now he only had the bottom of the barrel.

Corsair calculated how easy it would be to strip that number down by half or even two-thirds. At this point, he hadn't seen Mateo; he'd only heard him mentioned by Bella. But he was almost certain he'd picked out the individual the others deferred to.

This group was desperate, too. The soldiers shared expressions of fear, anger, and hopelessness. Forced conscription could cause that. If Mateo recruited others the way he'd attempted to do with Domingo, most of these soldiers weren't here voluntarily.

Caleb considered that as he watched the members of the camp move through their day. How many of the men he'd killed the other night were marching under coercion? How should he feel about that?

He searched his heart, looking for an answer. Caleb hoped it would come in Audrey's words and voice. But only silence reigned.

Voices caught his attention, and his head rotated left to see three men stomping through the undergrowth toward him. Corsair sucked in a breath and held it. The group appeared dirty and worn from the jungle. Caleb guessed by their looks that the trio hadn't slept indoors in a few nights.

He needed to move, but anything he did would draw their attention. Corsair's hand touched the FN FAL on the ground next to him. If he squeezed that trigger, he'd unleash hell for sure.

Keep it quiet. Caleb reached down for the Ka-bar knife on his belt. His fingers wrapped around the hilt, and he slid it from its scabbard. Corsair moved slowly until the tip of the blade came free. He squeezed the handle as the six feet stomped closer. They veered away from him so that they wouldn't walk across him. However, they would still be within a few feet of his hide. Unless the trio was as blind as the mice from the song, they'd see him.

The deciding factor in the next few seconds depended on Corsair launching an assault before they saw him.

He sprang to his feet, his mind racing as he calculated each attack. As close as they were to the camp, he needed to be quiet.

None of the men carried their weapons in their grip. Instead, they all hung on their backs, out of easy reach. That made Corsair's task easier.

The first kill was the quickest. As soon as Corsair landed on his feet, his left hand caught the nearest soldier by the hair, jerking him toward the assassin. The man's face turned, flashing a rather dirty and unfortunate-looking beard along with widened eyes. The Ka-bar blurred across his countenance, slashing through the sternohyoid muscle, severing at least six veins, and shattering the hyoid bone.

Blood slung off the tip of the Ka-bar as Caleb rotated around and drove the knife into the closest man's chest. His hands reached for the hilt as his heart stopped pumping.

The guerrilla's knees buckled, and his weight dragged him down to the ground.

The third man had taken the longest to react. However, whatever training he'd gotten was insufficient. Instead of distancing himself from Corsair and retrieving his weapon, he lunged for Corsair. Of the three soldiers, this one was the largest. What he lacked in strategy or even reaction time, he made up for with brute strength. He threw a jab that Corsair blocked. The next one came on the heels of the first. Before the assassin could get his arm up to block him, the balled fist struck him in the face.

For a split second, the world seemed to turn upside down. The guerrilla's punch knocked him off his footing and pitched him to the earth. Corsair rolled as soon as his shoulder slammed into the dirt. The guerrilla lunged at him with his foot as he tried to stomp down on his head. Both of the American's hands caught the massive boot inches before it crushed Corsair's face.

On the ground, Corsair wrenched the man's foot, pulling it as he twisted it around. The soldier lost his balance on the remaining leg, tumbling to the side as Corsair barreled away from him. If the pair ended up grappling on the jungle floor, Caleb knew the other man would dominate him on sheer strength alone.

Corsair, back on his feet and hands, scampered away, creating some space between the guerrilla and the American. The Brazilian soldier scrambled to his feet when he reached for the FN FAL strapped to his back. Caleb took two quick steps forward, driving his right boot into the soldier's face. Its impact spewed blood from the soldier's nose and sent him reeling backward. As the behemoth landed on his back, he squeezed the trigger. The submachine gun erupted into the air, missing Caleb by a long way.

Shouts erupting from behind Caleb signaled the gunfire had alerted the camp. Without looking behind him, Caleb leaped forward, slamming his heel down on the guerrilla's sternum before then kicking his gun up. The soldier on the ground continued to fire as the barrel aimed into the jungle.

The stomp to the chest caved the man's chest in, and while it didn't kill the man on impact, Corsair guessed the result was imminent. As Caleb stepped off the man, he drove his left heel down on the man's face. The blow crushed the guerrilla's skull, killing him.

More calls and wild gunshots came from the camp as more soldiers charged out of their tents. Caleb bent and jerked his Ka-bar from the second combatant's chest. The man's lifeless face fell to the side as the thick, silver blade retracted from his sternum.

Caleb sprinted into the brush as automatic gunfire peppered the trees around him. Branches and leaves fluttered down like snow as bullets ripped the limbs to bits. His feet pounded against the rainforest floor. Foliage smacked his face as Caleb dashed through the overhanging trees and underbrush.

Right now, he needed distance. The calls behind him suggested someone had discovered the trio of dead guerrillas. He didn't chance a glance behind him.

One of Hood's rules had been to never look back. "Unless your back is forward, don't turn around." When Hood first said it, Caleb thought it sounded idiotic. However, Hood was correct. If Caleb didn't plan to keep fighting his pursuers, he needed to regroup and strategize.

It was difficult to do that when being chased by armed hunters.

The terrain remained flat—a good thing, since it meant no random boulders or hills to maneuver around. However, it did allow for a dense growth of palms, brush, and bushes that might as well have been walls, given how thickly the vines and twigs intertwined.

Caleb assumed he could outrun almost any man in the camp. However, they would be far more familiar with the forest, canceling out any advantage he thought he had.

The assassin cut left behind a tree, his right foot landing in a nest of vines creeping along the dirt. The branches wrapped around his ankle like a shackle. Caleb came off his feet and slammed his chest down on the ground. Twisting, he slashed the tendrils with the Ka-bar while giving a backward glance. Seven men pushed through the jungle.

His pursuers saw him struggling in the brush and raised their weapons. The Ka-bar snapped through the fibrous strands as the enemy fired. Caleb rolled behind the tree and jumped to his feet. With another wall of growth shielding him, he sprinted ahead and wished he'd chosen the FN FAL instead of his combat knife.

His arms pumped as he dashed through more jumble of trees. Caleb skidded to a stop atop a bluff overlooking a tributary about fifteen feet below him. Without looking back, Caleb sheathed his blade and jumped from the cliff.

There was no way to see how deep the river was here. Caleb knew better than to attempt a dive, even though that could offer him a bit more speed in crossing the waterway. He hit the water in full cannonball mode.

When he was submerged in the water, he almost shouted for joy. Instead, he spun until he was parallel to the bottom and kicked hard. The width of the tributary was about two hundred feet, and he doubted he could cover the distance with one gulp of air.

He could feel the stream carrying him toward the main channel of the Amazon. His arms continued to breaststroke forward as the flow moved him downriver. When his lungs passed the point of burning, he kicked for the surface. With a quick porpoise-like movement, he burst out of the water, sucked in a breath, and dove back down, changing direction to swim with the current.

Caleb couldn't hear the gunshots under the water, but the bullets striking the surface made a distinct sound. With a lungful of fresh air, he let the flow drag him farther away.

When he resurfaced, he'd traveled a hundred yards downriver. Before the soldiers on the bank could locate him, he sank below the river and swam toward a wad of flotsam composed of decaying trunks and branches. He came up on the far side and grabbed a broken limb from the largest log.

As his feet pulled up to the surface, Caleb rode the river, hidden by the mass of dead trees.

31

"They didn't fly out," Sparr told Lee. "I'm positive. Garrett and I scoured the footage we got from Goodson Airport. No person fitting Khloe Evans's description flew out on any of those flights."

"She might have changed her appearance," Lee suggested.

"We assumed as much," Sparr assured her. "No one yesterday came close to matching a twenty-something and a toddler. In fact, we verified the only woman with a kid similar to Amanda Harrod's age was Belizean. So was the child."

"She's gone, then," Lee concluded.

"You sure?"

Lee nodded. "Have you checked buses or other public transportation?"

"The bus station doesn't have great camera coverage," Sparr answered. "Even the cameras on the cashiers only focus on the money and the employee."

"That's of no use. What about immigration?"

Sparr shrugged. "We aren't getting much help from the Belizean government. They're mostly stalling."

"Who asked?" Lee questioned, already guessing the answer.

"Pendleton," Sparr replied.

"Fuck," Lee moaned. "He has the charisma of a crab."

Sparr smiled. "That might be offensive to the crab."

"I'll try to call them," Lee offered. "Maybe I can make nice."

Sparr chuckled. "I'm sure Pendleton was super-pleasant. He only demanded help three or four times."

"Don't worry. He'll get promoted to my job before too long," Lee remarked.

"I hope not," Sparr said earnestly.

Lee didn't reply. Unfortunately, she suspected that could be the case. Winston's last few interactions with Lee had been short and blunt. Lee liked to think she was sufficiently competent to be competition with the older bureaucrat. After all, Winston had been helming the OOC since its inception in the early 2000s.

The Senate Oversight Committee had recently prodded into OOC affairs. The new senator from Wisconsin wanted to limit the authority of the office, something Carl Winston fought against. For the moment, Winston possessed the backing and support of enough lawmakers to keep his position. If that support faltered, he might topple.

For Lee, that might mean an advancement. But as long as she was under Winston, he found himself up for comparison with her. The main thing Carl Winston desired was to be compared to no one.

Lee suspected Winston maintained his status through coercion. Information and threats delivered by OOC agents kept Winston fed with the dirt he used to stay in power. Of course, proving that was a challenge. Winston held tight reins on most operations.

"What do I do?" Sparr asked.

"We're running out of time," Lee admitted. "If we don't trace a thread leading to Khloe or Corsair, Winston will pull us back. Take some photos of the girls down to the bus stations. Let's see if we can locate someone who spotted them. If we verify they're on a bus, we search along the routes."

"You are positive she's gone?" Sparr questioned. "This could be a ruse to send us after a ghost."

"It's possible," Lee confessed. "I doubt it, though. Corsair has instructed Khloe Evans, but this feels like something she did on her own. It might be well-executed, but if Corsair master-minded it, we wouldn't even have a clue."

"Could he be back?"

Lee shrugged. She didn't know. But without reporting her concerns, she was worried. Caleb Saunders had been out of pocket for too long now. It was impossible to determine if Khloe had remained in contact with him while he was in Colombia. If she'd contacted him, then everything could be a feint designed to mislead them.

But finding Khloe had to be the top priority. Every hour that passed gave her a bigger lead. Once they lost her, Lee worried she'd lose the only link to Corsair.

"I'm at a standstill," Lee told Sparr. "I'll go with you to the bus station."

Sparr nodded, and Lee followed the other agent out to the rented Toyota 4Runner. The bus terminal was in downtown Belize City. When they arrived, Sparr parked the SUV in front of the two-story yellow building. The words "Novelo's Bus Terminal" stretched across the front, on the same level as the second floor. Metal gates operated as barriers, easily opened when required.

Lee exited the vehicle and started toward the opened gate. Six locals sat on white twenty-liter buckets that might have once stored paint or spackle. The men were all over fifty, and they laughed amongst each other. All of them wore hats of different styles. Lee counted two straw cowboy hats, a well-worn ball cap with a Chicago Bulls logo on it, a soft-brimmed fishing hat, and what might have been a police or security uniform cap. All six men turned to appraise the pair of women as they approached.

One man in a straw hat mumbled something, and the other five laughed. Their gaze focused on the pair of agents.

"What did he say?" Sparr asked under her breath.

"I'm going to assume it was something neither of us wants to know or even think about," Lee answered.

Sparr shifted to examine the group. The one in the Bulls cap grinned a gap-toothed smile and winked at her. Sparr pivoted and huffed.

"Told you," Lee quipped.

"I wish there was somewhere men would have a modicum of decency," Sparr scoffed.

"Not in my experience," Lee countered. "At least not as a collective."

Inside the depot, Lee found a small lobby with a black-and-white tiled floor that gave her vertigo. Eventually, she oriented herself. Two double-sided wooden benches lined the middle of the terminal. Travelers filled each bench, waiting for their boarding time. Around the outside of the lobby, storefronts offered chips, snacks, and beverages to people loading on the long-distance buses.

"Let's split up," Lee suggested. "See if anyone recognizes Khloe."

"Okay," Sparr agreed.

As the pair of women separated, Lee walked to the booth. Behind the bars, a woman in her fifties cocked her head as Lee approached the window. The ticket seller scanned the OOC agent's attire, which, while not elegant, was professional and much nicer than what anyone else in the terminal was wearing.

On the other side of the counter, the lady looked to be chewing her tongue as she appraised Lee. "Can I help you?" she inquired.

Lee offered her a smile. "I'm looking for a woman who may have come through here in the last day," Lee explained.

"American?" the woman questioned.

Lee furrowed her brow. "Me or her?"

"You're obviously American," the ticket woman noted.

"She's American, too," Lee answered with a grimace.

"Haven't seen any Americans take the bus in a long time," the lady told her.

"Who else might have seen her?" Lee asked.

The woman reclined in her seat and shouted down the hallway, "Celeste!"

She turned her attention back to Lee and waited. The two women stared at each other for several seconds, and Lee wondered if she should say something else.

When nothing happened, Lee Hubbard glanced toward the passageway the other woman had just called down. Lee heard some shuffling over the din of activity in the terminal. A black woman was approaching them, wearing an over-sized dress that could have been a colorful tablecloth with a hole in it for the woman's thick neck.

"What's going on, Maya?" the woman asked.

"Dis lady looking for an American woman," Maya explained to the newcomer who Lee assumed was Celeste.

"Are you American?" Celeste asked Lee.

Lee nodded, not sure why it mattered.

"Why you lookin' for dis girl?" Celeste asked.

"She's in trouble," Lee told them.

"What kinda trouble?" Celeste inquired with a dubious expression.

"I can't really say," Lee said. She drummed both of her index fingers on the counter in front of her.

Celeste gave Maya a knowing look before she remarked, "Guess I can't really say, either, then."

"Listen, Celeste," Lee pleaded in a contrite tone. "I'm trying to find her before some evil men do."

"What kinda bad men?" Celeste asked, her tone hardening.

"She has a little girl with her. There are people who want to hurt her."

"Who are you?" Celeste pushed. "How do I know you will not hurt her, too?"

"So you saw her?" Lee asked.

Celeste shook her head again. This time, there was a bit of defiance in the woman's body language.

Lee sighed. "I'm with the United States government," she said. Lee removed her identity card from Homeland Security. While it didn't give any details of her position or the specific department she operated in, it did state "United States Department of Homeland Security" with her picture and name. She passed the laminated identification to Celeste, who pulled down a pair of half-frame reading glasses she'd been wearing as a tiara.

The transit employee peered at the Information on the card, glancing up at Lee every few seconds as she matched the image with the face in front of her. Lee thought she might not have given a passport the same scrutiny. After she finished studying the front, Celeste rotated it, both of her thumbs on opposite corners. When she studied the back of the card, she returned the ID to Lee.

"Is dis girl a terrorist?" Celeste asked as Lee replaced the card in her wallet.

"No," Lee assured her. "She's just in danger."

"I'm not sure," Celeste dithered. "Why is the Homeland Security trying to find a girl?"

"She's important."

Celeste shook her head slowly. "I don't know if I seen her."

Lee narrowed her eyes and tilted her head. Celeste stared back. If she was lying, Lee couldn't tell.

"You aren't sure?" Lee asked. "Can you take another look? This woman is with a three-year-old girl, and both of them are in danger."

"From who?" Celeste asked.

"American men," Lee said, hoping to keep it vague. She did not know how to explain to this woman the intricacies of Khloe's predicament. While Celeste's stance in protecting a girl she'd never met was admirable, it wasn't helping Lee at all. "They might be close to her now," Lee added.

Celeste pursed her lips and considered the request Lee made. After a long pause, Celeste announced, "I saw her last night. With a little girl."

"You did?" Lee exclaimed.

"Yes, dey took da bus to Flores."

"Flores?" Lee questioned.

"Guatemala," Celeste told her in a condescending tone.

"Are you sure?"

"Of course, I'm sure," Celeste scolded. "Twas de only bus last night."

"How full was the bus?" Lee asked.

"I tink about half-full, but more will board on the way."

Lee sighed. It gave her a start, at least. "Were there any other Americans on the bus?"

Celeste seemed to think before shaking her head.

"Thank you, Celeste," Lee offered before turning to see Sparr speaking to a transportation employee in a dingy, white button-down shirt.

Lee flagged Sparr over to her, and when the junior agent approached, she said, "Khloe boarded the bus."

"Yes, the porter identified her," Sparr told Lee.

"You had it easier," Lee noted, glancing back at the two women holding court behind the brass bars of the ticket window.

"He recognized her right away," Sparr explained. "He thought she was pretty."

Lee shook her head in disbelief. "Men," she muttered.

"His dick helped us this time," Sparr pointed out.

"Good, so they're headed to Guatemala," Lee said.

"Yes, but the porter told me something else," Sparr informed her superior.

Lee lifted an eyebrow.

Sparr continued, "There was another man who got on after Khloe."

"Who?"

Sparr shook her head. "No clue. He thought he looked Arabic."

"Arabic?" Lee questioned.

"His word, not mine," Sparr clarified. "Middle Eastern."

"Was he paying attention to Khloe?" Lee wondered.

"According to my new friend, he was trying not to pay attention."

"He said that?"

"The guy sees a lot, I guess," Sparr acknowledged.

"Great. So someone is on the bus with Khloe," Lee surmised.

"No confirmation, but I suspect so," Sparr agreed.

"We need to get ahead of that bus," Lee urged. "Fast!"

"Who is that guy?" Sparr asked.

"If I was a betting woman, I'd lay odds that Mahmoud Abbas has put a killer on Khloe's trail."

"Abbas?" Sparr questioned. "The arms dealer? Why?"

Lee nodded. Sparr wasn't senior enough to have all the details in Corsair's file. "Corsair killed Abbas's son. Now he wants vengeance on Corsair."

"You think that's who it is?"

"Look around. Do you see a lot of Middle Easterners?"

Sparr shook her head.

"I don't like the coincidence," Lee admitted. "We need to go now."

32

Khloe held Amanda's hand as they wove through the store toward the sign reading *Baños*. Her skin tingled, causing her to glance back. The two men on the bus watched her from two different points. Khloe resisted the urge to reach for the Karambit, but that meant releasing the child's hand.

Khloe pushed into the bathroom that stated *Mujeres*. She pressed her palm against the door and slid the slide latch over into the hasp.

"Where are we?" Amanda asked.

"I'm not sure, but we don't have a lot of time. We need to use the bathroom and get back on the bus."

The sleepy girl nodded. The restroom was what her mother referred to as a "one-holer," with only one commode and a small sink. Khloe pressed her spine against the door as Amanda used the facility. When she finished, Khloe chanced it.

No one kicked the door in. Khloe knew she might be needlessly stressed right now, but her sixth sense told her that wasn't the case. Those men were trouble, but how much they would cause was another thing.

In the dirty restroom, Khloe worried about what would happen if the men grabbed them. How would anyone know what happened to her? How would Caleb find out?

"Okay, wash up," Khloe ordered Amanda as she removed the Karambit from its place on her forearm. "I want you to hold on to me, sweetie. No matter what happens. Deal?"

"Deal!" the girl agreed.

Khloe tightened her grasp on the handle as she unlocked the latch. Again, no one tried to shove their way in. With her left palm, she grabbed Amanda by the hand and opened the door.

When she stuck her head out, a woman in her thirties stared at her.

"*¿Esta bien?*" she asked. Are you okay?

"*Sí,*" Khloe answered.

"American?" she questioned in thickly accented English. Nervously, Khloe nodded.

"*Cuidado!* Be careful. There are men out there who are —*peligroso.*"

"I saw them," Khloe confessed.

"They followed me," the woman told her.

"Want us to wait for you?" Khloe asked. "Were you on the bus?"

"*Sí,*" she answered.

"We'll wait here for you. If we all go together, it will be safer."

"*Gracias,*" the lady said before stepping into the bathroom.

"What are we waiting for, Klo?" Amanda wondered.

"We need to walk to the bus with that woman."

"I don't wanna," Amanda pleaded.

"It's okay, Amanda. We want to make sure she's safe."

"Protect her?" Amanda questioned.

"Yes. Just like your daddy would do."

"Daddy's tough," she stated.

The older woman nodded. "Yes, he is."

The door opened before anything more was said. The Latino woman exited the bathroom. "I'm Alyssa," she introduced herself.

"I'm Khloe."

"Who is this?" Alyssa asked Amanda.

"I not 'posed to talk to strangers," Amanda announced, puffing her chest out and clinching her fists. Khloe saw the girl tighten her hands into balls.

"It's okay, Amanda," she informed the child. "Let's get back to the bus. You hold my hand."

"'Kay, Klo," the girl agreed, reaching up and wrapping her little hand around Khloe's fingers.

The American woman held the Karambit under her shirt with her right hand as they started walking. They followed the path through the bags of chips and candy to the front door. When they stepped outside into the night air, Khloe sucked in a breath. One of the men stood only five feet from the entrance. His back leaned against the stone wall. He wore leather pants and motorcycle boots with a black t-shirt.

"*Hola, mi amiga,*" he rasped through yellowed teeth. His lips were white with spittle and dry skin.

Khloe turned from him, guiding Amanda toward the bus on the other side of the street.

"*¿Ingles?*" he asked, repeating in her own language. "English?"

"Come on," Khloe urged Alyssa and Amanda.

"I hear you," the man growled. "You don't want to talk to me?"

When he moved from the wall, his leather pants squeaked. Her first thought was that it was terrible attire for being stealthy.

"I'm talking to you," he snapped, moving closer.

Khloe let go of Amanda and spun clockwise, raising the Karambit. "Get lost!" she warned.

"Klo!" Amanda cried.

The woman whirled around to see Alyssa dragging the girl away. For a split second, she thought the other woman was trying to help. That was, until she saw the woman's eyes connect with the man in the boots.

"Let her go!" Khloe screamed.

A hand landed on her shoulder, and Khloe drove the point of the Karambit blade into the man's palm.

"Oww!" he howled. "*¡Maldita puta!*"

The man in the boots whipped his hand back, snatching the knife out of Khloe's grip. She ignored him and ran at Alyssa, who picked Amanda up and started running.

"No! Amanda!" she screamed as she chased after the woman.

A figure lunged at her from the darkness, and Khloe jerked away as the second man from the bus appeared from the shadows. He engulfed her with two enormous arms. Khloe kicked him in the shin and flung her head up to smack him in the chin.

He threw Khloe on the ground and spat out a wad of blood.

"Ha ha, she is a feisty bitch," the man in the boots laughed as he joined the other.

"Where's Amanda?"

"Oh, don't you worry, little *puta*. She is with our *amiga*." The man in boots bent to grab Khloe.

She scrambled away and kicked out with her right heel, catching him in the chest. The blow knocked him off-balance, and he rocked off his heels, landing on his ass as Khloe jumped to her feet and ran.

"Help!" she screamed as she searched the streets for Amanda and Alyssa.

The Latina woman carried the fighting Amanda to a van on the other side of the street. Khloe sprinted across the empty one-lane road. The bus rumbled like it was missing a cylinder, and its exhaust plumed out in black puffs. She charged through a cloud of fumes at the vehicle.

"No, no, no!" someone shouted as two hands grabbed her waist.

Khloe came off the ground as the second man twisted around with her. She had a second to register the fist flying at her before the man in the boots punched her in the face. The impact stunned her, and she felt a trickle of blood run from her nose or her lip. Everything swirled, and she heard some distant part of her brain yelling at her to get up.

Khloe's gaze rose to stare at the guy's yellow grin. "Don't try anything else," he threatened.

She shook her head and spat at him. The Latino man chuckled as the second one threw her down. This time, she hit the ground harder, and before she had a moment to curl up, a motorcycle boot struck her in the side. He kicked her again, and she rolled into a fetal position.

Rough fingers ran through her hair, catching a clump. Boots started dragging her along the pavement toward the van.

Khloe's hands flew up, smacking at his grip as all the

nerves in her head screamed in agony. She slapped at him, desperate for salvation.

Through the windshield of the bus, Khloe saw the driver watching the whole ordeal. His eyes narrowed, and his face was pinched. Yet, he only watched with a vague expression of sadness.

"Help!" she called again.

Across the asphalt, the bus's transmission shifted into gear with a whine. The engine roared as the driver pulled around the van and down the road. Khloe kicked her feet. The agony in her head hadn't stopped, but she pushed past it. She flipped over onto her stomach, reaching for her kidnapper's legs.

"Bitch, I told you to stop!" he shouted, driving the heel of his left boot down on her hand. She felt something break, and the pain that had been only in her scalp now resonated from her hand, too.

"What is going on here?" a deep voice boomed.

Boots stopped in his tracks, turning to the stranger who asked the question. He released Khloe's hair for a second, and she rolled away to stare at the person talking. He was a dark figure with a thick black beard. In the shadows, Khloe struggled to identify his features, but she didn't think he was Latino.

"Get lost," Boots ordered.

The second man advanced toward the newcomer, who now stepped boldly toward the trio.

"I think you should let the girl come with me," the newcomer said.

"Why should we do that?" Boots asked. Khloe could hear the smug grin in his tone.

"So I don't have to kill you," he replied.

Both of Khloe's kidnappers laughed, and Boots whipped

out Khloe's Karambit. "We'll see who ends up bleeding tonight," he growled.

Khloe crab-crawled away from the pair of men as they both stalked after her Samaritan. She bounced to her feet and ran from the men toward the van. She grabbed the side door, jerking it open.

Alyssa jumped out of the opening toward Khloe, but the girl was ready, catching her and flipping her in a self-defense move Caleb had shown her. The Latina woman slammed down on her back as Khloe threw her leg across her chest and straddled her. Relentlessly, Khloe pounded the girl's face.

"You fucking took my kid!" Khloe howled as she continued to belt Alyssa. The woman on the ground spat blood, or maybe she was trying to breathe through a mangled mess of flesh. Khloe broke her nose and both cheekbones, not to mention dislodging several teeth.

"Klo?" Amanda called.

Khloe turned to find the child in the doorway watching her. She pushed off Alyssa and grabbed the girl. Her hand was sending shards of pain through her nervous system. The adrenaline of the attack had masked the pain, but now that she was coming down, a wave of nausea hit her. Khloe put the girl down before hunching over and vomiting. It took almost a minute for the nausea to subside, and when it passed, she straightened up to see Boots and his companion sprawled in the dirt.

"Ladies, are you okay?" the man who just saved them asked.

"Yes, thank you," Khloe breathed with some relief. "You were on the bus?"

He nodded, pausing beside the unconscious Alyssa. He nudged the woman with his toe, and she didn't move.

"They left us," Khloe announced. She stopped to look at the man. In the light, she recognized him as Middle Eastern. Not Latino at all. "What were you doing on the bus?"

"Traveling, of course," he said in a prim voice.

"Thanks for your help. We're going to get on the next bus."

"That's in two days," he informed them.

"We'll go in the store, and they can call for the police," she suggested.

"That wouldn't be advisable," he told her. "These groups are often regional, but they are much larger than three people. Someone will be looking for their delivery, and these guys will not make it."

Khloe cringed. This man's English was meticulous, far better than Boots's or Alyssa's. She glanced at his watch—a gold Rolex President Day Date 40. Khloe recognized the timepiece from her stint working for Alejandro Valdez at his jewelry store in Puerto Vallarta. The timepiece carried a retail price tag of well over fifty thousand USD.

"Why are you on the bus?" she asked again.

"I told you, I was traveling."

She shook her head and grabbed Amanda, pulling the girl behind her. "No, really. Why?"

The man beamed. His white teeth gleamed through his dark facial hair. "I guess I'm here for you."

Khloe turned to pick up Amanda and run.

"Don't bother, Khloe," he said. "I have no plans to hurt you."

"What do you want?"

The man smiled broader. His eyes shone black. "I want Corsair."

33

Jason pushed through the foliage onto the footpath. The early hour held the temperature around the mid-eighties. Those numbers would only rise, so for now, it was moderately hot. The air still hung thick with humidity, but it always seemed that way in the rainforest. The best they could hope for was a shower that converted the moist air into rain. They'd end up drenched, but it would be a reprieve from the heat, humidity, and bugs. Once the downpour ended, they'd be soaked, hot, and fair game to the mosquitoes.

"How long did they say it would take?" Sophia asked behind him.

"Raul told me it was a day's hike, but he's going to be faster than us," Jason informed her.

"Right, he's on jungle time," Sophia quipped, referring to the idea that the people living out here lived on their own schedules, like the concept of "island time." No one hurried anywhere unless it was life-threatening. Even then, there was some unspoken agreement over how rushed anything should be. Life-or-death issues seemed to garner less priority over hunting or farming.

"I brought a hammock with us," Jason assured her. "I figure we'll end up camping out here tonight and finishing the hike tomorrow."

"Just one hammock?" Sophia asked, her tone rising with curiosity.

"It's a double one," Jason offered. "With a mosquito netting." He turned to see her face. She smiled at him.

"Good," she remarked. "I'll enjoy another night with the jungle sounds."

Most of the jungle sounds comprised bugs and birds, with an occasional howl in the distance. Until she came to the Amazon, Sophia had expected all sorts of dangerous wildlife. It turned out there weren't any large predators. Maybe some jaguars that might attack a child, but probably wouldn't. Even the idea that there were crocodiles in the Amazon River was wrong. She'd seen a few caiman, but the biggest one was four feet long. It was the small animals to worry about, like the bullet ant or the poison dart frog. A few other insects caused some pain, but most were treatable. Really, the malaria-carrying mosquitoes made up the deadliest creature in the rainforest.

Once Sophia realized there was less to fret over, the woman appreciated the wilderness more. The ayahuasca didn't hurt. Many of the villagers shared the drink derived from a few local plants. It had rendered the nights in the jungle even wilder for her. When she and Jason had tried it together for the first time, they'd shared an otherworldly experience. Sophia kept reiterating to Jason during that period that they were sharing a soul. At any rate, he believed it had sparked something closer between the two.

"Do you think we should have stayed?" Jason wondered.

"I worry about leaving them. Deke lost his friend, and Rick went off to scout the guerrillas' camp."

"It's okay to feel sad," Sophia told him. "But it's also okay to protect ourselves. I'm so sad about Don and Danny, but I don't want you to die, too. Or me."

"Me neither," Jason confirmed.

"Rick's actually kinda scary, too," Sophia noted. "He's hiding something."

Jason agreed, but he kept his thoughts to himself. Rick seemed like a likable guy, but when the raids happened, he'd become this killing machine. Jason didn't intend to get in his way.

"How long have we been walking?" Sophia asked.

Jason answered, "Two hours. Do you need a break?"

"No, I'm okay," the girl replied. "We can go another hour if you want."

"Be a good time to rest and eat," he agreed. "No point in killing ourselves if we can't make it today, anyway."

"We should have brought a tent," Sophia remarked. "We could stay a few more days."

Jason smiled at the idea. "What are you going to do when we get home?" he questioned.

Sophia shrugged. "Guess I'll go home. How about you?"

"I might travel a bit. I'm not sure I'm ready to be back in the grind of life," Jason said.

"Yeah, that would be nice," Sophia agreed.

"Soph, what if you came with me?" he asked.

The girl turned her head. "Travel together? Where would you want to go?"

Jason reached for her hand. "Anywhere works for me."

The woman grinned. "I'd like that."

She squeezed his fingers. Jason leaned in and kissed her. She returned the kiss, wrapping her arms around him.

"What will we do for money?" Sophia asked.

"I have some, but I can do odd jobs. It might be fun to see how we survive."

"You know, what if we find someone with a boat to take us to Europe?" Sophia suggested. "Backpack our way there."

"We should start a blog," Jason said. "Is that still a thing?"

"No, silly," Sophia corrected him. "We should do videos. YouTube, Insta, TikTok."

Jason beamed. "We should have been filming the shit with São Miguel. That would be an interesting start to our adventure."

"I got some footage," Sophia informed him, winking and grinning at him. "Does this make us... a couple?"

"We never defined it before," he advised.

"That's because we were the only two in the same age range. I wasn't about to fool around with Don or Bernie."

"True," Jason joked. "And Bella's too by-the-book."

"What if it doesn't work out?"

"It will still be a good story," Jason offered. "And we'll part as friends, right?"

She smirked and nodded.

Jason's head popped up. "Did you hear that?"

"What was it?"

"I don't know. It sounded like footsteps." Jason slowly spun in a circle, scanning the foliage around them. Nothing stood out in the rainforest.

He strained his ears, listening for anything out of the ordinary. The trees were quiet. Almost too quiet. The only birds chirping were in the distance.

"There's nothing," Sophia whispered.

"It's too quiet," Jason remarked.

"We were just talking," Sophia reminded him. "We scared the birds away."

Jason pursed his lips. That could be, but it seemed unusually still.

"Do you want to stop here?" Sophia asked.

Jason looked around. The narrow path meandered through a dense thicket of trees and brush. The encroaching growth choked out the sunlight.

"No, let's find a clearing," he advised. "Someplace to rest."

Sophia reached for his hand again, taking it gently in hers. Jason reveled in the cool touch of her skin. The sensation sent electricity through his arm, making his face break out in a broad grin.

Despite the euphoria overcoming him, Jason couldn't shake the continuing silence. If it was possible for stillness to be loud, it was doing so. The lack of sound permeated everything. Jason would have settled for a gentle breeze to rustle the leaves. Anything to diffuse the eerie calm.

Crack.

He froze in his tracks, and Sophia's eyes flicked to him. Something made that noise. A twig snapping underfoot. But under whose foot?

"What was that?" Sophia whispered so softly that Jason had to strain his ears.

He shook his head without uttering a word. Jason slid his hand up the small of her back, directing her to move along the footpath. She stared at him for a second, fear brimming her eyes.

As she passed through the thicket, he turned around, cradling the FN FAL he'd taken from the village. He swept the barrel across the path behind them. Nothing moved in his line of sight. It could have been a monkey or lizard creeping along the forest floor.

You're being silly. He worked to convince himself that his nerves had put his imagination in overdrive.

But Sophia had heard it, too.

There was nothing there, though. The rainforest was as still as ever. He turned back and stepped in line behind Sophia, clutching the rifle with both hands across his torso. Jason's head swiveled as they exited the thicket. The forest seemed to open up, allowing more sunlight to filter through the leaves far above the pair.

"There's no one," Sophia said with a breath of relief.

Jason nodded, but his uncertainty lingered. He would like to know what was out there. He turned again to check behind him.

The flash of movement almost escaped his eye. It was a branch springing back as if something pushed it out of the way and released it.

"Shit!" Jason hissed. He faced Sophia. "We need to run."

The girl's eyes widened. She spun forward and sprinted. Jason took off after her. He twirled back, searching for any pursuers.

No one was giving chase. Was he being foolish again?

He turned to tell Sophia he'd overreacted when he ran into her back. She'd stopped in the middle of the path. Jason lifted his gaze to where two men stood before them. Before he could pull up his rifle, he realized the men were aiming identical FN FALs at the pair.

"Oh no!" Sophia gasped.

"Stay calm," he whispered to her as he raised his hands.

"We didn't want any trouble," Jason said in English as he lifted the strap from the submachine gun off his neck. With slow motions, he tossed the weapon aside. "No trouble," he repeated in Portuguese.

One man sneered at him. "Too late," he growled.

"Please don't hurt us," Jason begged. "We were leaving them. We want no part of São Miguel."

"That depends on what the commander says," the sneering man offered. He stepped toward Sophia and touched her trembling cheek. "Perhaps he'll only want the girl."

"No!" Jason declared.

Before he could do anything else, the butt of the other's FN FAL struck him in the temple. He was vaguely aware of his knees buckling as the forest spun around him, plunging him into darkness.

34

Lee stood in the parking lot, if one could call the area of gravel a "parking lot." The majority of the rocks had long washed away. The red mud, now mixed with small pebbles of limestone, left a rusty residue on her shoes.

Sparr knelt beside a corpse wearing black boots while the PNC officer remained several feet back, talking on his cell phone. The *Policía Nacional Civil*, the state police in Guatemala, alerted neighboring districts of the killing in case the murderer was on the run. Although the *oficial primero*, the officer on the scene, had already classified this as a cartel hit.

"This one," Agent Gonzalez, the primary officer, said, "We want him for kidnapping. He's part of a trafficking ring."

"Were there any cameras?" Sparr asked the lead investigator.

He laughed. "No, this isn't like America. No cameras." He waved his right index finger in a circle in the air. "No internet here."

They were in the middle of nowhere. The stop on the side of the road was a tiny shop where passengers could buy snacks, but even calling the small shack a "stop" was an exaggeration.

"Did you speak with the owner?" Sparr asked, pointing a pen at the little store labeled "*Tienda*."

"Yes," the officer said. "The woman over there was with these two, but she approached another woman and a child, pretending to need help. Instead, she was helping the kidnappers."

Lee came to Sparr. "It looks like there are some tire tracks. A truck or van. Something bigger."

"Owner said it was a van," Gonzalez replied. "White."

"It's always white," Lee mumbled. "Any idea which way it went?"

Gonzalez shook his head. "I have someone finding the bus driver. The owner saw it pull away while the girl was being dragged to the van."

"They didn't do anything?" Lee wondered. "The driver or the owner?"

Gonzalez nodded. "Around here, it's better to mind your business."

"That's a shitty way to live," Sparr noted.

"Unfortunately, we don't have enough police to stop the criminals," Gonzalez explained. "They don't trust us to protect them, so no one wants to stand up to criminals."

Lee prodded the dead man in the motorcycle boots with the toe of her shoe. "Someone did."

Gonzalez nodded. "This man had his neck cut open with his own knife." He pointed at the bloody Karambit lying in the red dirt. "A bad man."

Lee crouched down. Gonzalez was correct. Whoever

killed these three was tough, but that only worried Lee more. Who was this person?

As Gonzalez directed his partner to collect some evidence, Lee flagged Sparr over to their car.

"Who did this?" Sparr asked.

"I'd bet your Middle Eastern passenger," Lee said.

"No one said his ethnicity," Sparr reminded her.

Lee nodded. "True, but this isn't a court of law, is it? We only need to find him, not prosecute him."

"Do you know who it is?"

Lee shook her head. "There are only a handful of people one could put up against Corsair. Even fewer from the Middle East."

"Where do we go from here?" Sparr asked.

Lee wasn't sure. Whoever picked up Khloe and Amanda had to get them out of the country. If he saved them, they might have made the mistake of going with him.

"*Señoras*," Gonzalez called from the edge of the road. "We found something."

Lee and Sparr walked over to where the officer stood. He stared down at his partner in the small ditch that ran along the side of the asphalt. The other official picked a shoulder bag from the gulch.

"Looks like someone threw it away," the officer told Gonzalez in Spanish.

"Can we look inside?" Lee asked in Spanish.

"Give it to me," Gonzalez ordered his subordinate.

The other officer passed the bag to his superior, who lifted it up for Lee to appraise it. It was a canvas bag with a name she didn't recognize. The quality appeared to match some of the cheap material coming out of China on any number of fast-fashion sites.

The *oficial primero* carried it to the hood of the 4Runner.

Without donning gloves, Gonzalez sifted through the bag, removing a laptop, several packs of various snacks, and two bottles of Coca-Cola.

"The computer has no power," Gonzalez noted.

"Can I see it?" Lee asked.

The police officer handed the laptop and cord to Lee, who carried it to the Toyota, where she plugged the laptop into an inverter that came with the rental. It took a minute for the computer to open. The screen opened, asking for a password.

"Dammit," she muttered. "I hoped it would just open up."

"Not much chance of that," Sparr commented. "Corsair has better opsec than that."

Lee shrugged. "I know, but imagine if we assumed that and Khloe was lazy."

Sparr nodded. "Had that happen last year in Morocco with Pendleton. He never bothered to check the phone that we picked up off this arms dealer. Turned out the damn fool didn't like dealing with the facial recognition and turned it off."

"Bet Pendleton felt like an idiot," Lee remarked with a mirthful grin.

"Oh, he blamed it on me," she told her.

The two women sat in the front of the Toyota, watching Gonzalez look around the crime scene.

"Will he get anywhere?" Sparr asked.

"Doubt it," Lee answered. "I'm going to make a call. We need to narrow down who our guy is."

"I'll stick to the officer," Sparr stated.

"Not too close," Lee quipped.

Sparr sneered at her. "I'm not sure I can get past the mustache."

Lee looked at Gonzalez and his bushy facial hair. "It probably has enough crumbs in it to feed a small family."

Sparr laughed as she got out. Lee dialed Angie's number at the OOC.

"Ang, it's me," she announced when her girlfriend answered.

"Why haven't you called?" Angie scolded.

"I've been busy. We had Khloe and lost her."

"Lost her how?"

"Someone grabbed her. We don't have much of a description. Middle Eastern man with a beard. Somewhere between thirty and forty. He's average height, so I guess 5'5" to 5'9". That's a wild speculation. He killed three human traffickers in Guatemala."

"You're in Guatemala?"

"Yeah, Ang. Khloe Evans and Amanda Harrod got on a bus in Belize City yesterday. They changed buses in Flores, Guatemala."

"Your unsub?" Angie asked.

"He got on the bus in Belize, too."

"Why did he wait so long to make a move?" Angie wondered.

"I bet he was just sticking to her," Lee explained. "Until Khloe ran into this gang. They tried to grab her, and this man intervened."

"Intervened?"

"Stopped it, I guess," Lee amended. "The witness saw the bus leave and this man kill two men."

"But you said there were three?"

"Yeah, a woman. Beaten to death. I'd guess it was Khloe who did it, though, not him."

"What makes you say that?" Angie asked.

"If he hit her that many times, she'd be unrecognizable.

Khloe has smaller fists and less power. It took more punches to beat her to death."

"Logical as always," Angie remarked.

"I need to figure out who this is," Lee said. "Can you help?"

"Hmm, Middle-Eastern? There was some chatter the other day. Omar Al-Farouqi popped up on our radar. Or at least, we think he did. Online. A user we believe is a pseudonym for Al-Farouqi reached out in a forum for Ifrit."

"Ifrit? I know that name," Lee said thoughtfully.

"That's all you've heard," Angie explained. "The man is a ghost otherwise. We only suspect he's Muslim based on a few snippets we've discovered. Plus, his pseudonym is Ifrit."

"What does it mean?" Lee asked.

"'Ifrit' is the name of a deity. I think it might be closer to a demon, like a genie."

"Al-Farouqi. Who is that?"

She could hear Angie's voice change as her girlfriend smiled into the phone. "Al-Farouqi is the recently promoted chief of security of Mahmoud Abbas."

"Oh, yeah?" Lee remarked. "You could have shared all this with me."

"You didn't call," Angie pointed out.

"I need all the information you have on Ifrit," Lee said, moving on.

"Sweetie, I just gave you everything we know about him. The only way to communicate with him is via this forum. You leave a message, and supposedly, Ifrit reaches out to you."

"What if he doesn't?" Lee asked.

"That means he doesn't want the job."

"Does he do that?"

"From what we've learned, that's the way he works—only on jobs he wants."

"He's good?" Lee questioned.

"Allegedly the best."

"Where would he go?"

"My guess," Angie replied, "would be wherever Abbas was."

"Do we have intel on that?"

"I'll see what we have. Taylor is the analyst tracking him."

"Get me that info ASAP," Lee demanded.

"I love you, too, boo," Angie said sardonically.

Lee smiled. "I love you, Ang."

"Hurry up and get home," her girlfriend urged.

"I'm trying," Lee replied, but she wasn't sure she believed it herself.

35

Sun-dried mud caked his body. His flesh stretched as the globs covering him shrank in the heat. Caleb started to scrape some off as he walked, but since it made for adequate camouflage, he left it on. After riding the current a mile downriver, Caleb had pulled himself up on the bank.

While he didn't want to take a direct beeline back to the village, he knew he should hurry. After Mateo's men gave up searching for him, they might proceed to São Miguel. After the fight the night before, he wanted to be there on the front lines to stop them.

Danny hadn't been the first person Corsair had lost in the field, but he had been the first one he considered an innocent. Except for Jackson and Audrey, of course. That wasn't in a war, though. At least, not until it sparked one.

He still felt guilty about Danny. Should he have sent the two American boys away? Perhaps he should have told Bella to take the villagers and leave. This wasn't a fight worth losing their lives over.

Did any conflict that existed deserve death? Caleb knew

the answer: plenty. He'd risk everything for far less than protecting his home. He would fight to the bitter end if it meant saving Amanda or Khloe. Hell, he considered Deke, Bella, and the rest of the villagers worthy of dying for them.

But Caleb Saunders was a different man than most. It wasn't that he always grasped what he was fighting for, but he appreciated the sentiment. That was part of what had offended him so much when he discovered Carl Winston had been farming him out on personal missions. Caleb could accept killing and dying to protect his country, but to find out he'd been doing it for years to line Winston's pockets? That cut him.

"What do I do, Audrey?" he asked, though he didn't need her to answer. Even her voice of reason wouldn't dissuade him. Although, knowing Audrey, she'd urge him to stand up for the people of São Miguel do Tapajós, just like she would tell him to protect their daughter.

"It's time to bring it home," Audrey informed him. That was something she said when she knew something had to be done. It was her equivalent of "just do it." She'd used that phrase when they were dating and found a stray dog that someone had clipped with their car.

"We need to bring it home," she told Caleb as he wrapped the injured animal in his leather jacket. That had been the moment he realized how much he loved her. She didn't balk at the hard things, and if she thought something was the correct thing to do, there was no stopping her.

"Did you know you ingrained that in me?" he asked her spirit.

Her face appeared in his mind with the same knowing smile she gave him when she knew she was right and he was wrong. "Why do you think I did it?" she asked. "I saw what you carried in you."

Caleb never understood if she really did. As he ran through the forest, he remembered the day he laid his soul bare to her. Despite having fought to the death on more than a few occasions, nothing had scared him more than telling Audrey he'd been a killer. He'd expected her to freak out and run. In fact, he'd already packed a go-bag, expecting to run as soon as she rejected him.

But she hadn't. It proved to be the toughest conversation of his life, yet she'd made it easy. He remembered her arms engulfing him as she swore to him that he possessed goodness.

He smelled the fumes before he saw the plumes billowing up above the treetops. While still two miles from the settlement, he picked up the pace. It took him fifteen minutes to run the last stretch.

Caleb stopped three hundred yards out from the village. The roar of fire echoed out here, and the undergrowth darkened with the smoke trapped under the foliage. He ran forward until he reached the edge of the village. Flames danced from the roofs of almost every hut. Bodies strewn across the courtyard appeared to be the few remaining villagers.

Caleb sprinted into the black clouds. He slid to a stop next to a prone figure. Raul. The other was Calvo. Both had bullets to the head. Neither had a weapon, either. Whoever shot them had stripped them of their guns.

Caleb straightened up and ran for Bella's hut. The entire stilted shack blazed. It might have been the first one the men had set fire to, because its walls were about to collapse.

"Bella!" he shouted. "Deke!"

Not a soul answered over the crackling flames. The wood screamed as the heat sizzled away any moisture in the grain. Caleb spun around, searching for more bodies. Most of the villagers had escaped yesterday, but the few who remained to defend their homes had been gunned down.

Caleb moved from corpse to corpse. None of the dead were part of Zion's Garden. No Deke, either.

Caleb stared at the burning wreckage of the village of São Miguel do Tapajós. In half an hour, the only thing that remained would be the smoldering remains.

This is my fault.

Caleb had likely spurred Mateo to attack after the incident at his base. Had he not engaged the three men outside the camp, Mateo wouldn't have launched a full-on assault. Whatever happened to Bella and Deke was his responsibility.

Caleb stalked through the settlement, searching for any weapons. If any had still been in Bella's hut, they were ruined. The ammo alone would have gone off in the heat.

Caleb coughed up some black residue as he marched to the edge of the village. When he reached the forest, Corsair stepped out of the curtains of dense smoke and into the verdant undergrowth. He pointed himself toward Mateo's camp and started walking.

Mateo thought he'd turned the settlement into a hellscape. He hadn't seen hell yet, but Corsair intended to send him there himself.

36

———————

"You can't do this to us," Khloe insisted.

Ifrit cocked his head at the audacity of the woman. She had her own cabin on the freighter, and so far, someone had catered to her every need. Yet, like most Americans, this bitch demanded more. The entitlement of all Americans nauseated Ifrit.

It wasn't that he didn't appreciate the woman's perspective. Even an ivory tower could be a prison, and nobody wanted to be trapped.

"This is how it is," Ifrit stated.

"Where are you taking us?" Khloe demanded.

"It doesn't matter," the killer informed her.

"The hell it doesn't!" the woman shouted.

"Klo, don't yell," Amanda Harrod urged.

"Sorry, sweetie," Khloe assured the child before turning back to Ifrit. "You're going to kill an innocent girl?"

"I'm not killing anyone," he promised her.

"Then what are you doing with us?"

"I'm only delivering you," Ifrit told her. "In somewhat pleasant conditions."

"Where are we being delivered?" Khloe asked.

"That doesn't matter," Ifrit explained. "There is no place you can go. We will be at sea for over two weeks. Unless you wish to swim a very long way back to shore."

"Who are you taking us to?" Khloe asked.

Ifrit grinned. "If I'm being honest, I'm not taking you anywhere. My employer only wants the little girl."

"You're using us for bait?"

Ifrit held the smile on his face. "In point of fact, I'm using the girl for bait. I suppose you get to stick around to keep her in line."

Khloe's eyes widened. "What does that mean?"

Ifrit shrugged. "It means that you are expendable. If you cause me problems, I don't need you anymore."

Khloe's head turned to stare at Amanda, seated on the other side of the cabin. She felt the color drain from her face as the realization hit home that she might not survive this trip.

"Look, Khloe, is it?" Ifrit asked.

The woman nodded.

"Khloe, it is unnecessary for me to hurt you or the girl," Ifrit explained. "How your journey goes is entirely up to you. Do you understand me?"

She gave a bob of her head.

"Good," Ifrit declared. "I will allow you to take your dinner in your room for now. This will be a long journey, so if you behave, I might allow you to roam the deck some."

Khloe blinked, not knowing how to respond.

"I'll leave you to rest," Ifrit stated as he started for the door.

"You mentioned Corsair," Khloe said. "That's Caleb?"

Ifrit turned back. He cocked his head and nodded.

"Do you know who he is?"

The hired kidnapper smiled. "I do. Do you?"

"He hasn't told me everything," Khloe admitted. "But it's been enough. And I've seen what he can do."

"Indeed?" Ifrit said.

"He'll come for her," she announced, jerking her head toward Amanda.

"We're counting on that," Ifrit informed her.

"I'm sure you are," Khloe said, steeling her courage. "But are you ready for him?"

"Ms. Evans, I doubt Corsair is prepared for what he's going to walk into."

She shook her head, forcing a smile onto her face. "You don't understand what he's done lately."

Ifrit grinned. "Are you trying to frighten me? Because I've killed quite a number of men like Corsair."

"I doubt it," Khloe said. "He tore through an entire motorcycle gang when they kidnapped her. Not to mention the mafia and cartel. I saw him. He should have been killed."

"My dear, I've seen his ilk before," Ifrit assured her. "Is he dangerous? For sure. In fact, the man is a legend. But he was a legend ten years ago. He's still formidable, but he is not in the same shape. I suspect he is not in the right mindset, either. He will react with emotion, and that will march him right into our trap."

"You keep saying 'our' or 'us.' Who are you talking about?" Khloe asked. "Do you have a vendetta against him?"

"Me? No. My employer does, though. Quite a big one. He placed a million-dollar bounty on his head."

Khloe sucked in a breath, and Ifrit could not resist flashing another grin at her.

"You think he's tough?" Ifrit said. "Wait until everyone comes after him for that money. If I fail, another will step into my place. I doubt Corsair will survive this. It might take more than me, but he'll fall. If you're lucky, you might escape this with your life."

"Really?"

Ifrit shrugged. "Perhaps. You have no intrinsic value to Corsair. He may come for you, but I think it's only because of the child."

Khloe glanced at Amanda again. "What about her?"

Ifrit raised his eyebrows. "What do you mean?"

"If you get Caleb—Corsair—will she be able to go free?"

The assassin gave the child an introspective stare. His pause was long enough to give Khloe a chill.

"She's just a girl," Khloe rasped under her breath.

"My employer desires his vengeance," Ifrit explained.

"He'll have Caleb. Isn't that enough?"

The man lifted his shoulders. "Who am I to say? He believes Corsair owes him a life for the one he took."

"Who did Caleb kill?" Khloe asked.

"His son," Ifrit answered. "My employer hasn't said, but I know how he thinks. If he has the girl, he'll want to dangle her in front of Corsair. I imagine he will take pleasure in killing her in front of her father."

"She didn't do anything," Khloe insisted, her voice full of anguish.

"It is not my place to say," Ifrit countered. "I'm only paid to deliver Corsair."

"What if you get Corsair without hurting her?"

Ifrit shook his head. "The die is already cast. I can't change a thing."

"Who is your boss?" Khloe demanded.

"That's enough questions," Ifrit ordered. "I've explained all I plan to."

"But—"

He cut off her argument with a single raised index finger. "I've said all I'm going to say," he repeated. "Do not make yourself a nuisance that I need to handle."

With that, Ifrit walked into the corridor and shut the cabin door.

37

The camp buzzed. Bella couldn't see what was happening. She lay on the dirt with her hands tied next to Deke, who was unconscious.

She thanked God that he was still alive, though. When the raiders stormed the community, they were all caught off-guard. Not to mention sorely undermanned. With only a small contingent left in the village, the plan had been to flee at the first sign of attack.

Bella begged Caleb—or Rick, whatever he wanted to be called—to stay in the settlement. They planned to bury their dead, including Danny and Don. She could see Caleb had been deeply affected by Danny's death. Not like Deke, who had been Danny's best friend since they were kids. Caleb blamed himself; Bella saw that in his expression. The die-hard killer thought he should have done something different.

What that was, Bella didn't know. She guessed part of it was a lack of knowledge. She suspected Caleb was a government agent of some sort. Given his secrecy, she figured he must trade in information. Not having that data made him feel unprepared.

While they interred their fallen friends, he'd vanished into the forest. Deke suggested Caleb had gone to find Mateo and his men. That seemed fair, and Bella secretly hoped the killer would act accordingly. Despite her belief that all life was precious, Bella hoped Caleb returned with Mateo's head on a spike. Even a scalp would satisfy her sense of justice for those she'd seen killed in the last few weeks.

The woman knew it was contrary to everything she believed in. If she purported to trust in the Almighty, that meant doing so completely. But it was Deke who'd asked her, "What if God sent Rick to save São Miguel?"

She confronted that idea now as she lay beside the barely conscious Deke. In the scriptures, the judges came to defend and fight for the Israelites. Perhaps Caleb was a judge delivered to destroy her enemy.

When she considered that idea, it comforted her. Although, with Deke hardly moving, she wasn't sure if Caleb would arrive in time.

A tent flap pulled, spilling light into the shadow interior. The thick canvas sides blocked most of the sunlight, and when the door opened, Bella squeezed her eyes shut against the sun beaming in.

"Bella?" a familiar voice questioned.

The woman bound on the ground blinked as the canvas closed again.

"Sophia?" Bella questioned. "Is that Jason, too?"

"Yeah," the male answered.

"I thought you left?" Bella asked.

"We did," Sophia remarked. She gasped. "Oh my God, is that Deke?"

Sophia knelt beside the injured man. The girl's wrists were bound behind her back. The guerrillas had tied Jason's behind him as well.

"What happened?" Bella asked the couple.

Jason bent his knees, lowering himself to the ground, the feat made more difficult without hands to catch his descent.

"They must have followed us," Jason said. "We'd gotten half a day away from the river when someone ambushed us."

"At least they didn't hurt you," Bella pointed out, glancing at Deke.

"What happened to him?" Sophia asked.

"We were burying Don when six soldiers appeared. Deke and I were on the eastern side of the village where the other graves are. More men must have stormed the village. I think they killed Raul and Calvo."

"No!" Sophia moaned. "Why didn't they just let us go? We were giving up!"

Bella shook her head. "I doubt they ever intended to let us go, or the villagers. Especially after Caleb—I mean, Rick —fought back."

"Where is Rick?" Jason inquired.

"He disappeared," Bella told them.

"Like, he left?" Sophia asked.

"I don't think so," Bella explained. "Some soldiers were talking about him. He may have killed a patrol earlier."

"Dang," Jason muttered. "I hope he's still out there."

"Why?" Sophia complained. "He caused all the problems. If he hadn't killed those men to begin with, we wouldn't be in all this mess."

"Not really," Jason reminded her. "They killed Bernie, remember? That was before Deke and Rick showed up."

"Don't forget Danny," a muffled voice said.

"Deke! Are you alright?" Sophia asked.

The other American wriggled against the straps binding him. "What happened?" he asked.

"You tried to fight six guys bare-handed," Bella replied.

"Shit, I seem to recall that," he murmured through a swollen jaw and bruised face. He groaned.

"Where does it hurt?" Bella asked, rolling to her knees so she could bend over him.

"I can't tell," he muttered. "Everything hurts. My side, especially."

"They kept kicking you," she explained. "Even after you were unconscious."

"Sophia, can you turn around and try to raise his shirt?" Jason suggested.

"I'll try," the girl said. She shuffled on her knees until her back was to Deke. "Don't let me hurt you more, Deke," she warned.

"Not sure I'd know," Deke croaked.

Sophia's fingers tugged at his clothing. The effort to lift his clothing took time as she moved slowly in the hopes of not causing more pain.

"I bet your ribs are broken," Jason told Deke.

"Yes, definitely," Bella agreed. "How is your breathing?"

"Hard but manageable," Deke wheezed.

"Hopefully there's not a punctured lung," Bella said. "Just keep taking slow breaths. Don't move."

"Can we do anything for him?" Sophia asked. "I can try to wrap him with a bandage."

"We have nothing to use," Jason pointed out.

Deke coughed.

"I told you not to breathe too fast," Bella admonished.

"I'm trying," he countered with a gasp.

"Rest, man," Jason urged. "That's all you can do right now."

"Sounds good," Deke grumbled.

"We need to get him to a doctor," Sophia stated. "Why don't they come help him if they're keeping him alive?"

"Why are they keeping any of us alive?" Jason asked.

"I'm guessing that we're bait," Bella speculated.

"That doesn't explain why they came after us," Sophia pointed out.

"You're bait, too," Bella told her. "But also, they might not want you to make it to Santarém to bring back Brazilian officials."

"Why not just kill us, then?" Jason asked.

"We never wanted to kill you," Mateo announced as he entered the tent. "We offered for the village to move, but you brought in—how do you Americans refer to it? Muscle? You brought in muscle to stop us."

"But that's not what happened," Sophia argued.

Mateo let the tent flap close. Two soldiers flanked him as they stepped into the shelter. With seven people in the canvas tent, the space grew tight.

"Can you at least offer him some first aid?" Bella asked, motioning with her head to Deke on the ground.

Mateo cocked his head and appraised the injured individual. "No, he will be fine."

"He's severely hurt," Bella argued. "It's your fault."

"No, *mi amiga*, it is your people's fault," Mateo said icily. "Who is this man you brought in to defend you? Where is he now?"

"He left," Bella stated. "And we didn't bring him in. He wandered in sick."

"Your sick comrade has killed a lot of my men," Mateo noted. "I'd hate to see him when he's healthy."

"Damn straight," Jason blurted out. "He's going to come for you."

Mateo motioned for one of his soldiers to silence the young man. The nearest guerrilla hit the defenseless man with the back of his hand. Jason, who had been resting on his knees, tumbled over under the impact.

"Jason!" Sophia cried.

"Quiet," Mateo ordered as Jason writhed on the ground. It took him several seconds to get back to his knees with his hands bound.

"Sir, we'll leave São Miguel to you," Bella told Mateo. "The villagers already left. We only wanted to bury our friends before we abandoned it, too."

"But you'd have reported to the authorities that we raided your village," Mateo pointed out. "That would cause more problems for us."

"No, we won't," Bella explained. "But someone will notice if we all vanish. Our organization expects weekly updates. We already missed one. If we miss another, someone will send people to investigate."

Mateo tilted his head as he stared at Bella. "When they arrive, our people will inform them you all left of your own accord."

"This is a global missionary group," Bella argued. "They won't buy that. And this isn't the first war-torn place they've put missionaries. It won't just be some church official who shows up—they'll reach out to the Brazilian government. Particularly The Ministry of Indigenous Peoples. That will bring in the federal authorities."

Mateo shrugged. "It will take time, though. By then,

we'll have established ourselves and rebuilt São Miguel. And we will have the gold."

Bella shook her head. "There is no gold," she stated. "If we found some, we'd be using it to help the villagers."

"Your not finding it doesn't mean it isn't there," Mateo said stubbornly.

Jason sat on his side, sucking on his busted lip. "Why are we still alive, then?"

Mateo smiled, spreading both hands out with his palms up. "I'm not a monster like you seem to think. I have people to take care of here."

"That doesn't answer my question," Jason grumbled, straightening up with more courage.

Mateo jerked his head, and the same soldier as before struck Jason again. This blow was stronger than the first, and Jason rocked over on his side. His face slammed into the dirt, and he spat out a mouthful of blood.

"Stay down," Mateo ordered. "Or the next one will leave you down permanently."

Jason didn't move, obeying the despot.

"To answer your question," Mateo added, "I don't need you alive."

He squatted down on his haunches, focusing his attention on Bella. "*Mi amiga,* I don't even care if your people send out an army. I'm going to have that gold. But for now, allowing you to live suits me."

"Until you find our friend," Bella pointed out.

Mateo lifted his eyebrows. "Exactly, which is why I have no intention of making your stay any more comfortable than it already is."

"You plan to kill us when you're done," Bella said.

"Let's just say I have no reason to keep you alive," Mateo remarked. He gave Bella an appraising look before turning his gaze to Sophia. "Now, my men might disagree with me. At least for you two." He scowled at the motionless figures of Jason and Deke. "My troops won't want them, though."

"You're a bastard," Sophia snapped.

Mateo leaned toward the girl, placing his face within inches of hers. "You are nothing more than a sow. If I choose to let you live, it will be for the benefit of my men. Perhaps I can breed an army from you. Or, I can butcher you now and save the trouble."

Sophia's cheeks reddened with outrage. When she spat in Mateo's face, Bella cringed. The leader of the guerrilla army smiled, reached forward, and grabbed the girl by her hair, jerking her close to him. With his hand full of her locks, he wiped the spittle off his face into her mane.

"Thank you for volunteering," he replied with a sneer. "Bento, why don't you take her to your tent?"

"Thank you, sir," the guerrilla who struck Jason replied in Portuguese before grabbing Sophia by the arm and dragging her to her feet.

"No!" Jason shouted, pushing his shoulders against the earth to lift his waist up. For a second, the man resembled an inchworm. That imagery ended when Bento slammed his left foot down on the back of his head. Jason splayed out on the ground, not moving.

"No!" Sophia screamed in a high-pitched wail as Bento dragged the woman from the tent.

Mateo, still on his haunches, peered at the livid expression on Bella's face. "You didn't have to let it come to this," he advised her. "Americans always think they have the upper hand. Foolish girl. When I'm done with you, you'll beg me to kill you."

Bella glared at the guerrilla, who flashed his tinted teeth at her.

His countenance twitched at the first sound of gunfire, and the grin on his face wilted in a second.

The corners of Bella's mouth rose in defiance. "Sounds like you're about to have your hands full," she remarked smugly.

38

Caleb stretched out in the brush, watching five men march Sophia and Jason at gunpoint through the rainforest. Neither of the Zion's Gardeners appeared to be injured, but both bore terrified expressions. Caleb had given Jason his blessing to escort Sophia to Santarém before he had set off to scout the guerrilla base.

The pair must have left after he did, and before the attack on the village. Otherwise, they would have already been taken back to the camp. He'd seen no sign of Bella or Deke in the settlement, which was the only hope he had that the two had survived.

Now, seeing Jason and Sophia captured, he felt some renewed confidence that Deke and Bella were still alive. He crawled forward to maintain a better view of the encampment, keeping his friends in his line of vision as long as possible.

As the soldiers escorted them through the grounds, he lost sight of them when they entered a maze of tents. Caleb pushed up on his hands and the balls of his feet to hurry through the undergrowth. When he reached the camp earlier, he'd given the perimeter a wide sweep, searching for a vantage point that didn't fall in the line of patrol. That wasn't a mistake he wanted to make again.

There were more troops on the base than he'd seen before. Two sizeable crowds clustered together under guard. A figure appeared at the edge of the two groups, and Caleb identified him as Mateo.

Mateo stood in front of the men, speaking in Portuguese. His words were too distant to understand, so Caleb only watched. Most of the people in both groups seemed frightened. They'd gone out and conscripted new soldiers. Caleb guessed they came from some surrounding towns and settlements.

That unsettled Caleb. The guerrillas he had killed so far were attacking the village or had the intent to. These new recruits had just now entered the camp. Caleb assumed it hadn't been voluntarily, either, considering their demeanor and how they'd been dragged in.

Each group had twelve to fifteen men. He had trouble keeping them all in view long enough to count without getting closer.

Round up, he told himself. With thirty men, this would be a lopsided fight. Even uninitiated troops with sufficient firepower were a match for Corsair. Nevertheless, this presented itself as an opportunity to take off the head of the serpent. While someone might try to fill Mateo's shoes, his recruits were already frightened of their new commanders. A little shock and awe could send them scattering before the soldiers had time to restructure.

However, shock and awe required both shock and awe. Neither commodity was in high supply for Corsair. He needed to arm himself before he did much of anything.

For the time being, he knew the general vicinity where the guerrillas held Jason and Sophia. He hoped it was close to where Bella and Deke were. Caleb also prayed the rest of the missionaries were still alive.

Corsair spotted a pair of soldiers patrolling. Two men weren't a problem for the assassin, but taking on both increased the risk that one would sound an alarm. The longer he was unnoticed, the more damage he could inflict.

Then he found his target. A brute of a man, but he was straying from the base toward the treeline. It took Corsair a second to figure out what he was doing. The guerrillas had dug a latrine outside of camp. It limited the odor of so many men's feces and urine in the camp itself, but it created a defensive nightmare. Something no one had taken advantage of, Corsair decided.

Without wasting time, Corsair, still on the balls of his feet and his fingertips, scampered across the ground like a monkey. He got behind the latrine, the aroma of raw sewage assaulting him immediately. The least Mateo could have done was have the men toss some leaves or wood chips in the holes. Instead, they were breeding bacteria as if it was livestock.

Caleb breathed through his mouth, attempting to lessen the scent. But now the air tasted of shit.

I'm not sure which is worse.

The latrine covered about twenty square feet. He guessed there was space for two or maybe three holes. He strained to listen, making out the splashing of piss in the hole. The brute would be done soon, and Corsair wanted to handle him out of sight.

The former OOC agent skirted the tent to the front, opening the door. What he thought was an atrocious odor outside the shelter became eye-watering inside the stifling hot canvas. Clear plastic panels in the roof provided dim lighting, in part because no one ever cleaned the acrylic. A greasy film covered the skylights.

A shiver ran through Caleb as he considered what was causing the residue.

In the darkened interior, he distinguished four temporary commodes lined along the rear wall. A wooden floor concealed the pit the guerrillas had dug out, and the toilets sat atop holes cut in the plywood.

With his chin pressed against his chest, he approached the man seated on the toilet, the man's fatigues pulled down to his ankles. The soldier rested his submachine gun against the back wall. On the man's belt, Corsair identified a Beretta 45 caliber.

Like most men, the guerrilla did his business within a bubble. His head was bowed as if he was in prayer, and his elbows were propped on his knees. Only when Caleb took two steps toward him did he look up, perhaps wondering why someone would choose the commode closest to him. Only, he didn't have time to form that thought. After he looked up, he had a split second of recognition to realize the newcomer wasn't one of his fellow soldiers. The next instant, his lifeless body slumped forward and rolled off the toilet seat, his neck bent to the side at an impossible angle.

Corsair scooped up the submachine gun, another FN FAL. He wondered if the Brazilian army was supplying Mateo's gang since they all carried the same rifles. While the military likely hadn't sold them the guns, that still wasn't a foregone conclusion. Plenty of corrupt governments funneled weapons to militias and guerrillas. Even more crooked supply officers made extra money selling surplus gear.

He removed the man's Beretta. Corsair wished he had a silencer, but that seemed unlikely. The soldier didn't have a knife on him, either. That surprised Caleb a bit, but he didn't linger on that thought before he started out of the latrine.

Caleb stopped. If anyone came in—and one had to assume this was a busy location at some point—the dead shitter would be easy to spot. He considered dragging him out through the rear wall, but that would take time to loosen the stakes and lift the side or cut out an opening. Since he lacked a knife, that option was out.

He could prop him on the seat and hope no one tried to engage with him. That wasn't viable, either. Even if a man came in with no intention of speaking, the literal dead silence might attract attention.

Caleb curled his lip and scrunched his nose up as he hooked his hands under the man's arms and dragged him toward the front of the tent. When he reached the edge of the wood, Caleb dug his fingers under the sheet and hoisted it up. A cross-section blank pinned the floor down, preventing him from opening the gap very wide. Instead, he lifted it about a foot. He dropped to one knee and used his shoulder to hold the wood up while he shoved the carcass into the pit. Unfortunately, he didn't drop the plywood fast enough to avoid the splash that spewed through the hole.

Corsair wiped his hand on his pants, reminding himself to wash his hands and burn his clothes at the first available moment. As he straightened up, the door opened, casting a beam of light into the latrine. Caleb faced the rear wall and lowered his head.

"Excuse me," a deep voice said in Portuguese.

Caleb spun around and struck the newcomer in the

throat. The resulting gasp came out in a hushed tone. As the man stumbled back, Corsair followed through with a blow to the nose, landing the heel of his right hand against the cartilage. The nasal bone broke under the impact, shoving pieces of cartilage into the man's brain. It wouldn't kill him, but he'd be unconscious for a while.

Unfortunately for him, he wouldn't wake up in time to not drown in the pit of shit.

The second splash was still faster than Caleb had been at dropping the wood, but he prepared for it, stepping back fast enough that only flecks of liquid sprayed his shoes.

Caleb didn't bother stripping the man of his weapons. He was too worried about another interruption before leaving. While the latrine was the perfect place to lie in wait for victims, it wasn't where he wanted to be.

As he lowered his head, he stepped out into the sunlight. Luck benefited him, and no one came toward the toilets, allowing him to slip back around the tent.

Thirty men to start. Now the count had dropped to twenty-eight.

If he had darker skin, he might blend in long enough to stroll through the camp, but it was hard not to identify him as Caucasian. If they were in Europe, he would have passed with no problem.

How much time did he have before his friends were in deeper peril? Time wasn't working on his side. If it had, he would have waited until the dead of night to enter the camp. But since he hadn't seen Bella or Deke yet, he didn't want to linger.

He retreated into the rainforest again, using the underbrush for cover. He moved around the camp's perimeter until he had a better view of the alley between the tents where he'd lost Jason and Sophia. Corsair located four tents from his angle that could house them.

Caleb crouched and waited. Before he charged in, Corsair wanted to know if they were alone or not. If not, how many guards were on them?

Two men stood like sentries between a pair of the canvas structures. One looked larger than the other. His instincts said that if Jason and Sophia remained prisoners, they wouldn't be in the bigger tent. Besides that, one tent backed up to another row of tents with a passage leading straight into the jungle. It created a defensive gap in Mateo's camp, and Caleb sought the advantage of it.

He marched down the corridor with tents bordering each side. While his head appeared to droop, Corsair scanned ahead by rolling his eyes upward. He located the bigger tent he'd identified as a possibility and squeezed between it and the neighboring one.

His vantage point now allowed him to see the smaller tent across from his concealment. The door flap pushed back, and a thick Brazilian man shoved Sophia out. Her hands were tied behind her.

"No!" someone shouted from inside the other tent.

"Let go of me!" Sophia screamed.

The Brazilian shook her violently before pulling her face close to his. He grimaced, flashing a mouth filled with rotting teeth. Sophia's head turned away, and the guerrilla grabbed her chin and yanked it to meet his gaze.

"I'm going to break you, you whore," he growled at her in Portuguese.

Tears welled in her eyes, but she pulled at his grip. The soldier let go of her and struck her with a backhand. The slap threw her across the clearing, where she fell into the dirt. Without her hands, Sophia landed on her face, unable to shield it from the ground.

The guerrilla grinned as he took a long stride toward her. His meaty fists grabbed her by the hair, jerking her to her feet as she screamed in agony.

Corsair bit the inside of his lip as he stepped out from his hiding spot, raised the Beretta to the back of the Brazilian's head, and squeezed the trigger.

39

———

Chaos reigned down on the camp as the gunshot echoed through the trees. Caleb wrapped his right arm around Sophia and dragged her back behind the tents.

"What the hell!" she howled before he covered her mouth.

"Shh!" he warned. "It's me."

"Oh, thank you, Rick," she blubbered.

"Shh!" he repeated, raising a finger to his lips. "Follow me," he mouthed, taking her by the wrist and pulling her deeper into the gap between the tents.

"Where are the others?" he asked.

"In that tent. That man was going to—"

"It's okay," Caleb assured her, turning her around and loosening the ropes on her hand. "Go out that way. Don't stop for anyone."

"Rick, Deke's in there, and they hurt him bad. I think they'll kill Jason, too."

"Not if I can stop them," he promised.

"The man in charge," she said. "He's very evil."

Caleb gave a nod.

"I don't want to be here," she moaned.

"Run. Get into the rainforest and hide. If I don't find you, wait a bit and head for the village. It's north of here."

She nodded.

"Go!" he demanded, pointing her down the alley. The girl sprinted. In fact, she was faster than Caleb thought he'd seen anyone run. In less than ten seconds, she was out of the camp and had disappeared from sight.

The rest of the encampment was alive and shouting. He needed to move before people would start searching everywhere for the source of the gunshot.

Caleb slid between the tents again and dropped to his knees next to the stake holding down one side. He loosed the strap, securing the canvas wall to the ground. After lifting it up, Caleb rolled under it into a bigger living space.

While he wouldn't have classified this as a luxury accommodation, it was among the nicer battlefield quarters he'd seen. In Iraq, he had been in the tent of a four-star general that had been more elegant, but that officer had enjoyed air conditioning and a fifty-inch flat-screen television. Still, this one had a couch and a queen-sized bed.

Corsair stood up. This was a commander's tent. Mateo's tent. His home. All Corsair had to do was wait for him to return.

Outside, a hubbub of activity had erupted. Men were shouting in Portuguese.

"Where is she?" someone called out. "Find her. Was she alone?"

As the voice trailed off, Caleb heard, "Hey, clean up Bento," before the words faded in the distance.

Corsair holstered the Beretta, lifted the FN FAL, and pushed the door of the tent open.

"What is going on here?" he asked in Portuguese as he stepped out.

The effect worked. Three men bending over the dead corpse of Bento looked up as Corsair let loose a burst of bullets, cutting them all down. The trio fell to the earth. Caleb opened the tent flap he'd seen Bento and Sophia exit from.

Huddled over two figures was a hog-tied Bella. She turned to see Caleb step inside.

"Oh, thank God," she praised. "They took Sophia."

He shook his head. "She's safe now." He crouched and untied her wrists.

"He killed Jason!" Bella cried, crawling toward the sprawled man. Caleb reached over, checking his pulse.

"He's still alive," he said. "But we'll have to carry him out of here." Caleb glanced at Deke, who was conscious but not moving. He added, "We'll need to carry them both."

"I can't lift them for very long," she informed him.

"See if you can help them," Caleb ordered.

"What are you going to do?"

"Look for some transportation," he told her. "If anyone comes back, play possum."

"What?" she asked, confused.

"Pretend to still be tied up," he replied. "If you need to run, do it. I'll return for these two."

"I'm not leaving them," she insisted.

Caleb gave her a half-smile. "I didn't figure you would."

He was out of the tent before she could reply. They required a vehicle, and he'd only seen two in the camp during his scouting runs the last two days. Both were small model trucks that had more rust than paint on them.

It wasn't just transportation they needed. Once they left, it wouldn't take long for Mateo to regroup and pursue them.

Caleb had to prevent that. The best thing he could do now was sow some chaos into the new recruits.

He slid between the two tents across from Bella's. In moments, he slipped into the gap and between another tent. The canvas created something like a maze effect as he zigged and zagged around the corners.

Caleb stopped at the border of a clearing where six guerrillas, now geared for battle, came stomping toward him. Hidden behind the tent, he let the unit march toward the edge of camp. Mateo knew he had an intruder, and he wanted to prevent Caleb's escape by increasing the perimeter guard—something he should have done before dragging the Zion's Gardeners in as prisoners.

Corsair stepped out from the niche where he'd been hiding and raised the FN FAL. The first rounds started on the left and ripped through the soldiers. Before he shot all of them, the two on the far right spun around and opened fire. He'd anticipated that, and while he'd expected both men to turn to the right, the man on the left surprised him by spinning the opposite way. Both fired without aiming, and Corsair dove into a tent.

As he stumbled into someone's barracks, he felt a burning sensation in his calf. With no time to inspect it, he hobbled for a second as he swung the barrel of his machine gun toward the opening and started firing.

The sound of bullets hitting flesh was distinct, but even Corsair couldn't hear it over the din of gunfire around him. When his magazine ran dry, Corsair charged for the back of the tent and hit the canvas wall at full speed. He rebounded off the rear section, but the impact dislodged the stakes that secured the tent to the ground.

Caleb lifted the bottom of the canvas, dropping his empty machine gun. As he rolled under the fabric, he came to his feet, his Beretta drawn and ready. The area was clear, and he dashed toward the center of camp. The Beretta wouldn't work for long if he ran up against more men with automatic guns. Corsair counted on his superior marksmanship against anyone in the camp, but each FN FAL held at least twenty rounds to the Beretta's fourteen-round magazine. He needed to get another weapon.

Shouts came from nearby, and Corsair ducked into a different tent. A man sat up on a cot, staring at the intruder in his quarters. He'd been sleeping—a miracle during a gunfight. The occupant blinked twice before some part of his brain triggered the fight-or-flight instinct. He reached for a Smith & Wesson nine-millimeter hanging in a holster off the left side of his bunk. His movements were still sluggish, and before his right hand crossed his torso for the gun, Corsair shot him in the forehead.

The man flopped off the bed, and Caleb winced to realize he'd been naked under his sheet. The assassin twisted back to cover the entrance. If someone had been nearby, they might identify the tent the last shot came from.

Seconds passed until they changed into minutes. Caleb relaxed. No one was coming yet, although a tent-by-tent search was inevitable. By then, he needed to be on the move.

In his head, he ran a quick tally. Two men in the latrine. Bento. The three guerrillas tending to Bento, the possibly six guards, and this sleeping bastard. Thirteen men—if he'd killed all six guards. The last two were unknown, but Caleb had still cut Mateo's troops down by almost half.

These soldiers were his veterans, too. The newbies had yet to experience the pressure of battle. Right now, they feared both the other guerrillas and whoever was attacking the camp.

Caleb inspected his leg. A red gash showed where a round had grazed his calf and tore through his fatigues. It needed to be cleaned, but the bullet hadn't punctured the flesh.

Caleb took the Smith & Wesson, slinging the belted holster over his shoulder. Beside the man's cot, he picked up a cheap switchblade with a "Made in China" stamp on the handle. The blade was thin, and while it had an edge, just one use might dull the blade irreparably. But one use was better than none, and he pocketed the knife.

He found a pack of Brazilian straw cigarettes and an inexpensive plastic lighter. Corsair stared at the light blue lighter in his hand, then turned in the darkened tent. Two lanterns sat on the ground. Kerosene lanterns.

Corsair scooped up the nearest lantern, pulling the hurricane glass off. The burner was screwed into the reservoir filled with fuel. Caleb gripped the burner with his palm and bent the thin metal until it ripped out of the container. In a rush, he doused the tent with the kerosene. With a flick of his thumb, he ignited the lighter, touching the flame to the pool of accelerant. Tongues of fire danced down the stream of kerosene.

Caleb palmed the lighter and escaped through the entrance as the flames filled the tent. The accelerant would speed the fire along, and Caleb counted on it, spreading to the other tents.

He sprinted toward the center of camp, the Smith & Wesson in one hand and the Beretta in the other. When he dashed into the open, he fired each weapon in succession at the four guerrillas closest to him. Each gun worked independently as he lined up shots with the Beretta and then the nine-millimeter. The rapid fire dropped the first four men and sent the other four running from the area.

In less than three seconds after arriving on the scene, he found the camp cleared. Caleb glanced at the four men on the ground, realizing too late that only one of them was armed.

"Shit," he muttered to himself. Caleb considered the new recruits to be innocents, but in the frenzy of battle, he hadn't distinguished them.

In his earlier career, Corsair had killed innocents. Even then, they were more collateral damage than intended targets, but he had acted under the impression that it was for his country. That had turned out to be a lie, and the realization now made him sick. These three, having been forced to be here, never had a chance.

It infuriated him. He wanted to find Mateo and make him suffer for what he'd done to these people. To his friends. To the villagers. He planned to send Mateo to hell himself.

Deke and Jason don't have time for that. The thought reminded the assassin that his two companions needed exfiltration soon, or they might not survive. He had to find the truck.

It took him a second to get his bearings. The two vehicles he'd seen were on the western side of camp. He turned to sprint across the clearing when a gunshot rang out. The shot missed him, but only because Corsair had already been moving.

Corsair dove behind a wooden table that the camp used for gatherings. He flipped it over as more rounds hit the wood.

"*Gringo*, you've been a problem!"

"Is that Mateo?" Corsair called back in Portuguese.

"We have not met yet!" Mateo yelled.

"Want to do it face to face?" the American shouted back.

"Don't do it!" Bella's voice cut across the battlefield.

Caleb turned to peer through the slats of the table. Mateo stood at the edge of the camp's courtyard with Bella in front of him, the muzzle of a Taurus PT92 pressed against her temple.

Corsair rose, training the sights of both weapons in his hands on the guerrilla leader.

40

"I've got something for you," Angie said on the other line.

"Good, because I'm stuck right now," Lee admitted. "I lost Khloe and Amanda. And I still have no idea where Corsair is."

"I suspect the girls are on a freighter," Angie informed her partner.

"Where?"

"It's not definite, but a freighter owned by Barzan Global left Costa Rica."

"How did you reach that conclusion?" Lee asked.

"The freight line offers some cabins to travelers, but this cruise canceled all passengers at the last minute."

"Hmmm. That's thin, Angie," Lee pointed out.

"Yes, but when they cleared out of Costa Rica, they listed two passengers: an Elizabeth and Shelly Carter from London."

"Do you have any other details?"

"I'm working on images from the passports they used,"

Angie told her. "However, cross-referencing with the UK, there are no records for either Carter over there."

"Where is the freighter going?" Lee asked.

"Saudi Arabia," Angie answered. "There's more, though. Barzan is owned by a conglomerate whose CEO is Rashid Al-Emadi, a close associate with Mahmoud Abbas. Our analysts concluded Al-Emadi is nothing more than a figurehead."

"Can we stop it?" Lee wondered.

"They're in international waters," Angie said. "We could, but we'd have to tear through a ton of red tape. I wasn't sure if you wanted that."

Lee stood up from the bed in her hotel room and started pacing. Her brain needed some exercise, and at the moment, she felt like the walls were closing in on her.

She began speaking her thoughts out loud. "Saudi Arabia. Is Abbas there?"

"Doubt it," Angie acknowledged. "His office is in Qatar. Saudi Arabia is likely a stopping-off point. They'll carry the girls from there to Abbas."

"Or someplace they can keep them," Lee surmised. "Abbas might not care to hold them in his house, if you know what I mean. He'll want them somewhere he can control the situation when Corsair comes calling."

"Where, though?" Angie asked.

"Sweetie, scrape the bottom of the barrel and uncover any place Abbas might have."

"If I don't, will you come home?" Angie implored.

"I think if I return now, Winston will attempt to railroad me. We need Corsair."

"Lee, I thought Carl ordered you back."

"Only if I found nothing. I'll make up something, but I need a genuine lead."

"On it," Angie assured her. "What else do you want?"

"An identification on Ifrit?" Lee asked.

"That's a no-go," Angie said. "The man is a ghost. Always has been, but he's beyond careful. Like Corsair was."

"'Was' is the appropriate word," Lee pointed out.

"Right. Let's hope this assassin also has a secret family and they out him somehow," Angie quipped. "I don't think you can wait on that. Besides, we at least knew what Corsair looked like. That's how we found him, remember? There are no images of Ifrit useful enough to identify him."

"Ugh," Lee groaned. She continued to pace. "If Abbas has Amanda Harrod and Khloe Evans, he has to send a message to Corsair. How?"

"One has to assume that Corsair set up some way to communicate with Khloe, right?"

"Yeah," Lee admitted. "That still leaves us in the dark, though."

"What about the mother?"

"Khloe's?"

"Yes. We've been watching them, correct? There's been no sign of them talking, but let's figure they are somehow. We know she called her parents from Puerto Vallarta."

"What's your point?" Lee asked.

"If Mom believed Khloe was in danger, would she give up how they've been communicating?"

Lee nodded thoughtfully.

"Are you with me, Lee?" Angie asked, breaking the other woman's train of thought.

"That's a good idea," Lee replied. "Can you go see her?"

"She lives in Cincinnati," Angie reminded her.

"Yes, but we can't send a local agent," Lee said. "Winston might hear."

"We have people watching her," Angie said. "They'd identify me if I showed up."

"That's easy enough. Just follow her into a busy public place. Like Walmart or the grocery store."

"Right, super easy," Angie said half-heartedly. "When would you expect me to do it? I have work, too."

"Call in sick. Tell them you got Covid. It's about a nine-hour drive," Lee suggested.

"You want me to drive?"

"If you fly, Winston will find out. Stay off the radar, though. Get to Cincinnati, talk to Haley Evans, and figure out how she and Khloe communicate. I'm betting it's similar to how she and Corsair do it. I'd guess a mail drop."

"Makes the most sense," Angie agreed.

"The Guatemalans retrieved Khloe's laptop, too. Sparr is working on it, but if they don't break it, we'll need to send it up to you. Or rather, to the guys in the Basement."

The Basement referred to the technical analysts at the Office of Compliance. Their tasks ranged from all types of information-gathering, and while they weren't in a physical basement, they were often relegated to their offices.

"I have something else for you, though," Angie added. "This might help you a bit more."

"What?"

"A very slim possibility of a Corsair sighting."

"What?" Lee exclaimed. "Why didn't you lead with that?"

"This is the longest we've talked in weeks," her girlfriend pointed out. "Besides, it's even less concrete than what I found about the two girls on the freighter."

"Spill it," Lee demanded.

"A villager in Brazil reported to Brazilian authorities that a group of guerrilla insurgents have targeted the village of São Miguel do Tapajós."

Lee frowned. "How does that apply to Corsair?"

"According to the villager, three Americans showed up to help fight off the guerrillas."

"Three?" Lee questioned. "That's too many. Corsair isn't working with anyone."

"True," Angie acknowledged. "However, there was another incident further upriver on the Amazon involving a small criminal gang. These are local thugs who specialize in ransom grabs. Anyway, local authorities found the entire group dead in the town of Juruti. They were all killed. Witnesses claimed three Americans stole a boat and escaped downriver. This was almost two weeks ago, though."

"And the villager who reported the guerrilla activity?"

"It seems the village abandoned their site and fled. Several went to the closest city, Santarém. They reported it to the local constabulary."

"What are the Brazilians doing about it?" Lee asked.

"Nothing as far as I can tell," her girlfriend replied. "I spoke with Damien over at the State Department—don't worry, I kept it low-key and explained to him it was background information. He informed me that the Brazilians are up to their eyeballs in criminal activity. It's nearly impossible to send out anyone to combat a small army."

"You're saying they won't do anything?" Lee asked.

"That's not definite, but Damien seemed to suggest it was a nonissue for the government. Especially if this isn't a large faction."

"I need to get to Brazil," Lee said determinedly.

"That's going to be hard without alerting someone here," Angie countered.

"Yeah. If we can't find Caleb Saunders, it's pointless. Carl Winston suspects I'm digging into him, and he's positioning me to take a fall for whatever the next big fuck-up is."

"I don't like you doing it alone," Angie stated.

"We have a new agent here who I trust," Lee assured her. "I bet Sparr will help me."

"Be careful, Lee. You can't be sure that she is really on your side."

"You're being jealous, Angie," Lee warned.

"I've met Tabitha Sparr," she reminded Lee. "She's good. But would she throw her career away for you?"

"I'm hoping she'll bet on me," Lee countered. "She could go a long way in the OOC."

"If you become director?"

"Well, Winston's too much of a misogynist to notice her."

"Right," Angie replied cynically.

"It's okay, Angie, I promise," Lee stated.

"I expect it to be," her girlfriend retorted.

41

———————

"Who are you?" Mateo demanded.

Corsair didn't answer. He focused his concentration around him. Mateo wasn't alone. Two men hung back on either flank. They weren't engaged, keeping their bodies behind the tents.

Overhead, black smoke billowed up as the fire that Caleb had started spread. Corsair's eyes darted quickly between his three potential targets.

"This will not end well for you," Mateo declared.

"Don't!" Bella shouted, and the guerrilla leader squeezed her against him, pressing the barrel harder against her temple.

"Shut up!" Mateo ordered.

"Let her go," Corsair commanded in a calm, serious tone.

"Go fuck yourself," Mateo blurted as the soldier on his left flank stepped from behind the tent.

Corsair's left arm rotated on an axis as he pulled the trigger. The Smith & Wesson barked. Before the figure hit the ground, the sights of the S&W retrained on Mateo. The leader's eyes cut to his fallen comrade, and he lifted an eyebrow, looking intrigued.

"Impressive shooting," he praised. "Tell me, who do you work for? CIA? DEA?"

"Neither," Caleb replied.

"Why don't you come work for me?" Mateo asked. "We will have untold treasures when we dig up that gold."

"You are a fool," Corsair scolded. "If you find gold, someone else is going to come in and take it from you."

"What makes you think they can?"

Corsair smiled. It was perhaps the most benign grin either Mateo or Bella had ever seen from him. Yet, it carried weight. The American didn't break eye contact with the leader of the now-defunct army as he pulled the trigger again. The soldier on Mateo's right hadn't stepped around the tent, but the nine-millimeter round punctured through the canvas corner and knocked the guerrilla off his feet.

"There's only one of me," he advised.

Mateo sneered at him. "For how long?"

"You have a choice," Caleb explained. "You remove that gun from her head and shoot at me. However, you must already realize that you aren't fast enough for that."

Mateo glared at him.

Caleb continued, "Or you can pull the trigger now, kill her, and be dead before her body hits the ground."

"You're cold," Mateo growled. "My men have you surrounded."

"I killed most of your men," Caleb barked loudly so that anyone in earshot could hear him. He spoke in Portuguese, hoping that his grammar wasn't rusty. "The next person who comes into view, I'll kill them before they get the first shot off."

"You are something," Mateo remarked. "Navy SEAL? Marine?"

"Just a concerned tourist," Caleb responded. "I was passing through."

"That's impossible," Mateo sneered. "You're a mercenary, then."

"Nope, I'm not getting paid anything," Caleb declared. "What I want is to put you on the ground so I can get out of this mosquito-laden hell."

"You dare talk to me like that?" Mateo shouted. His cheeks reddened as he stared at the defiant visage of Corsair.

"Dare?" the assassin laughed. "You're the one hiding behind a woman."

Bella's eyes remained frozen in fear. She blinked twice, and Caleb suspected she was praying for intervention.

"You mock me?" Mateo demanded.

Corsair smiled at him. It was a technique he'd learned from Hood—confidence in the face of trouble. It was all part of psyops. Mateo's world was unraveling, and while Caleb had experienced his own loss, he understood the wages of war. Mateo had been the ruler of his little domain for so long, he forgot it required blood to keep such a kingdom. The guerrilla leader had grown complacent in his position, thinking that he could rule with fear alone.

"You have no army left," Caleb pointed out. "The few men who stuck around are waiting to see how the die is cast."

Mateo wrinkled his forehead in confusion.

"How things are going to turn out for you," Caleb clarified.

"You think you'll walk away from this?"

"I'm positive I will," Corsair stated. "Do you think you will?"

Corsair caught the movement to his right, Mateo's eyes tipping him off as they glanced toward the row of tents to Caleb's side. The assassin slid his right leg back, angling it at ninety degrees from his front left foot. In the same swift motion, Corsair's arm swung around like the minute hand on a clock from twelve to half-past two.

Mateo aimed his barrel at Corsair, pulling it away from Bella's temple. The instant the muzzle cleared Bella's head, Corsair pulled both triggers. The forty-five caliber round exploded from the gun, crossing the sixty-five between Caleb and Mateo in less than a blink. Mateo's neck snapped back as the bullet shattered his skull, boring a hole through his brain before blasting through his parietal bone.

At the same instance, the nine-millimeter round punctured through the sternum of a guerrilla, still raising his weapon to fire on Caleb. The second target pulled the trigger on his FN FAL, sending a burst of NATO rounds into the dirt and spewing debris toward Caleb.

Bella screamed as Mateo's grip loosened and his body fell to the ground. Corsair, keeping both weapons in the ready position, rotated a full three-sixty degrees. No one charged out to open fire, but he heard the shouts as men vacated the premises.

"You okay?" he asked Bella without turning to look at her, still scanning the surroundings.

From the sobs she made between gasps of air, he knew she was at least alive.

"The others," she finally said. "Deke and Jason need help."

Caleb spun the Beretta around, handing the weapon's grip to the woman. "Go to them. I'm getting transport."

The missionary stared for a second at the gun before she reached forward and grasped it in her palm. "What do I do?" she asked.

"It's ready to fire. Aim it at something you want to kill and pull the trigger."

He expected her to make a comment about not wanting to kill anyone, but the woman didn't. She tested the weight of the Smith & Wesson in her hand and nodded to him.

"Don't think about it," he advised her. "Just point and shoot."

"Hurry," she urged, and Caleb dipped his chin in acknowledgment.

Caleb turned back to see the Toyota Tacoma he'd seen charging through the camp. The driver aimed the truck at him, and the engine revved as he drove it toward Caleb. Corsair raised the Beretta, firing into the windshield. He waited as the vehicle veered into a tent, ripping the canvas from the poles. The fabric covered the cab.

With the Beretta extended in his grip, Caleb moved to the still-running truck. He bent over and grabbed the corner of the tent, pulling it back while maintaining his gun at the ready. A young soldier slumped over the wheel. Caleb checked the man's—no, boy's—pulse. It was a pointless endeavor when Caleb saw the child's face. Three of the five rounds Corsair had fired into the window had destroyed his cheeks and punctured through his Adam's apple.

Opening the door, Caleb reached in and dragged the corpse out. This had been one of the new recruits. Whether he'd perceived Corsair as a threat or wanted to taste his own bloodlust, Caleb would never know. It didn't matter, and Caleb knew he did what he had to do. However, that boy's mangled visage would forever remain imprinted on his brain.

It took Caleb a minute to back the Toyota out and clear the canvas tent from around the wheels where it wound when it had plowed through the tent. The fire he started had now spread from tent to tent, engulfing a quarter of the camp. He steered the truck to the tent where Deke and Jason were.

"How are they?" he asked when he barged into the quarters.

"I don't know," Bella answered. "I think Deke will be okay, but Jason's still nonresponsive."

Caleb knelt beside Jason. His breathing was shallow, but he'd sustained a serious blow to the head.

"We need to hurry," Caleb agreed. "His injury doesn't look good. He could have some brain damage."

"This is terrible," Bella uttered.

"Just help me carry him," Caleb suggested. He ripped a side of the tent into a wide strip of cloth that he stretched out on the ground. The pair lifted Jason onto the tarp and carried it to the Tacoma. Once they situated him in the truck's bed, they repeated the process with Deke.

The other American roused as they picked him up. "Rick, you came," Deke muttered.

"I'm here, buddy," Caleb assured his friend as they moved him to the bed. "Get some cushions or mattresses," he ordered Bella. "We need to support them so we don't make it worse."

In less than five minutes, they converted the bed into a makeshift ambulance. As they pulled out of the camp, Caleb had Bella drive while he stood in the back with an automatic rifle ready for anyone to charge them.

Half a click from the guerrillas' base, Caleb spotted movement. He tapped the roof of the cab, signaling Bella to stop.

Corsair bounded out of the bed and sprinted into the trees. "Sophia!" he called, and the other girl stuck her head out from behind a tree.

"Rick?" she asked.

"Come on," he waved her toward them. "We need to get moving."

As he herded the woman to the Toyota, he glanced behind them at the camp. Flames devoured the tents, sending plumes of black smoke into the air. The haze filled the undergrowth as it tried to seep through the foliage.

Caleb jumped into the truck's bed with Sophia. As she watched the two casualties, Corsair rode along with his rifle raised on point.

There was no one left to fight, though.

42

It had been three days of water stretching around them. Khloe did not know their location, but she realized she and Amanda had nowhere to go. All the crew seemed to be Middle Eastern and only spoke what she guessed was Arabic. Whatever language they spoke, she couldn't understand it. Other than Amanda, her only point of contact was the man who had kidnapped her and Amanda.

She held the girl's hand as they strolled around the deck. Their kidnapper, whose name she hadn't learned, had finally allowed her to roam the decks—or at least the top two levels. He permitted her access to the ship's mess to get food, but nowhere else. If she tried to go to a different level, a deckhand would rebuff her in Arabic. Khloe suspected her captor had instructed the crew to keep her and Amanda corralled.

From the upper deck, they had a stunning view of the ocean. It beat the hours they'd spent in their cabin as the freighter chugged away from port. He wouldn't let her leave her room until they were far from other vessels.

While he didn't say why, she assumed he worried she might signal for help or perhaps jump overboard to swim for shore.

Khloe couldn't abandon Amanda, and trying to make it to land was a surefire plan for one or both of them to drown.

Now she stared across the blue water. The sun set behind them, and Khloe imagined the trip might be enjoyable under different circumstances. Given the sun's direction, she presumed they sailed on the Atlantic. Her prison guard hadn't given her an itinerary, so she wasn't sure which direction they were going.

When Caleb had planned their exit from Belize, he'd researched freighters like this one. Many would sail into the Mediterranean, making stops along the journey. As early as they were on their voyage, there was no way to tell. Khloe's only sense of direction came from the sun. Knowing it set in the west, she used it to gauge their heading. Even she realized that was a poor method of navigation, but she wanted any information she could glean.

"Why are they keeping us here?" Amanda asked her. "I want to go find Daddy."

"These are bad men. Remember, sweetie?" Khloe repeated to her charge. The man who brought them in liked to chat with the child, and Khloe attempted to get between them. With his amiable personality, the man seemed to connect with the girl. It made Khloe wonder if he had kids of his own.

She had tested that theory yesterday when she attempted to reason with him.

"She's just a girl," Khloe had argued. "Why don't you find her someplace safe and use me as bait?"

"Corsair won't be as motivated to protect you," he countered.

She shook her head. "He would still come," she assured him.

"Not my call. I'm only the hired help," he explained with a shrug.

"What if it were your child? What if someone wanted to kill her to get to you?"

"I would keep my daughter out of this fight. That's a father's job."

"Do you have a daughter?" Khloe questioned.

He shut her down after that, leaving her with Amanda. So far today, he'd stayed clear of the pair.

"Why do they want to hurt us?" Amanda asked.

Khloe shrugged and lied. "I don't know."

"I hate them," Amanda growled, baring her teeth.

As Khloe walked around the upper deck, she searched for anything to help them get away. If they were crossing the Atlantic as she thought, they'd have several days before any attempt to escape was viable. Attempting an escape now only put the pair in the middle of the ocean with no help to be found. If they reached port, she would need to be ready to react. There might not be a lot of time when that window opened, and Khloe intended to take advantage.

She bent down and looked at Amanda. Khloe had waited until they found themselves alone on deck to talk to the child. She already struggled enough with communicating to Amanda the importance of her doing exactly what Khloe told her. The girl was only three, and she struggled to pay attention to anything in general.

"Amanda, remember these people want to hurt us," Khloe explained to Amanda. "If I tell you to do something, you have to do it."

"Yes, Klo," the child responded, but she was already

losing focus as she stared through the railing at the waves in the distance. "It's a lot of water."

Khloe nodded. She struggled to fight back the tears. How would Caleb find them? She assumed her kidnapper or his employer would send a message to Caleb—if possible. From the way he talked, the man seemed to have figured out how they communicated. He'd taken her laptop, but she guessed it was long gone now. If he was smart, he would assume Caleb could track it.

Did the crew have computers? Or phones? She'd been forbidden to go anywhere beyond the mess, and Khloe had found nothing useful in there. She thought there must be a communal hall or someplace for the off-duty crew members to hang out.

Khloe observed how the deckhands looked at her. After all, Khloe was a young, attractive woman on a boat full of men. If she found a way to use that to her advantage, she would.

The problem seemed to be when to act. Khloe guessed from the man's comments that the trip at sea took two weeks. If she tried something too soon, she'd cause trouble. The man had already assured her he only allowed her to stay around to watch Amanda. If she became too much of a nuisance, he might toss her overboard.

As she stared across the ocean, Khloe worried that there was no veering off this path. She lifted her eyes to the cumulus clouds gathered over the horizon.

"Caleb, where are you?" she asked the puffs of white, hoping for an answer that she knew wouldn't come.

43

___

"Wait, you're saying that our boss is crooked?" Sparr asked Lee.

The two sat in the rear seat of a Gol Airlines 737 aircraft. Most of the seats were empty as the plane taxied down the tarmac at La Aurora International Airport in Guatemala City.

"Very," Lee explained. "Understand that I have no evidence yet, but I know Corsair will provide it."

"And you don't believe Caleb Saunders is a traitor?"

Lee shook her head. "No. The only person who can prove he was seems to be Carl Winston."

Sparr wrinkled her nose. "What is he doing? Director Winston, that is."

"I suspect he used OOC resources, like Corsair, to perform assassinations for hire," Lee told the junior agent. "That might be why Corsair went to ground a decade ago."

"But you have to find Corsair to get that proof?"

Lee shrugged.

"What happens if we can't find him?" Sparr asked.

"Worst case is Winston sends the OOC after me,

claiming I'm a traitor," Lee replied. "Don't worry, I'll swear you were here under my orders. However, I'm betting it will only end my career and let Winston move someone he can control into my position."

Sparr cocked her head and studied her superior. "Why bring me in?"

"I trust you," Lee explained. "I'm not ordering this, understand? If you want out, I'll put you back on the next plane to D.C."

"Oh, no, I'm in," Sparr insisted. "I've read all about Corsair, and the details seemed sketchy at best. Is anyone really as good as he was? Some of those files read like they were legends."

"No, he is that good," Lee corrected her. "I'm not saying he hasn't lost an edge since he vanished underground, but remember, Corsair was a beast before."

"You think?"

"I saw him in Mexico," Lee told her. "He was riddled with bullets and still took out the head of the Cincinnati mob and a corrupt FBI agent. Like I said, if he lost anything, the man was short of unstoppable in his heyday."

"What is our plan, then?" Sparr asked. "Fly to Brazil and find him?"

"I'm hoping we catch a break," Lee admitted. "Otherwise, this will be a pointless trip."

"The laptop?"

Lee nodded. "I have someone looking at it. If they can get inside, we might find a lead."

"You're sure it's him in the Amazon?"

"I'm betting my career on it."

"Good," Sparr replied. "I guess I'll be throwing in with you."

"Thank you," Lee told her junior partner.

The 737 picked up speed on the runway, and Lee gripped the armrest like she did every time a plane took off. As the wheels came off the ground, she breathed a sigh of relief. Somehow, it was only taking off that scared Lee, although she knew planes crashed more on landings. For Lee, once the flight started, the hard part was over.

She hoped that worked in all situations.

44

———

"Do you plan to drive back?" Bella asked Caleb.

The pair sat in the truck's bed, surveying the ruins of São Miguel do Tapajós. Most of the huts were nothing more than blackened hulks, the stilts charred. The main buildings had burned completely, and with no one to extinguish them, they had continued to smolder for days.

Sophia was on the bank, watching the green water of the Tapajós River flow by. With all her belongings smoldering, there had been little for her to pack. She hadn't talked much since the medics arrived. Caleb had used the Toyota's CB radio to reach emergency officials in Santarém. Unfortunately, the medevac chopper reached them half an hour too late for Jason.

The young man never woke up, and Caleb guessed they'd find that some swelling or an aneurysm killed him. Sophia had cradled his head when he passed, and since then, she'd been inconsolable. All she had done was sit alone and cry.

Deke, on the other hand, had serious injuries but was

still alert and somewhat mobile when they flew him to the hospital.

"I should have gone on the helicopter," Caleb admitted.

Bella motioned her head to a Brazilian agent who had come in with the medics. Several of the villagers, including Joanne, had left Leandro and Davi's group to travel on to Santarém, where they had alerted authorities. Now the Brazilians wanted answers, and this agent was the only one assigned to the case.

"It must have been important," Bella had replied wryly when Agent Gutierrez told her why he was there.

"Can you take me to the city?" Caleb asked Bella. "You can check on Deke."

She nodded. "I'd like that."

"Are you coming back?" he asked.

She shrugged. "I don't know. Perhaps I'll go home for a bit. Help Deke get Danny's body to the States, if that's what his family wants."

"You do good work here," Caleb pointed out.

"Want to stay and help?" she asked.

He exhaled with a smile before shaking his head. "No, I have other places to be first."

"Right," she replied. "But what if there is gold here?"

"Don't mention it to him," Caleb warned, gesturing toward the Brazilian agent. "The government will take over this entire area, and the villagers won't get a thing."

"There's nothing here, though," Bella reminded him.

"Nothing you found yet," Caleb corrected. "It might be worth setting up a small panning operation. If you find nothing, it's only a waste of time."

She nodded. "We'll see how things turn out."

Caleb watched the woman. The missionary didn't have

the same spirit he'd seen days earlier when he first woke up in her hut. Losing friends had weighed on her.

"Besides, it depends on what Zion's Garden does," she explained. "This will have serious repercussions with them. Leadership might pull any aid Saõ Miguel is getting for safety."

Caleb shook his head. "Doesn't seem like there's much to worry about there anymore."

"Gutierrez wants you to take him to see the camp," she told him. "He's supposed to ask you to go tomorrow."

Caleb nodded. If he hadn't already decided to leave, this would have clinched it. He didn't intend to get any closer to the agent than he had to. He did not want the agent to send out a report that included Caleb's description.

"No, I'm leaving this afternoon," Caleb announced.

"Really?" Bella questioned. "You just said I could drive you."

"You still can," he reminded her. "Sophia might want to go, too."

"I need to stay until Leandro or Davi get back."

He nodded in understanding.

"Do you think it could have been avoided?" Bella asked him.

"In the whole scheme of things, yes," Caleb responded. "Although I'm not sure if we could have done anything different. Those men thought they could take something that wasn't theirs. I don't know if there was a good solution to all this."

"That doesn't really help, does it?"

Caleb shook his head. "It rarely does."

"What are your plans, Caleb?"

"I have to get home," he replied.

"Who are you running from?" she asked.

"Some days, it seems like everyone," he responded. "But today, I'm running to my daughter."

Bella smiled. "That's nice. Do you plan to tell me who you really are, Caleb?"

"I'm nobody," he explained as he stood up from the Toyota's bed.

"Would our Brazilian friend agree with that?" Bella asked pointedly.

Caleb lifted both eyebrows. "I'm hoping by the time he reports my presence, I'm already out of the country."

Bella nodded. "Why don't you take the truck, then?" she suggested. "I will occupy his time."

Caleb dipped his head. "I'll see if Sophia needs a ride. Will you tell Deke bye for me?"

"Of course," Bella agreed as she hopped off the tailgate and hugged Caleb. He returned the embrace before pulling away.

"Take care of yourself, Rick-Caleb," she said.

The American left Bella and walked to Sophia, who stared bleary-eyed at the water coursing past.

"Sophia, I'm leaving. Do you want a ride to Santarém?"

She lifted her head to stare at him before nodding.

"If you want to say goodbye, avoid the investigator. He might not want us to leave yet."

"Thanks, Rick," she mumbled.

"We'll head out in fifteen."

The jungle road was little more than a wide footpath, complete with gigantic potholes and gullies carved by rain run-off over the years. While it was less than twenty miles from São Miguel do Tapajós to Santarém on a map, the trip required a jaunt south through the trees before Caleb found the state roads, which were only graded gravel drives.

It was a six-hour journey, and Caleb felt like he might

as well have been by himself. Sophia stared out the window, crying between moments of silence. He didn't fault her. Everyone dealt with trauma in their own way, and at one point, she leaned over and rested her head on his shoulder for about ten minutes. It wasn't a moment that needed to be spoken about, and he understood her emotions.

Somehow, he wondered if he was correct when he told Bella the conflict was inevitable. If he hadn't been in the village, would they have fought back? Would so many have died?

Mateo's death had been anything but justice. As he reflected on it, he replayed the instant Mateo died. It was fast—too fast to equal the pain the guerrilla leader had caused so many. His demise did nothing for Danny or Jason. It wouldn't comfort Sophia or Bella. Not in the long run of life. Nothing brought back those that they had lost.

"Do you need a place to stay?" he asked her when they reached the city limits.

She nodded. "Someplace close to the hospital," she replied. "I want to check on Deke."

Those were the most words she'd spoken in the last six hours. Caleb agreed and found a pinkish building that read "*Casa do Ivo*" on its side.

"This will need to do," he told her. "Do you have money?"

She nodded. "Are you staying here, too?"

"I'm a little short on cash," he confessed.

The girl pulled the small backpack off her back and dug inside, producing an American Express card. "I can cover you," she told him.

"Thanks," he said. "I can't stay, though. There are people depending on me."

"Would you stay for a bit?" she begged. "I'm not sure I'm ready to be alone."

He nodded. A few hours to regroup would help. He needed to plan his next moves. What he told Sophia wasn't true. He had some money—more than enough to get him anywhere. However, he needed to avoid leaving a trail, and a hotel that likely had cameras or at least a desk clerk not used to seeing Americans was not ideal.

And cash didn't buy airplane tickets. Not on commercial airlines, anyway. With some luck, he might find someone who could fly him out for an under-the-table payout. That would take some time.

Sophia got the last room available, a comfortable efficiency with a double bed and a single wooden chair. It only cost her eighteen dollars a night. Once in the room, she found the bathroom to take a hot shower, and Caleb wandered down to the lobby.

"Do you have a computer where I can check my email?" he asked the clerk in Portuguese.

"No, sir," the employee responded. "There is a restaurant down the street with internet. Cyber Sonic."

"Thanks," he told the man before walking two blocks to the café.

He found a small storefront with a blue sign reading "Cyber Sonic" with an image of the titular hedgehog. Inside the shotgun-style shop was a long green counter opposite twenty partitioned stalls with older Dell PCs.

"How much for an hour?" he questioned the woman behind the desk.

"A hundred reals," she informed him.

"Will you accept US dollars?"

She jutted her bottom lip out and nodded. Caleb peeled a twenty-dollar bill from his pocket and slid it across to her.

He pulled another one and stacked it on the first. It was almost double the rate, but he figured she would take it. If she wasn't the owner, that second bill might slip into her own pocket. In which case, the woman would not want to discuss the American who came in for fear that her boss might discover she'd taken a cut off the top. There was no guarantee that would work, but Caleb thought it was a bit of insurance.

"Pick a stall," she told him.

Caleb chose the farthest desk from the clerk and logged onto his email. Caleb straightened up, his eyes widening as he saw Khloe's last message. It was a long one with several addenda she included with dates. There was an additional draft in the folder.

Caleb selected it.

"Corsair, I've been looking forward to meeting you face-to-face. For the moment, your daughter and friend are safe and in my care. If you would like them to stay that way, you will contact me. You have one week to respond, or repercussions will follow."

Caleb stared at the screen. Anger rose in his gut. How had he allowed this to happen? He'd been too busy protecting people who weren't his responsibility that he'd let Amanda and Khloe get taken.

Who was it? Nothing in the text clued him in on the kidnapper.

He started to type a response, but paused. This message was only a day old. He still had six of them to answer. Caleb needed more information, and if he replied to this draft, this person's instructions—and he knew those would come in the next communication—might prevent him from putting a rescue in motion.

Plus, a tech-savvy operator could ping his IP. So far, he

hadn't clicked on anything, but that didn't mean there weren't new ways to track people. The former agent suspected that as soon as he responded, the receiver would tag his location.

Especially if the OOC was behind this.

Corsair signed out of the computer. He regretted he couldn't say goodbye to Sophia, but Amanda needed him. The clock was ticking.

He opened the browser and searched for pilots in the area. Hoping to find an aircraft to fly him out of the Amazon, he discovered a courier who ran daily flights between Santarém and Macapá. He jotted down the number on a scratch pad next to the terminal before closing the window and wiping the history.

Caleb was two blocks away when he found a payphone and called the number. Thirty minutes later, he reached the airport, a shack with a short tower and a single runway. The only traffic in and out of this airfield were small private planes. He saw the plane waiting on the tarmac, and Caleb drove the Toyota up to the aircraft. Another half hour, and he was airborne.

45

———

"You think he'll be here?" Sparr asked.

"Macapá is logical, although he could be in Belém," Lee considered. "If he's leaving the Amazon on a boat, those are the closest ports."

"Both have cruise ship ports, too," Sparr suggested. "Easier to blend in with tourists."

"That's my thinking."

The pair sat in an outdoor café. Lee sipped on a coffee with milk while Sparr indulged herself in a *cafezinho*, a beverage similar to espresso but sweeter.

"How do we find him, though?" Sparr questioned. "This isn't a large city, but it's too big to expect to run into him."

"We need our people to break Khloe's computer," Lee admitted. "Otherwise, we might be wasting our time."

"How much time until Winston or Pendleton calls?"

Lee shrugged. "Hours? Days? Whatever it is, it won't be long enough."

Sparr nodded as she drank the rest of her *cafezinho*. "I'm going to the port," she announced. "Perhaps someone in security will help us identify him if he gets off a boat."

Lee agreed. There was little else they could do. She'd already reached out discreetly to the local police, but the captain she'd spoken to had been less than helpful. Without giving the details that the man they were searching for was an assassin, she only requested some assistance to locate a fugitive. The officer didn't care, complaining he had too much on his plate keeping law and order in his town to worry about American fugitives.

Sparr left Lee to her coffee, and the deputy director took out her phone. She dialed Angie's number.

"Tell me you got into Khloe's computer," Lee said when Angie picked up.

"Hello, dear, I'm good. I love you, too," Angie retorted.

"Angie, I'm dangling out here. This is a wild goose chase."

"Then you will not like what I have to share," her girlfriend replied ominously. "Khloe's laptop was worthless. She must have wiped the history after every use. They were careful. The guys in the Basement are working on it at a deeper level, but the word is it might be hopeless. I think Damien said the best case was retrieving an old solitaire game."

"Great," Lee moaned. "Guess I'll be looking for a new job. Wonder if I can get into corporate espionage."

"That will pay better," Angie pointed out.

"That's assuming Carl Winston doesn't hit me with treason charges," Lee reminded her.

"We won't let that happen," Angie assured her. "Besides, you're being hyperbolic. He'd have to manufacture some crazy bullshit to try that with you. And you have enough friends in D.C. to shield you."

"Let's hope," Lee said. "Find anything on the freighter?"

"Just tracking it. It's en route to the Mediterranean."

"Please keep an eye on it."

"You realize it will be over a week until it reaches its destination. That's a long time for you to be AWOL."

"I realize that," Lee said with a sigh. "If I can't find Corsair in the next few days, it will all be over. I'll come back to D.C., and we can send some agents to meet the freighter when it docks."

"You don't sound like you're resting," Angie scolded.

"I'm on my fourth cup of coffee today," Lee advised. "If that gives you an idea of how it's going."

Angie sighed. "Lee, you need to slow down."

"But I might miss him. Then it will all be for nothing."

"Just take care of yourself," Angie implored.

"I'll try."

"How's the new partner?" Angie asked, and Lee didn't miss the hint of jealousy in her voice.

"She's good," Lee said vaguely.

"I looked her up," Angie informed Lee. "She is also quite attractive."

If Angie had been there, Lee would have cocked her head and scoffed at her girlfriend. Which, of course, would have been a feint because Lee had also noticed how appealing Sparr was.

Instead, Lee responded, "Don't be silly, Ang. This is professional."

A figure slid into the chair next to Lee, and she turned with annoyance to the newcomer invading her space. She met the muzzle of a Beretta Px4 pressing into her side.

"Hang up the phone," Caleb Saunders growled. "Now!"

"I got to go, Angie," Lee said, disconnecting the call.

She looked at Corsair. His facial hair had weeks' worth of growth, and the man looked and smelled like he hadn't showered in a while.

"Caleb?" she replied, not knowing what else to say. Lee Hubbard had been chasing him for over a year, and just like that, he'd approached her. "What are you doing?"

"Do you have Amanda?" he asked. His eyes stared at her like black pinpoints.

"No, I don't."

"Khloe messaged me. She warned me you talked to her."

Lee nodded her head. "I did, but that was weeks ago. I'm not the one who took her."

"You told her you wanted to speak to me about Carl Winston," he stated.

"Yes. He has labeled you as a traitor. I don't believe him."

"You shouldn't," Caleb replied. "He's the traitor." He narrowed his eyes. "Does he have my daughter?"

"No, and he doesn't know she's been taken yet," Lee explained. "I came down here looking for you. If I'm going to take Winston down, I need you."

Caleb shook his head. "I don't care about that," he told her. "Not while Amanda's in trouble."

"I know where she is," Lee said, wincing as he drove the barrel into her more. "It's Abbas, not us."

"Of course it is," Caleb growled. "Where is she?"

"We believe she's on a freighter to Saudi Arabia."

"We?" Caleb demanded.

"Me and a close confidant in the OOC."

"Would this be your partner? Angie Callahan?"

"Wow," Lee said, impressed despite herself. "You're thorough."

"I also know you don't want anyone at the OOC knowing that you are in a relationship with another woman."

Lee shrugged.

"Where's my daughter?"

"In the middle of the Atlantic. So is Khloe Evans."

"And Abbas has them?"

"Ever heard of a man named Ifrit?" Lee asked.

Caleb shook his head.

"Not surprised," the deputy director said. "He was just a kid when you were active. Now he's what you once were—a hired gun, but a very good one."

"Who is he?" Caleb inquired.

"A complete ghost," she told him. "No pictures. At least, nothing usable. No contact. We think he is either Syrian or Lebanese, but that's just a guess based on a few jobs attributed to him."

"He's taking them to Abbas, then," Caleb stated. "Where is this ship?"

She nodded. "They are a week from the Mediterranean."

"Makes sense," Caleb noted. "He gave me a week to respond."

"Hmm," Lee mused.

"What?"

"How did he contact you?"

Caleb gave her a half-grin and shook his head.

"You realize I am on your side," Lee argued. "You don't need to hold me at gunpoint."

Caleb lowered his chin and gave her a hard look. "Fine. But if you try anything, I'll kill you on the spot."

"Understood," Lee replied calmly.

The Beretta vanished, and Lee allowed her shoulders to slump in relief.

"I'm just guessing that he used the same mail-drop method as Khloe, right?" Lee asked. "We found her laptop."

Caleb didn't reply.

"Look, Caleb, Ifrit suspects you were off-grid, and while he's not completely off-grid, he is unavailable until the freighter reaches the Strait of Gibraltar. I bet his deadline is arbitrary."

"Not while he has my daughter," Caleb said.

"Listen, there's time, is all I'm saying. If you come to D.C. with me, we can take down Winston. Then, with your name cleared, I'll back you with the force of the OOC."

"Not a chance," Caleb answered tersely. "My score with Carl Winston can wait until Amanda and Khloe are safe."

"There might not be time for that," she warned.

"I've been out from under the wing of the OOC for over ten years. I don't need you now."

"It's not that," Lee argued.

"No, it's that you're out on a limb," Caleb guessed. "You want to take down your superior, and without me, you can't. Fine, but not until Amanda is safe."

Lee Hubbard bit her lip. "I'll help you, but I can't do it as the OOC."

"How are you going to help?"

"You need to travel without being seen," she advised. "I'm the person who has tracked you the most. I can divert attention from you."

Caleb leaned forward. He stared into Lee's face, searching for the lies.

"No, I need more than that," Corsair declared. "If Mahmoud Abbas wants a war, I'll deliver it to him."

"What?"

"I must contact Ifrit within six days. We start now."

"Start what?" Lee questioned.

"Dismantling the Abbas empire. In the next six days, I will lay waste to everything Abbas owns. If you help me, I'll return to the States with you to confront Winston."

Lee reclined in her chair. For the first time in months, she saw the end of her journey. She also realized the tremendous risks involved. Despite Caleb Saunders's skill, Mahmoud Abbas held an intricate empire that spanned the globe. While at the forefront of multiple investigations, not only in the OOC but also in the FBI, CIA, and DEA, Abbas remained free to distribute arms, drugs, and slaves across the globe. His criminal enterprise was such that no intelligence organization had all the details.

Yet, a coup like this might cement her position after she removed Winston. It would take timing. And, above all, success.

The deciding factor was that Caleb Saunders would go after his daughter with or without Lee Hubbard's help. At least if she helped him, he would repay her by getting Carl Winston out of the OOC.

"Okay, we do it," Lee agreed. She jutted her hand out to shake Caleb's, but the former assassin only glared at the proffered palm.

"What about your partner?" Caleb asked.

"Sparr?"

He shrugged. "I don't know her name."

"I bet she'd back my play," Lee told him.

"If she gets in the way, I will remove her," Corsair promised. It was the kind of threat he'd made over and over in his past life, but not one he'd thrown out arbitrarily since Audrey's death. While Lee Hubbard didn't catch the significance, Caleb Saunders did.

He did so with the image of Amanda's face lingering in his head.

"Trust me, we'll make this work," Lee assured him.

"Fine. I'll contact you in two hours," Caleb stated. "I need the most comprehensive list of suspected targets. Anything that Abbas has his hand in, I need that information."

Lee nodded.

"Two hours," Caleb repeated before sliding out of his chair and vanishing into the crowd of people milling along the sidewalk.

Lee rose to her feet, searching the streets for Corsair, but he was gone.

She checked her watch. Two hours. Time was ticking, but she couldn't resist cracking a smile.

She had Corsair now.

ALSO BY DOUGLAS PRATT

The Chase Gordon Tropical Thriller Series

Diamond Reef

Dark Cay

Deep Gold

Runaway Tide

Devil Water

White Coral

Shark Pass

Gator Alley

Havana Sunrise

Gulf Dreams

Red Light At Night

Green Flash

Dead Slow

The Corsair Novels

La Playa de Los Muertos

Midnight Dance

Guerrilla Gold

The Jay Delp Mystery Thriller Series

The Woman Under the Bridge

The Girl on the East Beach

The Rikki Talens Adventure Series

Crossbones

Lost Cause

The Greene/Wolfe Series

Missing in the Keys

Missing in Zanzibar

Missing in Hawaii

The Max Sawyer Mystery Thriller Series

Blood Remembered

Baptism of Blood

Blood Stained

Crimson Blood

Blood River

Blood and Roses